Tales from Faer Ri

Dawn of the Druidae

C. L. Hurst

Tales from Faer Ri

Internal illustrations: Zach Castedo

Saturn's Moon Press is an imprint of Cactus Moon Publications

For information address Cactus Moon Publications, LLC, 1305 W. 7th Street, Tempe, AZ 85281

http://www.cactusmoonpublishing.com

First Edition

ISBN 978-0-9996965-1-4

Acknowledgments

A huge 'Thank You' to all my friends, family, and students who have supported me in following my passion of writing. Special thanks to Zach and Emilia for their artistic skills in bringing my ideas to life.

Finally, I'd like to dedicate this book to my amazing children and loving wife, who pushed me to share my stories with the world, and have always believed in me, even when I didn't believe in myself.

FAER RI

Dearmed Skerries
Fells of Beag Cairdeas
VLOORHAVEN GLEN
Domhain Bay
He-lush-Ka's Camp
ÆLFHEIM
TALAMH GLAS WOODS
Ramsebo Outpost
RUINS
The Wastes of Magadesh
Skregmore Reeks
Ba'asada
Sera Ke Dante

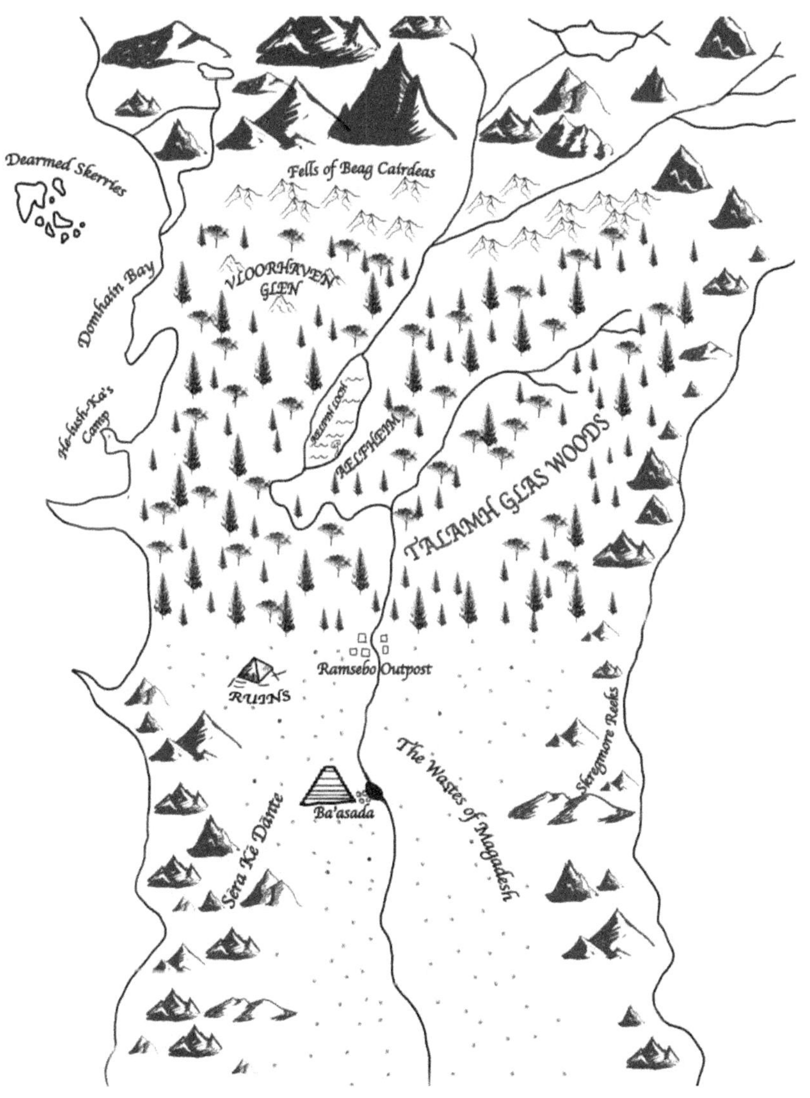

One

A light mist shrouded the stones, causing the massive titans to glisten with wet beads of crystal that traveled along the fissures until they gathered together and cascaded to the ground. Ganju adjusted his cap and pulled the string of his rain poncho a little tighter as he approached the ruins. His olive-hued skin was worn and weathered from years of sun exposure and the elements, but he still felt the chill of the soggy air. Short in stature, he was strong for his age, and still very capable.

For seven years he had worked for a private security firm contracted by English Heritage, the organization that supervised the UNESCO site. The company he worked for liked recruiting former Gurkhas, and getting a work visa to come here from Nepal was a great blessing. He had spent the last two years walking rounds at one of England's most popular destinations. It was a far cry from the tours he had served in Afghanistan. The park closed in the evening, and so his job was fairly quiet and solitary. There was the occasional incident with some local kids trying to vandalize the monuments, but for the most part it was peaceful. For Ganju Pun, Stonehenge was the perfect assignment.

During the graveyard shift Ganju and his partner took turns walking the park, and keeping an eye on the entrance. Trevor was new to the job and Ganju found himself having to wake Trevor from time to time. After a few weeks his body would adjust to the overnight work schedule, but until then it would be difficult for Trevor to stay alert.

After checking his watch, Ganju examined the outer ring of the stone circle. In two years he had not paid much attention to the rings. Frankly, he had little interest in a bunch of old stones that happened to be placed in a circle by some long dead civilization. And yet people travelled from all around the world to see this wonder. He just didn't get it. Tonight, as he did every night, he merely checked to see that nothing had been written on the surfaces by groups of tourists that had visited the ruins that day, in the unlikely event that they had crossed over the rope boundaries unseen.

He switched on his radio to let Trevor know that he had found nothing. "All clear at the outer ring, Trevor," he reported. There was no response, Trevor was most likely sleeping.

He finished his patrol and began the long march back to the car, musing about how he would frighten poor Trevor. Suddenly a bright light surged behind him followed a few seconds later by a loud crack. Ganju fell forward with the force of the blow. Did something strike one of the stones? Had the wet ground given way, causing one of the monoliths to tumble into another? Or was this Trevor's way of spooking him?

As his eyes slowly adjusted to the returning darkness, he turned and searched for the source of the noise. Although there was a road nearby, no lights were visible, and the fields were empty in all directions. The area nearby was used by the military for training, including Special Ops groups, but he had no notice of any exercises for tonight.

Having seen nothing from the roads or fields, Ganju pointed his torch back at the stones. There, in the center of the three concentric circles, was a black, huddled mass. As he watched, the mass seemed to detach itself from the center of the circle and slowly spread into the surrounding shadows. Not quite understanding what it was he was seeing, he eventually made out the dimly lit forms of what appeared to be people wearing dark cloaks. He had been warned about groups sneaking in to perform what they felt were sacred rituals in the rings, but this was his first encounter.

"Oy, you lot! You can't be here after hours! You best get moving before I have you arrested!" The figures didn't pause as they continued to spread like a dark mist throughout the ruins.

He grabbed his radio and called for Trevor. "Trevor, wake up lad. We have some trespassers. Trevor? Trevor!"

Fine time to be dozing off! He drew his tactical baton, but soon realized that there were too many of them for one security guard to scare off. He would have to run back to the car and call the authorities. He turned and started to run down the road when a shadow emerged from behind a stone.

"You'll be spending the night in lockup if you and your friends don't leave this instant," he said with a determined look in his eye. His grip tightened on the baton and he flicked the telescoping end out to show he meant business. The figure continued to walk toward him slowly. It seemed to be cloaked in a deep hooded gown, making the face impossible to see. The dark specter before him gave off an eerie presence mingled with a dusty, moldy stench of decay.

"Last warning . . . " Ganju mumbled feebly as the figure reached him. He had never felt such intense fear. Gurkhas were known for their nerves of steel, and yet he couldn't move. The hooded figure raised what seemed to be an immaterial hand and extended the palm towards Ganju. A strange sickening pulse racked his body, only for a moment, but it was enough to cause him to fall to his knees. He looked up into the cowl and saw a swirling mass of dark matter with a vague outline of a face. Two dark orbs that could have served as eyes focused on him as he knelt before the strange visage. What this was, he had no idea, but it was not human.

Paralyzed with fear Ganju tried to consider what he should say or do. It was then he noticed a dark curved blade emerge from behind the figure. With a silent motion the creature lifted the scythe and brought it down on the man. The blade, made of the same dark swirling matter as the being, passed through him. He felt the black sickening feeling as before, but this time it disappeared almost instantly. The strange sensation that had held him captive was gone, and he tried to stand up as the figure walked away. Something was different, unusual in the way his limbs moved. He looked down at himself only to see his body swirling and spinning, spiraling in on itself. He turned again to look at the strange figure as the light around him grew darker and darker until Ganju saw and felt nothing.

***

The car rocked side to side as a loud crack thundered in the distance. Trevor woke with a start and shook his head to clear his mind—he didn't want Ganju to catch him napping. He sat up and checked the time. Ganju should have been back by now. Trevor tried reaching him on the radio, but hearing no response, he got out of the car and began walking towards the park, pulling out his torch as he approached the entrance. He looked down the path and noticed something shining on the ground ahead of him. Tentatively he approached the objects on the ground. As the light found the source of the reflection, Trevor's eyes finally made out an odd assortment of metallic items on the ground: a belt buckle, keys, buttons, a torch, and a baton—Ganju's baton!

Trevor ran to the car and called the authorities as a shadow slipped from behind the vehicle and into the Bath countryside.

Two

Brendon's mother was packing his lunch as he came down the stairs. His younger brothers, Conall and Donovan, were already eating a breakfast of pancakes and sausage. The first day of a new school year was one of the few times he and his brothers would get a home-cooked breakfast, since both mom and dad had to leave for work early in the morning. Mom, who worked as a nurse practitioner, had the tradition of scheduling herself off on the first day of school in order to see her boys on and off the bus. Kaitlynn Baird had a hard time coming to grips with the fact that her "babies" were now fourteen, twelve, and eight, and were, therefore, more than capable of getting on and off a school bus on their own, but they appreciated the love behind the gesture.

Brendon hurried to grab some pancakes off the plate in the middle of the table before Conall could reach them. Though Conall was younger than Brendon, he had experienced an early growth spurt making him a little taller than his older brother, and it was well known that he could eat more than both his siblings combined. Brendon was able to snatch the plate just as Conall was reaching for more, his mouth dripping with syrup and crumbs. He made a mock sad face as Brendon shook his head at him. Brendon forked several of the golden treats onto his plate and looked for the syrup and peanut butter. He smeared on the peanut butter before drenching the pancakes with "sugary goodness," as Conall liked to call it, and then handed the syrup back to Donovan (who was still trying to perfect the sausage to syrup ratio on his plate by adding some of one, and then the other).

Brendon and Conall were often mistaken as twins, due to their proximity in size. Both had brown hair, both had green eyes. But Conall had slightly bigger ears and a face full of freckles, messy hair and some serious swagger for a boy entering middle school. Brendon, on the other hand, was more reserved and a little self-conscious about his looks. He had spent a fair amount of time on his hair today, trying to get it to not stick up. He had used gel, then pomade, and then rinsed both out and tried gel again. He couldn't seem to find the part, and each pass of the brush created a new problem. Eventually he had settled on "good enough" when he had heard his mother call him down for breakfast. His freckles had faded away during middle-school, and although he didn't know it, the girls in his class found him to be fairly handsome.

Donovan looked nothing like his brothers, or the rest of the family for that matter. He had auburn red hair and very fair skin. His amber eyes looked almost like a tiger's eye, his face like an upside-down tear drop. Of the three boys he spoke the least, and he had a kindness about him that was unmistakably a trait from his mother who was known for such. Being the youngest, she doted on him much to the chagrin of his brothers, who claimed she was spoiling him.

Dad was on a diet again, which meant he would be coveting the delicious smelling breakfast until it was consumed, so the boys did their best to make sure there was no temptation for him when he came downstairs. As they ate, their mother came around and filled or refilled their glasses with milk. Then she poured herself some whole-grain cereal and sat down to eat with them. Mom did not need to diet, but she did what she could to support her husband.

"So, Brendon, are you excited?" she asked. "First day of High School!" she said with a smile. She had such a beautiful smile, the kind that could instill a sense of peace and confidence in oneself, as if you were the most important person in the world at that very moment. Her long brown hair was tied back in a pony-tail while she was cooking, but she usually wore it down.

"Not really," replied Brendon. "I'm a freshman, the lowest of the low. I've gone from being the oldest and tallest, to the shortest and smallest. I am the bottom of the food chain."

"But you have made lots of new friends at cross country practice. And this year you will have Mr. Dabir for social studies. I would think it would be nice to have a friend of the family as a teacher."

Obviously, she was a little confused about the social networking "no-no" of being "chummy" with a teacher. Not to mention that fact that Mr. Dabir was perhaps the most eccentric man he had ever met in his life. He had dark skin for an Iranian, and he chose to keep his mustache big and bushy while keeping his beard neatly trimmed. He was balding and so kept his remaining hair very short. Often Mr. Dabir wore outdated clothes that looked as though they came from the previous century, and he always carried a gnarled, twisted cane (even though he had no need of it). Brendon's parents were the first to welcome him into the neighborhood a few years back, and he had since been over for dinner on a number of occasions. When he became excited he spoke with a thick accent, his native Persian dominating the formal English he had learned in school.

Iranian by birth, Mr. Farzan Dabir had spent his formative years growing up in an English boarding school, followed by eight years at an Ivy League school in the States. He then spent another thirty-four years teaching at the college level before taking a job at Bridgerton High School in southwestern Michigan. Why he would give up the prestige and salary of his university career was beyond Brendon, but his parents decided he had wanted to find a quiet town away from all the noise of the big cities. New Haven was about as quiet and out of the way as Brendon could imagine.

At that moment Brendon's dad came down the stairs and kissed his wife on the cheek. "I'm late, so I'll just eat my lunch for breakfast and then come home for lunch," he said as he grabbed one of the bags off the table. He gave each boy a hug, and then headed to the garage. Alistair Baird was an insurance claims adjuster, and his hours varied from day to day depending on what he had to do and where he had to travel. Mostly he worked from home, but lately he had been traveling more and more, which was making it hard to have family time together. He had been an athlete in school and had pushed the boys to be involved in sports. Though supportive of Brendon, he was not a fan of cross country. But he had promised to come to more meets this year if he could.

They were pretty close knit, as far as families go, and Alistair and Kaitlynn Baird had originally joked about having nine kids—"from A to K" they used to say. So far it was only A through D, but that was enough for Brendon, even though it would be nice for mom to have a little girl to love on.

Brendon and his brothers finished their food and gathered their belongings as they headed out the door. Their mother gave them all a kiss on the forehead (which Brendon hoped nobody saw) as they left the garage, and the boys walked down the driveway and boarded the bus. Brendon sighed as he sat down towards the back, away from his brothers, and stared out the window. School—the killer of summer fun, and the bane of the existence for all children everywhere. One hundred and eighty days of grueling torture.

As the bus pulled away, Brendon felt an odd sensation of anxiety—not the kind you get when you are going to a new school—the kind you feel when something is . . . wrong. Out of the corner of his eye he thought he saw a shadow slip into the front door of his house. The bus turned onto the next street and Brendon dismissed it as light reflecting off the bus windows. His first cross country meet was after school today, and he needed to start focusing on getting through school and preparing for the race. He ran his hands through his light brown hair, thinking it would have been nice to get it cut before the race, but the weather had been mild, so it wouldn't be overly hot anyway.

***

The Bridgerton Bison had no chance of winning. There were only seventeen runners on the entire boys' team, most of which were incoming freshmen, and their opponent had an army of juniors and seniors at their disposal. To make matters worse, the course was unfamiliar to Brendon, and it was heavily forested. The older boys had joked that one wrong turn would take you straight into Canada. Brendon wasn't worried, he had a great sense of direction, and if he kept one of the experienced runners in sight, he should be fine.

Bridgerton was a newer school, with wide hallways and lots of technology in the classrooms. The lockers were still clean, and the building was in good shape. For the most part, his classes had been easy that day, the teachers focused on passing out syllabi and going over class rules. He did have a few friends in each class that he knew from eighth grade, and his schedule didn't seem that difficult. The hardest part of the day was remembering the combination for his school locker and not mixing it up with his cross-country locker combo. The easiest part of the day was Mr. Dabir's class where they had a substitute teacher due to a last-minute family illness. Interestingly, Brendon was under the impression that Mr. Dabir had no immediate family. Aside from that, it was a pretty normal "first day".

As the bus pulled into the parking lot of the state park where they would be running, Brendon noticed dark clouds threatening on the horizon. The coach had told them it would not rain until later that night, but the clouds seemed to disagree. Brendon exited the bus, removed his blue and white joggers and matching team jacket, and began to stretch. He was slight of build, but not skinny. His coach told him he had a good body-type for running, and that when he started growing again his legs would be longer and his times would be faster. He looked around at the runners from the opposing team. The North Central Cougars were a contender for the cross-country state title this year. They had two brothers, Gustavo and Martin Neruda, who were already ranked and had offers to run in college.

The wind began to pick up and the leaves began to rustle as the trees swayed overhead. You could hear parents and other spectators gathering at the finish line on the far side of the parking lot, along with the sound of cars and busses being parked and turned off. There was a peculiar stillness to the woods that made Brendon feel uneasy.

Having met with the course officials, Coach Haskins returned to where his teammates were stretching and told the captains to begin the warm-up. Brendon only half-listened as Coach Haskins tried his best to buoy them up, his attention instead directed at the swirling clouds in the sky above. Moments later they came together and gave a team cheer before heading to the starting line. As the contestants lined up he was jostled a bit and found himself toward the back of the pack. The course official blew the whistle and the race began.

Brendon quickly found himself falling behind. The Cougars had started with a brisk pace and his teammates had decided to break pace to keep up with them. Brendon remembered what coach said about that and tried to keep to his original plan. As they moved towards the trees an ominous feeling came over him. It was an irrational fear that he could not explain, and he shook his head to overcome the sensation of gloom seemingly coming from the dark and foreboding trees ahead of him.

Within seconds he entered the woods and the feeling of dread increased. To his left he saw movement and it startled him out of his gait. When his eyes returned to the path he realized he had lost track of the back of the pack. He slowed his pace and began to look for the markers that were placed by the course official. The path turned to the left around a large hedge and when it straightened once again it forked in two directions, neither of which seemed to be marked. He stopped to look for the marker and listen for the pounding of feet.

Silence.

Brendon decided to turn to the right and stay close to what he thought was the center of the park. After a few yards it began to narrow and eventually thinned into a small game trail that led nowhere. Frustrated and embarrassed, Brendon doubled back and took the path that had led to the left. He picked up his pace to catch the tail end of the pack. After running for another few minutes, the trail again forked, and again Brendon saw no sign of directions. The clouds overhead made the course very dark, and the wind began to howl. It was clear that the rain was not going to hold off for much longer. He decided to go right again, but after another few minutes he began to doubt his decision. Slowing down and stopping, he realized that he had to make a choice—either continue running down this path and hopefully come out at the end of the course, or he could return down the path he had come. He knew that if he ran back the way he had come he would eventually make it back to the starting line. But what if the finish line was just ahead? It would be embarrassing not to finish.

Movement out of the corner of his eye caught his attention. But when he looked there was nothing. Those feelings of anxiety began to return, and he decided to run back towards the starting line. As he turned, he jumped back in fear as a large dog stared at him from the path he had just come from. Brendon was not afraid of dogs, but this was a large animal—some sort of husky perhaps, with large paws and a wolf-like appearance in his muzzle. Its head was down, and it was panting heavily, eyes fixated on Brendon. Brendon started to back away slowly, not wanting to startle the animal, and walked backwards until he could no longer see it. Once clear he decided to follow the path until he emerged at the other end of the course.

As he began to run again, cold droplets of water fell from the heavy storm clouds. Wishing he had his jacket and joggers, instead of a tank top and shorts, Brendon tried not to think of the cold. Instead he ran even faster now, hoping he didn't ruin his new shoes in the mud that would shortly begin to form on the ground. To his left he heard a rustling noise. He looked through the drizzle and undergrowth and could almost make out the form of another runner who must have been on a parallel path.

"Hello?!" he called out, but received no response.

Almost immediately, he felt that dark presence he first experienced when entering the woods. It was closing in on him from behind and Brendon wondered if that large dog was following him. Would the dog actually attack? What if it was wild? What if it had rabies? Brendon would be known as "the kids with rabies" for the rest of his high school life. Just what he needed…

At that moment, something sprang at him from the trees, and he ducked as a feathery blur flew just over his head. He wheeled around to see an enormous bird (was it a hawk?) coming towards him again.

Brendon jumped off the path and began to run with his face buried in his arms to block the thin branches as they whipped by, as well as prevent injury from the bird whose nest he must have disrupted. He couldn't shake the fear that gripped him and he felt that at any moment whatever was chasing him from behind would catch him. He called out for help and again heard no answer. He leaped over a small creek, churning his feet in the wet leaves and soil on the far side of the ravine. Using his hands, he clawed his way up the embankment until he reached the top and began to run again—this time with all his might. It felt as though his heart was about to burst out of his chest, but his fear and adrenaline kept his feet pumping. The rain was falling in earnest now and his vision was limited to a few feet in front of him. The undergrowth began to clear, and he thought he saw some lights up ahead when suddenly something grabbed him from the side.

"Brendon! Where have you been?" yelled Coach Haskins through the pouring rain. "Never mind. Are you alright? You totally scared us, man! I mean, seriously! What were you thinking? We've been searching for you for over an hour."

Relief washed over Brendon as his coach led him back to the parking lot at a light jog. Had it really been an hour? It seemed like it had only been a few minutes. Disoriented and exhausted, he climbed the stairs of the bus and flopped down in an empty seat while the other guys teased him about getting lost. Once the "search party" had been recalled, the bus and athletic staff pulled out of the parking lot and headed back to school. Brendon knew this would be all over school by tomorrow, but he couldn't shake off the horrible feelings he had felt while lost on the course. How long had he really been gone? It didn't seem like it was that long, but the others said they had been searching for at least an hour. *I just want to crawl into bed*, he thought as he took out his gym towel and did his best to dry off.

Three

The rain had slowed, so Brendon had sat on the curb and waited for some time, but when it became evident that his parents weren't coming, Nate Yoder's mom had offered to take him home. Brendon got out of the car and said thanks to Mrs. Yoder for dropping him off. His parents had apparently forgotten about the meet and failed to pick him up after the team returned to school.

He closed the car door and waved goodbye as he walked up the driveway towards the open garage door. Both cars were here, which meant both mom and dad were home. Brendon felt a little angry that they hadn't come for him, and was preparing a little "pity party" for himself for when he entered the house.

But as he maneuvered around his mom's white van he noticed that the door to the kitchen was ajar. Confused, he walked up the step and into the kitchen. The lights were off, and flipping the switch brought no results. Power outage due to the storm, thought Brendon. He walked around the kitchen island to the drawer where they kept the flashlights, but as he reached for the knob a hand shot out of the shadows and jerked him to the ground. A second hand, rough and calloused, covered his mouth as he tried to yell out.

Looking up at the face of his captor he saw a flash of fear in the eyes of Mr. Dabir, who was supposed to be tending to a sick relative. While keeping a firm grip on Brendon's mouth, Mr. Dabir released Brendon's arm and put his finger to his lips indicating the need for silence. He then uncovered Brendon's mouth and motioned for him to stay put. Sweat dripping from his dark face, Mr. Dabir picked up his twisted cane and began to crawl around the corner of the island, past the dishwasher. Brendon looked around the kitchen in a panic, trying to grasp what was taking place and why Mr. Dabir was in his house. Where were his parents? Where were his brothers? He wondered if something terrible had happened to them. Then, as if in response to his query, he noticed two sets of eyes peering out from the food pantry across the room from where he was crouched. Conall and Donovan were hiding from something, and they were trying to be as silent as possible.

Brendon rotated his body away from the pantry and rose a little higher to peer over the counter at the living room. One of the chairs was flipped over, and he noticed that a set of keys and loose change were sitting in a pile in the middle of the room.

As Brendon scanned the scene wondering what had happened, that horrible nauseating feeling of dread returned and he spun around in time to see a dark figure entering the house through the garage. It seemed to look right through Brendon, who froze in fear, and then it pulled a large pole with a curved blade attached to it from under its cloak. Brendon knew he should move, but he couldn't bring himself to do it as the blade rose and began to fall towards him. At the last possible moment, he heard a thud as Mr. Dabir flew from behind the counter and swung his gnarled cane at the would-be attacker.

The man in the robe staggered and crashed into the sink with the force of the blow. Redirecting itself towards Mr. Dabir it raised a hand as if to command him to stop, but without hesitation Mr. Dabir swung his cane again—this time at the face hidden in the deep cowl. A flash of green light was followed by a wretched screech of pain as Mr. Dabir's glowing cane found its mark. The dark figure fell *through* the wall . . . causing Brendon to gasp in awe at the now vacant space by the sink as the dark cloak swirled through the backsplash and out of view.

"Come children!" cried Mr. Dabir as he ushered Donovan and Conall out of the pantry and towards the front door. Brendon stood there, transfixed. "You too, Brendon. It is *not* dead, and it is *not* alone," he said as he pulled Brendon out of the kitchen.

"What do you mean '*it*'?" asked Brendon.

"Thees eez not thee time to explain!" Mr. Dabir bellowed, his Persian accent getting the better of him. He looked furtively at Brendon and his brothers, then gathered himself and knuckled his mustache on either side. Returning to his calm British demeanor, he continued in his normal voice. "Suffice to say you and your family are the targets of a 'Reaper'—more than one reaper if I am not mistaken, and I rarely am. It is time to leave," he explained with resolute dignity. It was surreal how he could muster such composure, especially in contrast to his mood only seconds before. But Brendon wasn't convinced.

"Not without my parents! Where are they?! Their cars are here, so they can't be at work! What have you done to them?!" yelled Brendon, tears welling up in his eyes and a lump in his throat.

Mr. Dabir paused and looked at Brendon with deep sadness in his eyes. "I am very sorry, Brendon. Your parents have been taken. Most likely they are still alive, but I am sure they would want you to avoid capture, so we really must be going."

What did he mean 'taken'? What was going on? Brendon didn't know what to think, but he did know what his parents had taught him to do in an emergency and he ran to the phone to call the police. He picked up the phone and began to dial as Mr. Dabir began to walk towards him in protest, but at that very moment the dread feelings returned, and Brendon looked up from the phone to see the dark figure re-emerge from the wall above the sink, while two more cloaked figures entered through the wall of the family room. They were nearly surrounded. There was no way for Brendon to get to the door before they reached him. He threw the phone at the nearest apparition only to have it pass through the hooded face and against the wall at the far side of the room. It was as if they were shadows or ghosts. The only thing that seemed to affect them was Mr. Dabir's cane, which was once again glowing with a dark green hue around the knotted end.

Hopelessly outnumbered, Brendon didn't know what to do. He looked at his younger brothers who crouched behind Mr. Dabir. He wanted to protect them, but he felt completely helpless. He turned to face his attackers, ignoring the lump of fear that caught in his throat, and summoned the courage to shout at the top of his lungs, "GET OUT!"

The creatures paused and seemed to wither slightly under his command, but they regained composure and renewed their slow, deliberate path towards Brendon. The two closest to him raised their hands and spread their palms outwards facing him. He felt a convulsion of sickness and pain wrack his body, his vision began to blur, when the sound of glass breaking disrupted the advance of the reapers. A massive hawk flew into the room and dove at the reapers. Before reaching the first hooded figure, it shimmered, like a mirage on hot pavement, and a bull elk appeared where the hawk once was, it's antlers tearing into the first reaper eliciting a scream followed by a flash of light and then nothing. The elk shimmered and then became an old man, dressed in jeans and a flannel shirt.

He had long white hair, and several feathers hung from multiple piercings in his right ear. His skin was brown and leathery, his nose hooked and protruding like that of an eagle. His dark obsidian-colored eyes were like two small marbles set deep within his face.

"Quit stalling Farzan, and get these boys out of here! There's an army of reapers bearing down on this home, and I can't fight them all!" cried the newcomer as he shimmered and then became a wolf-like dog that snapped and drove one of the reapers down the hallway and into the back bedrooms. Brendon recognized the dog as the one who had frightened him during the cross-country meet.

Mr. Dabir turned and held his cane like a sword at the remaining reaper. He motioned for Brendon to join his brothers and make their way to the front door. Sounds of a struggle emanated from the back bedrooms and Brendon could only imagine what might be taking place. The remaining reaper seemed hesitant, glancing first at Brendon and then at Mr. Dabir. Brendon and his brothers opened the front door and stepped out onto the lawn. Mr. Dabir followed walking backwards, his cane an ardent green flame pointed directly at the reaper as it followed them through the door.

The sky overhead churned with dark sinister clouds, the wind tore through the branches, shattering limbs as the storm began to renew its strength. Lightning flashed from behind the neighbors' homes followed by the low rumble of thunder. In the distance a car alarm sounded, followed by another. The rush of the storm surge caused the trees around the house to tilt as roots strained to keep their mammoth trunks from ripping them from the earth. To their left, two bodies crashed through the vinyl siding of the house as an enormous bear pushed itself off of a reaper and brought its massive paw down upon the cloaked chest. There was a flash of green light and the figure disappeared. The bear looked up at Mr. Dabir and shimmered into the old man again.

"What are you waiting for, Magi? Finish him!" he yelled.

The sky grew darker and more ominous still.

"I am WORKING on it!" barked Mr. Dabir, with a look of intense concentration on his face. The remaining reaper seemed to recognize that something was about to happen and launched itself at Brendon with all its force and fury. From out of the sky a bolt of lightning struck the reaper in mid-flight, causing another eruption of light followed by the clap of thunder. It happened so fast Brendon didn't even have time to flinch. Mr. Dabir was breathing heavily as his eyes met with Brendon's.

"Well it's about time. I thought I was going to have to do all the work," said the old man.

"You try summoning lightning sometime. It's not as easy as you may think, and I am not as young as I once was!" replied Mr. Dabir. He turned to Brendon, "There is so much to tell you, but we really must go," he said wearily, "My car is just around the corner. We have to get you to the reservation."

"Reservation?" asked Brendon.

"The Pokagon Potawatomi reservation outside of Dowagiac," answered the old man, "It's near where I live, and one of the few places the reapers cannot enter. By the way, since Farzan has forgotten his manners, let me introduce myself: Kiwidinok Taylor, but you can call me Kiwi." He extended a hand which Brendon shook, dumbfounded, and then started off towards the direction of the car Mr. Dabir had indicated earlier.

Mr. Dabir muttered something about having more manners in his little finger than Kiwi had in his entire body, and then motioned for Brendon, Conall, and Donovan to follow. Brendon nodded and helped his brothers, who were still in shock, towards Mr. Dabir's car. He had a lot more questions, but knew they would have to wait.

Four

The children sat quietly in the back seat of Mr. Dabir's car as he and Kiwidinok spoke in hushed tones with one another. It was obvious to Brendon that they didn't agree on the next course of action, and equally obvious that they did not want the children to hear as they would occasionally look over their shoulders to be sure the children weren't paying attention before continuing their conversation.

Brendon pretended to look out the window at the rolling pastures and small farm houses, while straining to make out pieces of the conversation. So far, he had gathered that they were heading to a local Native American reservation where they would be safe, and that Kiwidinok would have to get permission from the tribal elders for the rest of them to come on the reservation (unless there was an official pow-wow open to the public, the lands were protected by tribal police and off limits to those who were not Native American). In the meantime, they were going to wait at Kiwidinok's house, located a few miles away in Dowagiac. Mr. Dabir would make them some dinner and wait for Kiwidinok to return. More than that, Brendon could not make out.

Kiwidinok was a strange fellow. His long white hair reached his shoulders, and was tucked behind the feathered earrings he wore on his right ear. There were five piercings, Brendon noticed, and each feather had a piece of rawhide attaching it to the earlobe. His blue jeans and flannel shirt were faded and looked well-used. A small piece of jewelry hung around his neck, but Brendon couldn't tell from where he sat what it was. He also wore a silver bracelet with a large turquoise stone in the center. In contrast, Mr. Dabir wore brown dress slacks, a blue oxford dress shirt, plaid bow tie, and a tweed vest. Unlike the tall and lean Kiwidinok, Mr. Dabir was shorter and a little thicker in the middle. He too was older, but his face was not as weathered. His British accent combined with his clothing and demeanor made the unlikely pair even more curious. How did they know each other? What was it Kiwidinok had called him? Magi?

They hit a pothole and his focus turned to the back seat of the car. His brothers were still in shock. Conall, his green eyes red from tears, was simply staring out of the opposite window, and Donovan had his face buried in his black t-shirt, a tuft of red hair peeking out of the collar. Every so often his shoulders would shudder which, as Brendon knew, meant he was crying. He wanted to tell him everything was going to be alright, but the truth was he didn't believe it himself. His parents were gone. How did Mr. Dabir put it? *Taken*? But for what reason, and why did these reapers want him as well? More importantly, what were they? It was overwhelming, and he did not know what to believe. What he saw that afternoon was like being in a movie, an intense movie, and it hardly seemed real. But here they were, living through a terrifying experience.

Kiwidinok began to give Mr. Dabir some directions, and it was apparent that they were nearing his home. A few moments later they pulled up to a small single-story brick ranch where a couple of dogs ran from behind the house to bark at the car as it came to a stop. Kiwidinok got out and greeted them with tender eyes and then whistled for them to hop in the back of his green truck. He opened the front door of the house before returning to the truck, and with a quick wave, got in and drove back down the driveway.

Mr. Dabir and the kids got out of his car and headed into the house. It was tidy but modest, with only sparse pieces of furniture here and there. The kitchen only had two chairs, so Mr. Dabir grabbed a couple of milk crates from the pantry so that everyone would have a place to sit. He found a few cans of soup and an aluminum pot, and began to heat their dinner on the stove. A second foray into the cupboard produced some bread, a jar of peanut butter, and some honey which he asked Brendon to prepare into sandwiches. In a matter of minutes, they were seated and eating dinner. At first the brothers shied away from the meal, but hunger drove them to partake and they began to relax, if only a little.

"I suppose you are wanting some questions answered," said Mr. Dabir. The boys nodded.

"And I shall give them. I know this must be hard, and I know that what I am about to say will be difficult to believe, but I ask you to trust me and allow me to explain.

"The first thing you should know is there are more worlds than the one in which you live. One such world is known as the Land of Faer Ri. It is from this world that many of what we call "fairy tales" originated. In fact, you are descendants from a race known as aelfin, or aesir, to use the old tongue. A more modern name for them would be 'elves.' I know that sounds strange, what with all the stories and myths about elves, but you need to understand that there is a reason those stories exist in the first place—as distorted as they are, they are all based on a real people who came to this world as refugees from a war they could not win."

"*This* world? What, are they aliens? Did their 'spaceship' crash?" piped up Conall, in an obvious attempt at sarcasm.

"No, No," replied Mr. Dabir, "As you no doubt saw today, magic is very real, and the aesir, or elves, were practitioners of that magic. *I* am a practitioner. An *elf*, like you."

The boys looked at him curiously.

"A practitioner means I study and use magic," explained Mr. Dabir.

"Kiwi called you 'magi.' Is that what you are, a magi?" asked Brendon.

"Yes—and no. Let me explain a little more: The aesir were a race of magic users who lived in a great city known as Aelfheim. Unlike the myths, they were not diminutive creatures who went around fixing shoes. In fact, they were very much like humans in their appearance. They studied and practiced magic, but in a way that benefitted their communities. They lived in peace with nature and the other races of their world—that is until the Naga Invasion. But I am getting ahead of myself.

"When children reached about 12 years of age, and showed potential for magic use, they were given the opportunity to choose one of three disciplines: Chaldees, Saami, or Druidae. The Chaldees study the stars and the science behind the elements. With great effort and years of practice, they can become 'magi.' It has been said that a true magi is a master of *time* and *influence*. He can predict future events, and influence the weather. They are the historians and scientists of the aelfin society. Kiwi called me a magi, but in truth I do not deserve the title. There are very few magi in the world, and much of their knowledge has been lost."

The boys continued to eat their dinner as Mr. Dabir continued.

"The Saami are the Healers of the aesir. They use what is known as "shift magic" to help heal wounds and communicate with animals. They spend their lives studying nature and the spirits of the animals that reside therein. When they can use the shift magic to change shape and/or to heal, they are known as shaman. Kiwi is a shaman, a very good one at that. Shaman are more common, but they are seldom willing to leave the protection of their sacred lands. The reservation where we will be staying had been created by a group of shamans over a thousand years ago, and was only recently re-acquired by the Potawatomi nation in the past century. It is a great advantage for us, if we can reach it in time. I fear you three are quite the prize, and I doubt the reapers will simply give up," Mr. Dabir said with concern in his voice.

"Why should we be so important? We're just kids," asked Brendon.

"Ah, well you see that leads me to my next point. The third group, the Druidae, were the most powerful of the aesir. They studied the earth—plants, trees, rocks and streams. With their voice alone, they could control the world around them. It was the Druidae who were the greatest protectors of the aelfen people when the naga invaded. The great Warrior Bards kept the enemy hordes at bay for two years while the council prepared for the exodus of the aesir. It was the High Bard, Caedmon Anluan himself, who discovered the magic of a realmlink between this world and theirs. Several months and all three disciplines of magic were used to create a portal between the city of Aelfheim and our world. When completed, the aesir left their homeland, with the intent to return when it was safe to do so. But there were complications. When they tried to build a realmbridge in our world they were unable to open the portal. After many centuries they gave up and settled into the societies that existed in that day. The only remnant of that first civilization visible today is a portion of the realmbridge itself. We know it as Stonehenge."

"But that doesn't explain why they took our parents, or why they want us," said a timid voice. It was the first time Brendon had heard Donovan speak since breakfast that morning. There was a great sadness in those golden hazel eyes that made Brendon feel sick at heart. He had no idea what to do and where they could turn for help. It was too much to think of at the moment.

Mr. Dabir smiled kindly at Donovan. "You are right, Donovan, I have neglected to share that piece of information. Forgive me. You see, your grandfather was the very last of the Druidae, or druids. He never became a bard, and he kept the history of his family a secret from his children. There had been so many disappearances of Druidae over the years that he felt your father would be safest if he didn't learn magic. He sent your father to the States to keep him away from the realmbridge.

"But before he died he called an old childhood friend of his from boarding school—-me. It was then he confided in me his secret, and entrusted in me his most valuable possession. I promised I would watch over it and your family, and so I gave up my university position and took a job in South Haven."

Mr. Dabir walked over to the doorway where he had propped the cane. He picked it up and brought it back to the table. "This shillelagh belonged to him, and is reputed to have been created by Caedmon Anluan himself. It will work for anyone with aelfen heritage, however it can do much more in the hands of a descendant of Caedmon Anluan," he paused, "I know your grandfather would want you to have it."

"I don't want it," said Brendon. Conall eyed the ebony knotted stick longingly, but a glance from Brendon caused him to look at the ground. Donovan slowly shook his head.

“That’s fine,” said Mr. Dabir softly, “I’ll just hold onto it in case you change your mind. After all, you won’t need it once we arrive at the reservation.”

More silence, and then Conall’s head jerked up. “If our grandfather was an elf, why did he die? Don’t elves live forever?” he asked.

“The stories about ‘elves’ being immortal stem from the somewhat longer lifespan that the aesir enjoyed compared to that of their human counterparts thousands of years ago. A typical aesir lives for about two hundred years, but as their numbers dwindled and they intermarried with humans, their lifespan decreased. There are no pure aelfen bloodlines in the world today. Only hints and whispers of what once was.”

“And the reapers? What are they?” piped up a nervous Donovan again.

“Now *that* I do not know. They have been around for centuries. We know they come through the realmbridge, and we know that they use some distorted form of shift magic, since the bodies and clothes of their victims are taken, but those objects that are not organic—metal alloys, plastic—are left behind. We also know they have been searching for and capturing aelfen descendants in all parts of the world, and we know that they are difficult to harm—only aelfen magic, or things created by that magic, can touch them. Why people are taken, and for what purpose we do not know. And until we know, we are doing our best to locate and protect as many families as we can. Unfortunately, this attack took us by surprise.”

“Who is this ‘us’ you keep referring to?” asked Brendon.

“Chaldean historians like myself. We research genealogies and do our best to keep track of . . .”

The children jumped as the door to the house was flung open. It was Kiwidinok, and his face was scratched and bleeding.

"We must go. The elders were unable to meet with me, but we can't wait any longer. There are reapers all around the reservation, and they are growing more numerous by the hour. We will have to enter through the woods to the south of the bridge that leads to the main entrance. The creek is narrow and not very deep. Crossing will not be difficult, but we must leave now."

Mr. Dabir and the children stood up and followed Kiwidinok to his truck. Brendon and Mr. Dabir got in the back with Kiwidinok's dogs, while Conall and Donovan sat in the cab next to Kiwidinok. The engine roared to life and dirt sprayed from the back tires of the vehicle as they made their way towards the reservation. It was dark now, and only one headlight was working, so it was difficult to see where they were going. At least Kiwidinok's dogs were friendly, as they curled up next to Brendon.

Within a few minutes they passed a few road signs designating the upcoming reservation, and Brendon began to feel that sensation of doom that had been all too prevalent today. He wanted to say something by way of warning to Mr. Dabir, but the look in his eyes told Brendon that he had felt it too. The truck slowed, and then turned off the road onto a dirt path into the woods. It was bumpy and Kiwidinok had to slow down even more to prevent his passengers from being thrown from the back of the truck. Tree branches began to get lower and lower as the truck entered an area not meant for vehicles. Finally, they came to a halt. Kiwidinok cut the engine and Brendon heard the sound of water flowing. They must be near the stream.

The moon was not quite full, but it illuminated the scrub around the truck as Brendon and Mr. Dabir climbed out of the bed. Noticing his interest in the moon, Mr. Dabir stepped closed and whispered.

"Waxing Gibbous," he said matter-of-factly. When Brendon gave him a bewildered look he pointed at the moon. "It will be full in three more days or so," explained Mr. Dabir with a hint of satisfaction.

Kiwidinok shook his head at his old friend's completely ill-timed lesson in celestial bodies and motioned for the boys to follow him. They walked about thirty paces before Kiwidinok stopped them and crouched down. The dogs began to growl, and as Brendon squinted he could make out the shapes of reapers moving towards them from the water's edge. His heart began racing, and he felt panic as he looked left and right. They weren't only in front of them, they were all around them. At least a dozen reapers were converging on their location, and there seemed to be no escape.

"Mr. Dabir and I will hold them off. You boys run to the stream. Once you are across you will be safe. We will join you as soon as we can," said Kiwidinok. "Mr. Dabir?"

Mr. Dabir loosened his bow-tie and removed a pocket watch from his vest. "Will you hold this for me?" he said giving the watch to Brendon, who nodded silently. "All right lads, we'll see you in a moment. Don't look back—just run!" He turned to Kiwidinok, "After you, Mr. Taylor."

Kiwidinok just grunted and then shimmered into an enormous elk which sprinted towards the stream to clear a path for the boys. Mr. Dabir lifted the now glowing shillelagh and spun to face his attackers, motioning again for Brendon and his brothers to run.

With adrenaline kicking in, Brendon took Conall and Donovan by their hands and pulled them towards the stream.

The sounds of shrieking and explosions of light were all around them, as the magi and shaman fought furiously to defend the young children. The sound of rushing water was getting louder, and Brendon felt as though they might make it, when a black shape appeared just to the right of them.

Brendon was so startled he couldn't think of anything else to do but yell. There was such terror and fear in his voice, he felt ashamed. But there was anger too, and for a moment he thought he saw the reaper shrink back. Mustering his courage, and placing himself in front of his brothers he roared at the top of his lungs, summoning all his anger and fear of having lost his parents. This time the creature did move back, for some unknown reason. Brendon didn't question, he just continued backing up towards the stream. The ground began to slope downward, and Brendon felt his shoes slosh in the muddy banks of the stream, his brothers by his side, and the reaper advancing slowly. Sounds of battle still emanated from the woods, but soon they would be safe. Just a few more steps.

Behind him Donovan gasped, and Conall screamed, "Look out!" And then everything went black as a glowing blade passed through his midriff from behind. Turning he saw two more reapers lift their scythes and sweep them through his brothers as the darkness slowly blurred his vision into nothingness.

He had failed.

Five

Brendon awoke to the sound of strange voices. As he blinked himself awake he coughed at the musty odor surrounding him. His eyes adjusted and he found himself in a small stone cell with dirt and straw strewn about, a slatted wooden gate that reached from the floor to the ceiling offered the only source of light. The cell was too small for a grown adult to stand up in, but Brendon was able to walk hunched over to the gate. He tested the handle, but found it chained and locked from the outside. He peered through the gaps only to see strangely painted men with spears conversing one with another. Something about them seemed different, but he couldn't make it out at first. And then Brendon noticed the eyes—the eyes were small slits, almost snake-like. The men were also bald, completely devoid of hair—even on their arms and legs. Their bodies were either covered in thick paint or tribal tattoos that made all sort of designs which flowed from one to another. They wore only loin clothes, but carried a spear and a short knife at their waist. As if noticing his scrutiny one of them looked directly at him and commented to the others. They moved away from view and towards an opening of the enclosure that housed his cell.

Suddenly a thought occurred to him and he cried out, "Conall? Donny?"

Silence . . . followed by a faint groan from the right of his cell. He tried again, "Conall? Donny?"

This time he heard someone stirring and a small voice answered, "Brendon?"

Relief. "Yeah, Donny, it's me. Is Conall with you? Can you see him?" he asked.

A pause, and then, "Yes. I can see him. He's in a cage across the room from me. Where are you?"

"I'm in a stone cell, probably built for animals judging by the size of it. I'm to your left . . . near the light," responded Brendon. "The gate is locked from the outside. Can you get out of the cage?"

A different voice responded, "No, we're locked in too," answered Conall, who seemed to have been awoken by the sound of their voices.

The light from the left was broken up by shadows as a group of the snake-eyed men walked back into the room. They spoke with one another, but it was unintelligible to Brendon. Two of them unlocked his cell while the other four opened the cages of his brothers. Rope was tied around his hands and a thin silver chain was attached to a collar placed around his neck and the necks of his brothers. A piece of cloth was then placed in Brendon's mouth. The foul smelling fetid taste caused him to gag multiple times before he mastered his resolve and blinked back the tears. His brothers' eyes were wide with fright, but he could see a little anger in Conall's face. Of the three brothers, he had the shortest temper, and he didn't like seeing Brendon mistreated. Strangely Conall and Donny were not gagged, though they were similarly bound.

The boys were led from the gloomy, damp room towards the light. The brilliance of the sun made it difficult for their eyes to adjust, but they soon saw that they were being led from a stable of sorts towards a series of buildings. It was obvious that at one time this city had been a beautiful architectural wonder, with trees growing in and around buildings, gardens on rooftops, and wide tree-lined roads with ornamental shrubbery and statues. The white marble buildings would have been a glorious vision to behold in their day, the sun giving luster to the chiseled polished stones. But years of neglect had turned it into a crumbling waste, with roots tearing apart the structures they were once so harmoniously enmeshed, while grass, moss and other undergrowth covered the paving stones. Debris littered the streets, and the once grand estates seemed unfit for habitation. Brendon felt a strange sadness overcome him, as if something close to him had died.

Their captors led them down the street and then turned right at the intersection of a plaza surrounded by large misshapen trees and four spacious buildings. As they made their way down the wide boulevard, the largest of the buildings loomed just to the right of them, dark and ominous. To the left there seems to be the remnants of a park, only the grass was overgrown and had been trampled flat in some areas. To Brendon's amazement, a large ring of mammoth stones surrounded by a smaller ring of greenish-gray quartz lay in the center of the grassy mall. Brendon had never been to Stonehenge, but he had seen pictures. These stones appeared to be laid out in the same pattern and design--just like the books he had read, only it was perfect—no gaps missing or stones at crooked angles. And then it came to him; this was the "realmbridge" that Mr. Dabir had been talking about. Or rather, this was the "other" realmbridge . . . the one the elves had built in order to escape. Somehow, he was in their world now. And maybe that meant his mother and father were here as well. For the first time since his parents went missing he felt hope. Hope that they were still alive and ok. In that moment, Brendon decided that he would do everything in his power to locate and rescue his parents. He felt emboldened for a fourteen-year-old kid trussed up and being dragged through the street, but he would do anything for his family.

The man leading him tugged on the silver cord around his neck and he returned his attention to the road before him. Just then, a stomach curdling screech arose from the ring of stones. The snake-men spoke to each other and three of them left at a run towards the center of the plaza, spears in one hand and short knives in the other. Brendon watched as a cloaked form detached itself from the gap between two of the large stones in the ring and fell forward, charred and smoking. Another scream followed as a second dark form emerged from the rings, this one bleeding from a deep gash across its chest as it staggered towards the large building near Brendon. The snake-men ran up to it and helped support it on its feet. As it rose to full height Brendon could see that it was a reaper, only it looked like a man rather than an ethereal spirit, as they had in his world. It coughed and then pointed a thin shaking finger at the ring of stones.

As Brendon watched, a group of men emerged from the building to his right. Unlike the tattooed handlers they had seen up to this point, these men wore full armor of overlapping metal plates from head to toe. The armor looked almost like scales of a fish or some reptile, and the painted designs made them look like large lizards running through the ruins. Each carried a long pole with a curved blade on the end, as well as a long, curved sword on their back. It was reminiscent of a samurai, only the armor was not the same and the helmet was pointed at the top.

The soldiers drew their weapons and entered the ring. Immediately the sounds of battle ensued. Metal scraped stone and cries were heard as bright flashes of green escaped through the gaps in the realmbridge. A deep throated growl shook the plaza and several men were flung from one of the apertures as a massive Kodiak bear exited and rose to its back legs, roaring a deafening challenge. At its side was a diminutive man, leaning heavily on a twisted wooden cane. Mr. Dabir! Somehow, he had managed to find them. And the bear protecting him must be Kiwidinok. By their haggard appearance they seemed to have been fighting for some time, and Mr. Dabir was using the shillelagh as a crutch, rather than a weapon.

The soldiers encircled them and issued commands to one another. A quick series of attacks, feints, and retreats were harassing the weary shaman, and it seemed Mr. Dabir lacked the strength to do anything but back away from the attacks. Finally, outnumbered and without hope, Mr. Dabir whispered something to Kiwidinok who shimmered and became himself once more. The soldiers moved forward quickly to grab them, but at the last moment Kiwidinok spun around, took the shillelagh and shimmered into a fierce looking bird which took flight and soared out of view. The tattooed men tried to hit him with their spears, but the target was too small and too quick for them. Kiwidinok had escaped.

Brendon felt a little resentment towards him at that moment, having left them all in the hands of these strange men, but he could understand. Left with the option to run or be captured, running was a sensible choice. But without Kiwidinok, they had no chance of escape.

The soldiers examined Mr. Dabir, and questioned the reaper, who looked more and more like a frightened servant. Were these soldiers its master? Why did it not appear as formidable here as it did in Brendon's world. Within a few moments there was a bright flash of white light and several more reapers emerged from the ring. They gathered their fallen comrades, picked up the smoldering remains of the others, and then walked towards the disheveled building next to Brendon and his brothers. As they neared, one of them looked up at him; its timid furtive glance met by Brendon's stern glaze lasted only a moment before it quickly averted its eyes. Behind them came the tattooed men supporting Mr. Dabir between them. His leg had a long gash just below his knee, and was losing a lot of blood. The men set him down and one took out a leather pouch which he opened and placed his log knife inside. He extracted the knife and a pink viscous balm covered the blade. With the flat of the blade he smeared the balm over the wound, which began almost immediately to seal itself. In moments, the wound scarred over, still red and tender looking, but it was no longer bleeding. Mr. Dabir was restrained, bound, and gagged like Brendon, and they resumed their march through the city.

As they left the plaza the road turned again to the right. Here were the remains of other large buildings, their purpose buried in the years of vegetation as nature worked to reclaim its own. Brendon was hungry, and the gag was causing his jaw muscles to burn with discomfort. He wondered why they had not gagged his brothers although he was grateful they had not. Donovan was sniffling again, but Conall had grown quiet and sullen. Brendon knew this was typically a precursor to a tantrum or other explosive outburst. He just hoped that Conall had the sense to remain quiet until they had a chance to figure things out.

The road now veered to the right again and began a downward slope. The buildings were smaller and closer together, and Brendon had the sense that these may have been dwellings at one time. There were many of them that had been built around trunks of trees, incorporating nature into the design. But without the careful hand of the gardener, the trees had overcome the edifice and all that remained were the foundations and a partial wall here and there.

Stepping over a large stone that had fallen from a nearby structure some time ago, the group moved slowly down the path. At the next intersection they turned left, still descending, and in moments Brendon saw a vast body of water spanned by a small bridge that ran from the end of their road to the banks of the shore on the other side. It took them much longer than he thought to reach the bridge which, it turns out, wasn't so small. Constructed of stone with arches below for support, the overpass had three main sections connected by platforms evenly spaced between them.

As they approached the gateway on the near side of the bridge an old man, painted much like the others, exited the gatehouse with three golden amulets in hand, placing one of them around the neck of the tattooed snake-man in the lead. They spoke a few words in the nondescript dialogue of theirs, and then the party moved forward while the man with the amulets returned to his post.

Brendon stepped onto the bridge and observed that it was in good condition, perhaps one of the few things maintained by these strange people. As they left the city and trekked across this section of bridge, Brendon noticed a slight ripple in the water. Without warning an enormous yellow and red eye opened and peered up at him from out of the water. The eye was nearly as big as his kitchen table, and two sets of eyelids opened and closed from opposite ends as the iris widened and narrowed. Searching among the group it focused on the amulet the leader wore before blinking once more and submerging once again. It gave Brendon the shivers to think how big the creature must be given the size of its eye!

At the first platform they turned slightly to the left and continued forward, the snake men pulling on the silver chains to keep the boys from lagging behind. Brendon looked behind him at his brothers and Mr. Dabir. They seemed to be doing well, although Mr. Dabir was limping. He looked back at Brendon and winked. What did that mean? Maybe the stress of battle had addled his brain, but Brendon was distracted by what he saw behind Mr. Dabir.

The city they had just left was actually on an island in the middle of a lake. Dilapidated as it was, it was still breathtaking and beautiful to behold. The white marble structures seemed to gleam as they reflected the light of the sun, their dirt and filth not as noticeable from such a distance. What a shame it had fallen into ruin. He could just make out the streets he had walked down as they sloped upward towards the central plaza where they had been held. If that was the realmbridge, they would have to return to it one day in order to get home. Brendon decided to pay extra attention to their route, so that he would be able to follow it back.

As they passed the second platform and turned to the right this time, a breeze from the far shoreline reached the group. It smelled of pine trees and wildflowers, but it was chilly, and Brendon began to shiver in spite of the bright sun. After a few more minutes had passed they finally approached a gatehouse on the far side of the bridge where another painted man waited to remove the amulet and place it into a wooden chest for safe keeping. The group leader stopped the procession and went in search of something in an adjacent building. Moments later he returned with four soldiers dressed in that same metal scaled armor and a large wicker basket. Brendon and his brothers were untied and Brendon removed the gag. The soldiers gestured with their spears that they should sit down, and the basket was passed around among them. Inside he found stale bread and some dried fruit. Brendon was too hungry to turn it down and he began to eat, as did his brothers. The bread was dry and rough, and it made his throat hurt to swallow it, but he was hungry. The dried fruit wasn't so bad, but it was very tart with a bitter after taste. It looked like a prune or dried apricot, but was a translucent yellow in color. After a few bites he looked around and noticed that neither the soldiers nor the tattooed men offered to untie Mr. Dabir, who had been placed a short distance away from the children. Brendon felt sorry for him, but he just looked at Brendon and winked again. What was wrong with him? What was he trying to say?

Brendon had no time to think as he and his brothers were hefted up off the ground and bound once again. This time when they gagged Brendon they did not push the gag in as far, and he was able to bite down on it to prevent it from choking him as it had done before. Three of the tattooed men stayed with the group, as well as the four soldiers, while the other tattooed men returned to the bridge. They spoke in that strange dialect once again, the soldiers giving the orders this time, and then he was pulled forward by the silver chain along with his brothers, and Mr. Dabir. As they left the compound of small out buildings (most of which were comprised of stone and timber and had crumbled in upon themselves) and entered the dense forest, Brendon couldn't help but to feel caught up by the natural beauty of his surroundings. He had never seen trees this tall in his life! Trunks the width of a car, and towering over the forest floor like giant wooden pillars capped with an umbrella of dense green foliage. Here the sun could no longer be seen, and were it not for the small breaks in the forest canopy from time to time, they would have been plunged into complete obscurity, wandering in the darkness.

The four soldiers took up positions in the front and back of the procession looking warily from right to left. It took Brendon a few minutes for his eyes to adjust to the shadows of the giant timbers. The trail was wide and there were paving stones visible at times, but years of neglect had covered the path with dirt and fallen needles. All around them the sounds of the forest hinted to the abundant wildlife. Amongst the tall stately trees and bordering the path were countless wildflowers that managed to sustain themselves with the small patches of sunlight that dappled here and there in this serene woodland setting. The slight stirring of a crisp breeze would shift the light patterns and swirl them around in a surreal living kaleidoscope of white and green light. Again, Brendon was enchanted by the magnificence of this strange land.

Hours went by as the group marched through the woods. Donovan was tired, and every so often his captor would have to push him forward to keep up, which caused more flashes of anger in Conall's eyes. Brendon was grateful that, to this point, he had been able to keep his cool. Up to now they had been treated well, except, of course, for Mr. Dabir, and it would do them no good to try and fight. They were only three children and an old man. Running cross country had taught him that sometimes slow and steady wins the race, and so he waited for the right time to try and escape from his captors. Only he wouldn't leave the others behind, he thought ruefully of Kiwidinok.

***

At first Kiwidinok had flown high above the island, keeping an eye on his friends from above. Mr. Dabir had told him that the shillelagh could not fall into the hands of the Naga, and that he would need to take it and use the shift magic to carry it away. Reluctantly, he had complied, but now he needed to find a way to rescue the boys and free Farzan Dabir. Farzan was a good friend, and without his knowledge of the history of Faer Ri, they would not survive long. The boys, those poor boys, would be difficult to save, but he would not leave them to a life of captivity. Who knew what purpose these strange men had in mind for them? And then there was the matter of the Prophecy, not that he was as convinced as Farzan that these boys were the "foretold". But either way, he would not fail them.

Just before the group had entered the forest he had shifted into a tree squirrel, allowing him mobility and stealth among the dense woodland. This way he could listen to them and keep an eye on the children while he came up with a plan. It would be dangerous for him to try and free the captives by himself. The snake men (he believed them to be the Naga referred to in the tales he had heard about Faer Ri) could easily kill any one of them before he managed to free all of them. He needed to find a distraction; a large animal or other diversion that might allow him the time needed to free Mr. Dabir. The two of them could then free the children, that is, if Mr. Dabir could summon the weather. Interestingly, the Naga had gagged him, incorrectly assuming that a magi used his voice to control the weather. Much like a shaman, he would only need to will it into being.

However, in the moment they had allowed themselves to be taken by the reapers and transported to this world, he had felt a change in Mr. Dabir, as if he were not "connected." Perhaps his injury was preventing him from concentrating. Regardless, Kiwidinok knew that he needed to find an answer soon. When the Naga stopped to feed the children, he had been in a shifted form, and therefore was able to overhear and comprehend their plans to deliver the prisoners to a larger group a day's march into the forest. At that point the children would be sent down river to a sea port where a ship would take them to the heart of the Naga Empire. Mr. Dabir and the other adults recently captured would be sold as slaves to the sagittaries. Divided thus, it would be much more difficult to free them. No, he thought, he needed to act now.

Kiwidinok drew himself away from the path and shimmered into his human form. It was difficult to perform two magics at once, and he needed to concentrate to accomplish his next task. He knelt and dug his fingers into the rich fertile soil of the forest bed. Closing his eyes, he reached out with his thoughts, connecting himself to the spirits of all living creatures within several miles. He felt a plethora of wildlife and insects, but nothing so large as a badger. He extended his reach even further, nearly exhausting his abilities, when he felt them: a fair sized group of creatures, maybe fifteen or sixteen of them, due east. They did not seem very large, but perhaps they would suffice as a distraction if he could herd them towards his friends.

Changing into a raven, Kiwidinok flew towards the direction of the creatures. As he approached the group he lighted on a nearby elm branch and observed. These weren't animals, as he had first suspected, rather they seemed to be diminutive men. He had never before felt this life essence and was intrigued by them. Thinking quickly about what he had learned about the land of Faer Ri, he deduced that these must be gnomes. But from what he knew of gnomes, they were a peaceful race. Stories passed down to him by his grandfather described them as intelligent and resourceful. Supposedly they had lived harmoniously with the aesir, and when the aelfen people had escaped the land, several tribes of gnomes had followed. Plenty of "fairy" tales include stories of the little people, typically portrayed as outlandish and silly. However, his grandfather had taught him that they were a noble race, good at heart and trustworthy.

These gnomes looked a little different than those he had imagined. For one thing they did not look very benevolent. They were dressed for combat, with dark studded leather gambesons and thick leather helms. They carried an assortment of shields and weapons, but the blades had been covered in moss and dirt to prevent the metal from reflecting. This was no mere "outing"; this was a hunting party. Benevolent or not, these gnomes looked as though they expected trouble.

He waited for them to approach before shimmering into his human form. Surely, they would recognize the shift magic and see him as one of the aesir their people had once trusted. Holding aloft the shillelagh, he hoped they would be able to understand him. Curiously the shillelagh glowed green for a moment in his hands and then returned to normal. Ignoring the strange glow, he decided to do his best to sound like a noble warrior from a play he had once seen.

"Behold the Blackthorn Shillelagh of Caedmon Anluan," he cried out, "All who would call him friend come now and save his children, the last of the Druidae! Come, for they march . . . nigh . . . unto this very glade bound and shackled and without hope of rescue! Er . . . Come and free the 'Hope of the Aesir'!"

They looked at him in bewilderment. Did they even understand him? What language would they speak and how would he be able to communicate with them if they didn't know English? He had tried his best to imitate the formal speech of Mr. Dabir, but it appeared to have not taken effect. The gnomes eyed him suspiciously and began to pull even more weapons from their sheaths. This wasn't going as well as he thought it would. The largest of them stepped forward. Like the others he was dressed for combat, and carried a large cudgel of sorts. There was something regal about his mannerisms and Kiwidinok assumed this must be their leader.

He directed his words the gnome that had stepped forward, this time without embellishment, "Please, friend, if I may call you such. I am a shaman, as you have witnessed, and I need you and your men to help me free my companions."

"Yer friends are in trouble and you be wanting our help?" asked the large gnome who had taken his place in front of the group. His voice was deep and gruff, and the words that Kiwidinok heard didn't quite match those coming from his lips. It seemed as though he spoke with an Irish brogue, only somehow not the quite the same. Almost like a foreign movie that had been dubbed.

"Yes," replied Kiwidinok relieved that the man had understood.

"Am I to assume that th' Naga have taken them?" the leader asked again.

"Bald guys with tattoos and soldiers with scaly armor?" asked Kiwidinok. The gnome nodded and Kiwidinok continued, "Yes. About seven altogether."

The leader thought for a moment while his men began to spread out and take up defensive positions. "You appear to be an aelfen shaman. Are you one of Bidzil's servants or did He-lush-Ka send you?" he asked.

"I know not these people whom you have named. But I am a descendant of the aelfen shamans who passed through the realmbridge. My name is Kiwidinok, and I am alone, save for my friends who have been captured." Again, he tried to sound formal, assuming it would make him sound more credible.

"You say you have come through th' realmbridge? Then you would have been taken by th' reapers and woken up in chains. How is it that you have escaped?" interjected a lean and muscular gnome standing to the left of the leader. He had a grim countenance and carried a staff with a curved half-moon blade at the tip.

"Did I not show you the Blackthorn Shillelagh? It is truly the same used by the High Warrior Bard himself, or so I am told. With it my companion and I were able to overcome the sorcery of the reapers and remain awake as we passed through the realmbridge. I escaped so that I might in turn free them," asserted Kiwidinok in a voice one would expect to hear during a Shakespearian festival.

The gnomes whispered to one another, and the leader spoke up again, "You mentioned children. 'Tis not often that th' reapers capture children, as they are not suitable for th' slave trade. Are they truly, as you have claimed, the last of th' Druidae?" he asked.

"I believe it to be so, or rather my friend does," he added softly. The gnomes looked at one another quizzically. It seems they didn't trust him. Then, fearing they would deny his request, he again assumed his natural voice, pleading with them. "Please. I need your help."

The leader retreated and spoke in hushed tones with his men. One of them shook his head emphatically, but a look from the others caused him to throw his hands in the air and walk away from the discussion. A moment later the leader returned to declare their intent.

"It just so happens that we are returning from a raid on a Naga outpost. th' fork-tongues killed two o' my men before they turned tail and ran. Perhaps this will help us to grieve our losses. Lead th' way, shaman."

Kiwidinok shimmered and took flight. He remained just ahead of the group to help guide them. With luck, they would get to the captives before they reached the river.

***

As the afternoon wore on, Brendon tried not to think about how tired his feet were by instead focusing on the armor of the man in front of him. Like those in the plaza it was a series of overlapping metal scales, like a fish or lizard. They seemed to be lightweight, and they made no sound as they moved up and down in fluid motion. They were composed of a sort of greenish metal, much like aged copper that you sometimes would see on the roofs of old buildings back home. The soldier's entire body was covered with the interlocking scales, while large breastplates and shoulder plates covered the torso and upper arms. Around the waste they wore a leather girdle along with leather gloves and boots protecting the extremities. A domed helmet of a bright gold hue and a pointed top along with the same metallic green scales draped from its base protected his head and neck. It would be difficult to land a blow without hitting some sort of armor.

Just then the soldier stopped, and the rest of the group stopped with him. The forest had grown quiet, almost eerie. Brendon looked around but saw and heard nothing. The soldiers motioned to each other and the tattooed men pulled Mr. Dabir and the boys to the ground while standing over them to protect them or prevent escape. Above them a raven cried. The men looked up at the bird and at that moment a dull flash of metal gleamed from beneath the undergrowth and burst through the brambles towards the first soldier in line. He drew his sword but was met with a flurry of spinning knives that bit deep into his armor, penetrating the metal and ending his life in the blink of an eye. Standing over his "once captor" was a small man, perfect in proportion but only waste high to an average adult. Without pausing, the short man dressed in dark leathers and draped in moss launched himself at the next soldier.

Looking back towards his brothers Brendon saw an army of child-sized warriors hacking and slashing with a ferocity that caused the armed soldiers and tattooed men to drop their weapons only to have their lives forfeit before they could plead for mercy. Brendon quickly covered his brothers' eyes to shield them from the scene, but out of the corner of his eye he saw the man nearest him fall to the ground with a blank stare on his face, his hand clutching a wound at his side until he shuddered one final time and became still. Only then did Brendon shut his eyes, trying to banish away the brutal scene he had just witnessed.

In moments the ambush was over, and Brendon's hands and neck were being loosed. A powerfully built warrior, no taller than Brendon, walked up to Mr. Dabir and spoke in that strange language, to which Mr. Dabir replied as though it were of no consequence. Had he known what they were saying all along? Avoiding the bodies lying around them the boys walked towards Mr. Dabir.

"Mr. Dabir," Brendon coughed and spit as he tried to get the bits of rag out of his mouth, "What's going on? Who are these people? Why didn't you tell me you could speak their language? Why. . ." He stopped mid-sentence as a black raven flew from the canopy above and shimmered into Kiwidinok.

"One question at a time, young Druidae," he said smiling.

Six

Kiwidinok took the boys further on down the path away from the fallen soldiers and tattooed men, while their rescuers did their best to conceal the remains. Brendon had questions he wanted answered, but waited to ask realizing that it would be less traumatic for his brothers if they did not have to continue to see the dead bodies. Brendon himself did not want to look.

Kiwidinok held the twisted cane that had once belonged to Mr. Dabir. "We will answer your questions, but first, take hold of this . . . all of you. It's yours after all." He held out the shillelagh that had belonged to their grandfather. Begrudgingly, he and his brothers took the twisted blackthorn stick in their hands and instantly Brendon felt a connection—a connection to all the world around him. An emerald light surrounded the shaft. He felt alive and full of life. His despair waned, and his hopes flourished. He felt . . . power, power to do anything he wished, know anything he wished to know, do anything he wished to do. The sensation faded and he and his brothers released the shillelagh. Brendon lowered his arm and turned towards Mr. Dabir and the leader of their rescuers.

"And these younglings really are th' last o' th' Druidae?" asked the leader. Brendon blinked in amazement as he realized he had understood the man. Had the shillelagh done this for him? Then, as if waking from a dream, he noticed for the first time that all the voices her heard were speaking English. No, that's not it, their mouths were moving differently and he could almost hear a second language being spoken at the same time. He was merely hearing them in English, the other language too muffled and subtle to make out. The shillelagh must have allowed Mr. Dabir and

Kiwidinok to communicate with their rescuers as well. He looked after his brothers, checking to see if they were alright, while Mr. Dabir and Kiwidinok spoke to a man who seemed to be the leader of the band of diminutive fighters.

They were led down the trail in the same direction they had been headed for another few hundred yards. Mr. Dabir continued to talk with the leader. Stopping for a moment under a small group of pines, they were offered water. Brendon drank deeply before returning his attention to the conversation between the gruff warrior and Mr. Dabir.

"Yes, sadly they are the last of the Anluan bloodline. And they bear his blackthorn shillelagh. I believe they have returned to fulfill prophecy, only much sooner than expected," explained Mr. Dabir. What did he mean by prophecy? Mr. Dabir noticed him listening and changed the subject, "Brendon, allow me to introduce Cian Torin, our gracious liberator and leader of the gnomes of Vloornhaven Glenn." The leader bowed slightly. "Over there, carrying the half-moon staff is his oldest son, Quinlan. And there, talking with the older gnome is his younger son, Girvan," said Mr. Dabir indicating the two gnomes who stood a few feet behind them.

Another gnome, larger than the others, made his way towards the company having finished placing leafy tree branches on the fallen enemies. It was the same man who had taken out Brendon's captor with the flashing twin knives. He walked up to Cian Torin and whispered something in his ear. Cian Torin nodded as the man walked away, and then looked up at Brendon.

"That be Risteard, my lieutenant and champion," said Cian Torin, "He has been my friend since childhood, and there be no greater warrior in th' entire gnome race. He reports that these men bear the markings of the royal house of Amararaja, the Naganese Emperor. He believes you boys were to be delivered directly to th‘ palace. If this be true, they will be searching for us.”

“I believe I can confirm his suspicions,” chimed in Kiwidinok, “I overheard the Naga discussing sending the boys toward the sea port at rivers end, while Farzan here would become a slave for the sagittaries,” he said indicating Mr. Dabir.

“What are sagittaries? And what’s this about Naga and Emperor Amar-whatever? Please, tell me what’s going on. I don’t understand any of this,” pleaded Brendon. His brothers walked up and stood next to him.

Mr. Dabir looked at Brendon with compassion in his eyes. “You deserve to know everything, but there just isn’t time,” he said with sadness. Then, as if reconsidering, “Perhaps I can just shed a little light on the situation before we have to move on, enough to resolve your immediate concerns. Brendon, you and your brothers are the last of the Druidae, as you have no doubt overheard. And yes, there is a prophecy given to the Magus Supreme in ancient days, before the exodus of the aesir, which speaks of the return of the Druidae and the fall of the oppressors. It also mentions that magic lost will be found again, and that the finding will destroy the aesir, only to give birth to a new age and the death of the old world. It’s very cryptic, as prophecies often are, but the first portion is what we believe you are to fulfill—the return of the Druidae and the fall of the oppressors.

“For thousands of years the aelfen people desired to return to this world, but their magic users could not duplicate the process, even when all the stones were exact in size and material to this world—a labor that took decades to create. Those who remained behind on this side to guard their escape were to seal the realmbridge from this side in order to protect them from the invaders. Sadly, they failed in the attempt. For centuries, raiding parties and Naga armies came through the gate. Creatures both great and powerful were sent through to hunt and devour the aelfen people. Eventually the elders chose to abandon their attempts to return, fearing that it would mean inevitable death and a premature end to the Druidae lines. After some time, the attacks stopped, only to be replaced by reapers—who seemed not to kill but to capture, or at least that is what those who practice the shift magic claimed. By then the aelfen race had mixed with the humans of earth, and much of the teachings and secrets were lost. For the Chaldees and their Magi, the prophecy was merely a hope to be handed down from generation to generation.

"When I agreed to watch over your family, I did not realize then that I would see the prophecy come true. Neither Kiwidinok nor I knew how we would get you here in the first place. By taking you, the reapers have brought you to the one place that we needed you to be, albeit earlier than we had wanted. We had hoped for you all to be of age and to have been trained. But in its own way and time, the prophecy has been fulfilled. Once you were taken, we decided to let the reapers take us so that we could protect you."

"And our parents?" asked Conall, "Were they part of your plan?"

Mr. Dabir thought for a moment and chose his words carefully. "Your parents were not aware of your aelfin lineage or theirs, and we had not yet discussed how we would convince them to allow you to train. It appears they were taken when you were targeted, merely because they were in the wrong place at the wrong time. Your father, apparently, never exhibited any signs of his magical heritage, so he would not have been considered a threat. Cian Torin has informed us that many adults who are taken from our world are sent to work as slaves for the sagittaries, a race of creatures that are part lion, part human. According to the histories passed down from the magi, they were neutral in the war between the aesir and the Naga Empire. But from what Cian Torin tells me they seem to have created some sort of trade agreement with the Naga. For what purpose they do not know, but the sagittary are no longer neutral."

"There was a large group o' people being held at th' outpost we attacked," offered Cian Torin, "When th' 'snakes' ran from us they took their captives with 'em. We have done our best to free slaves in the past, but we were unable to do so this time. He-lush-Ka's camp has a few o' yer people, as he and his warriors also fight to free captives. Perhaps he has rescued yer parents."

"How can you be sure? They could be with the group that you let get away!" snapped Conall. His temper was finally getting the best of him.

"Aye, they could be," replied Cian Torin, "I am truly sorry for yer loss. If they have been taken by th' sagittaries, we can do nothing. We are too few, and they are too powerful. We can only hope that He-lush-Ka has found them. We were headed to his camp for supplies before meeting with Kiwidinok. 'Tis a three-day trek, but we will be safe there. He-lush-Ka leads the last of the aesir shaman, though they be but a few. We could take you with us."

"I am afraid that we cannot do that," answered Mr. Dabir, "We must follow the prophecy and train the boys in the ways of the Druidae. It is the only way we can end the oppression of the Naga. If we go with you we put them at risk of being discovered."

"We don't care about your prophecy! We just want our parents back!" cried Conall.

"He's right. All this talk of magic is more than we can deal with at the moment," said Brendon. "We need to figure out where my parents have gone and how we can get them back. That is our only priority. We need to find them and return home."

There was silence as all the group stared at Brendon. He felt a bit sheepish, and wondered if he had offended them.

"Perhaps Bidzil would know," offered young Girvan, smallest of the gnome hunting party. The old bearded gnome with whom he had been speaking looked at him crossly.

"Who is Bidzil?" asked Kiwidinok.

"A powerful magic-user, and no friend to the Naga. An aesir most assuredly, but he travels with huldrefolk and firbolg, and although He-lush-Ka respects him, he is not welcome in the camp. But Bidzil does have ways of knowing things, and he often strikes out at the Naga. Some say that he is a great magi, others a shaman. Some even say he is a Warrior Bard, foolish as that may be. We have not seen him for years, but we do see signs of his passing through th' woods—trees repaired, rivers diverted. It may be that he can help you find yer parents," continued Girvan.

"You say too much, young leprechaun! You only suggest him because you desire his help in increasing your magic!" scolded the older gnome. His cheeks flushed, and he turned to Cian Torin, "I apologize, my Lord. I have only concern for yer son's safety."

Cian Torin frowned. He looked at his sons and then at Brendon and his brothers. Stepping away from the group he consulted with Risteard. Brendon wondered what the old gnome meant by calling Girvan 'leprechaun.' Surely, he didn't mean the kind that hops around on cereal boxes and throws marshmallows.

Most Irish fairy tales made them out to be silly and mischievous, not to mention much smaller. These gnomes were somber and stout of heart.

It must have been mid-afternoon by now, Brendon thought looking up at the light filtering through the trees. He wasn't as cold as before but when the sun went down it would be much cooler. Then, as he looked at his brothers, it dawned on him that they must be worse off than he was. When they had left their home, they hadn't time to grab a jacket, and only wore jeans and a t-shirt they had worn to school. Brendon felt awful for being self-centered.

"Conall, Donny, are you guys doing alright? Are you cold?" he asked.

Donovan shook his head and Conall replied, "I'm fine." Brendon didn't believe him.

Glancing back at the band of hunters he watched as they cleaned their weapons and repositioned their packs. The older gnome with the thin gray beard was whispering in a stern voice to the king's son…Girvan, was it? Other than that, the rest of the men were silent, their eyes scanning the path in both directions, wary of Naga patrols.

Eventually Cian Torin returned to the group. "I have decided we will help the young boys find their parents. But we must move with haste, and divide our forces. My son Quinlan will take Kiwidinok and travel south. They will attempt to catch up with th' slaves and soldiers from th' outpost. If they have yer parents perhaps they will be able to sneak in at night and free them. If they use stealth and speed, they may be able to rescue them in time.

"Risteard and Girvan will head towards th' wilds of Fenian Chase at th' northern end of Skregmore Reeks in search of Bidzil.

If they can find him, and he knows anything, they can report back to us at Vloorhaven Glen. Meanwhile Mr. Dabir and th‘ children will pass through He-lush-Ka's camp with me and th‘ rest of my men to gather supplies. We can check for their parents and then make our way to Vloorhaven Glen as well."

"How will Kiwidinok and Quinlan recognize our parents?" asked Brendon.

"And how can we train the boys if we are enmeshed in a rebel camp that's on the run from enemy patrols?" asked Mr. Dabir.

The older gnome with a beard also looked as though he wanted to say something, but a glare from Cian Torin held his tongue in check.

"Alright," responded Cian Torin, "Conall, is it?" Conall looked at him and nodded slowly. "You will go with Kiwidinok and Quinlan in order to identify yer parents. Donovan will come with us to th‘ camp, and we can look for a suitable place for you to train him once we find his parents. Brendon, you will go with Risteard and Girvan, my younger son who is about yer age. And yes, Scioldmed, you will go as well." The old gnome did his best to hide a relieved smile.

Mr. Dabir began to protest, stating that this plan would be placing the boys in harm's way, but Cian Torin pointed out that they would be in danger regardless of their destination—no place was truly safe anymore. And before Mr. Dabir could say anything more on the subject Cian Torin called for his men to distribute supplies and packs. In moments the parties were equipped, and Brendon was saying goodbye to his brothers. It happened so fast, Brendon could hardly object. But he felt as though he had no choice but to trust his newfound companions.

"Conall, pay attention and listen to Kiwidinok. Do what he says and don't cause trouble. Donovan, you will be OK. Mr. Dabir will look after you; it sounds like you will have several shaman to protect you."

"What about you, Brendon?" came Donovan's small voice. "Who's gonna look after you?" he asked.

"Don't worry," Brendon whispered jerking his thumb over his shoulder at the three gnomes that he was to follow, "I've got 'Mini-Muscles' and 'Mr. Happy' with me. I'll be fine," he quipped referring to Risteard and Scioldmed respectively. They gave each other a hug, and then separated for what they hoped would only be for a short while. Mr. Dabir offered the shillelagh to Brendon.

"I know you don't want it, but it belongs with you," Mr. Dabir urged. "It may even help you in your search for Bidzil," he added. Brendon looked at the gnarled old walking stick. He didn't know the first thing about it, but he felt that he should accept it regardless.

"Thank you," he murmured. With another quick glance at his brothers, and a reassuring nod from Kiwidinok, he turned and followed Risteard.

Seven

The first thing Brendon noticed about his new companions was how very unalike they were. Risteard had a wide, muscular build, short cropped blonde hair with a small tuft of a beard, and was very soft spoken. His quiet nature made him seem distant and aloof. On the other hand, Scioldmed was older, smaller, and much thinner. He had wisps of hair on the top of his head (which was usually covered by a brown leather cap) and a long thin beard that looked more like a cobweb that had somehow become attached to his chin. Scioldmed had an opinion on everything, and chose to express his opinion whether or not it was solicited. Risteard continuously reminded him of the need for stealth, which would cause him to restrain himself, but only for a moment. Girvan, however, was a little of both. He was young and well-built, but smaller in stature. Whereas Risteard came up to Brendon's chin, Girvan and Scioldmed came only up to his chest. Like Scioldmed, he was more talkative, but not overly so, and certainly not as annoying.

Their attire was also different. Risteard wore a leather gambeson, with hundreds of metal rings that interlocked with each other and covered his torso. The metal seemed to be a dark iron alloy, and was fastened tight to the leather in order to prevent them from jingling. His legs were covered in thick leather as well, with heavy boots hobnailed with a small black spike on each toe. His arms were adorned with black metal braces. He carried two long knives at his waist and one small knife in his boot. In contrast, Scioldmed wore only his leather cap as protection. His long brown tunic, ornamented with dark green scroll work on the cuffs and hem, flowed to the ground where small leather boots would occasionally peak out as he walked. Girvan seemed to be an amalgamation of both as he wore a black leather vest with dark iron studs, and a short tunic underneath that reached just below his knees, leather breeches covering his legs. He too carried a knife in his dark black boots, but never seemed to use it.

Brendon, still wearing his blue and white track suit, used the shillelagh as a walking stick in order to keep pace with the shorter (but much heartier) gnomes, and gradually moved himself closer to Girvan. He hoped to be able to gather more information about where they were, where they were going, and a little about gnomes in general. Girvan was happy to comply.

"This region is known as the woods of Talamh Glas, where th' aelfin people once lived. Its chief city was Aelfheim, where you entered through the realmbridge. When th' Naga drove th' aesir from the realm, they retained th' woodland as a 'protectorate' of their empire, though few Naga choose to live here these days. For years after th' exodus, those of the Druidae, Saami, and Chaldees who had chosen to stay behind sent their bards, magi, and shaman into th' city in an attempt to close th' realmbridge. Those who were not killed or captured either escaped through th' realmbridge or hid in th' forests, only to be hunted down like wild animals. It is believed that th' last of th' Saami shaman fight with He-lush-Ka to free those captured by th' Naga. There are rumors of Chaldean magi living on an island in th' western sea, but we have had no contact with them. The Druidae, as you have been told, are no more. That is, until you arrived," explained Girvan.

"And who is this Bidzil? Is he a shaman? Why does he not fight with He-lush-Ka and the others?" asked Brendon.

"Because he is a savage!" shouted Scioldmed, "He associates with huldrefolk and lives in th' wild forests northeast of the woodland. Those who have seen him claim he is aelfin in appearance, only wild and hairy, with long nails and sharp teeth. His magic is like nothing they have seen. I for one do not think he is aelfin, rather some supernatural creature of the forest. Stories of his exploits go back for centuries—much longer than an aelfin lifespan. Some say he is a spirit, a ghost of some dead warrior. Others tell of a mournful cry that wracks their soul and causes th' very earth to shake. This is th' one we seek out, if he exists. Mark my words, it would be better that we left him alone."

"Those descriptions become more terrible with each telling. And besides, surely a gifted leprechaun like yourself isn't afraid of a little magic," quipped Risteard, who had barely spoken since they had departed.

Flustered, Scioldmed sputtered, "It is not my safety for which I am concerned . . . Girvan is still an apprentice, and has not yet mastered th' basics of gnomish magic. It is a risk to endanger th' Cian's son on such a journey, unproven as he is."

"Where I come from we have stories of leprechauns," said Brendon, quickly changing the subject. "They are supposed to play tricks on humans and have pots of gold which they hide at the end of rainbows."

The three gnomes stopped and turned to look at Brendon. They stared at him with blank looks on their faces. "Do yer people not know that rainbows are caused by a refraction of light through tiny drops of water in th' atmosphere?" asked Girvan.

"Well, yes. But leprechauns are mythical creatures, so they can do the impossible in the fairy tales I have heard," responded Brendon. This seemed to anger Scioldmed.

"Do I look like a myth?!" he asked. "Am I not standing here in front of you? You discredit th' gnome race by mocking those fortunate enough to be born leprechaun. 'Tis a rare and wonderful gift that is only bestowed by nature once every generation. Girvan has spent many years learning to use his gift, and when I am dead he will take my place as th' clan leprechaun. We don't use our magic to 'play tricks', and we certainly don't bury our treasures with a rainbow as a marker!"

"Come along, Scioldmed. th' boy did not mean to insult," said Risteard. The group resumed their march, and Brendon fell silent, obviously having put his foot in his mouth.

As the sun began to fall, the travelers looked for a place to make camp. Brendon was exhausted and hungry; having not eaten since his Naga captors had fed him that morning. He had wanted to tell his gnome escorts he was hungry, but had been afraid to offend them further. Risteard had run ahead of the group to scout out a good site, so it was just Girvan, Scioldmed, and himself. Girvan glanced at him several times in the last few hours, and Brendon got the impression that he had wanted to say something but was resisting out of respect for his tutor. If there was something positive that came out of his faux pas, it was the silence of Scioldmed for an entire afternoon. It was almost worth it.

Risteard returned at a quick jog. "There's a small stream up ahead and a clearing in which we can rest for th' night," he said to the group, and then turned and led them to the indicated camp site. They were too close to the Naga outposts for a fire, but the dried meat and fruit they offered Brendon was very tasty and renewed his energy. Unlike the dried fruit from the Naga, this was succulent and sweet, and tasted like a chewy strawberry. The meat was savory and not too tough. Brendon wasn't a fan of beef jerky, but this was tender and really “hit the spot”. He had hoped to probe Girvan for more information, but as he rested between the roots of the large tree he felt his body give in to fatigue, sleep overcoming his desire for more answers.

***

Brendon awoke to the sound of a slight popping noise. His eyelids fluttered awake to see three mushrooms rise from the forest bed to hover a few feet off the ground. He turned to see Girvan staring intently at the mushrooms as they slowly made their way towards his outstretched hands. Scioldmed was whispering instruction to him so as not to break his concentration. Within a few moments the mushrooms reached his hands and he relaxed as they fell into his palms.

“Well done, young Girvan. Those appear to be very large and tasty mushrooms,” commented Scioldmed. Brendon thought to himself that it would have been easier simply to pick the mushrooms, but refrained from saying anything, having learned his lesson from the day before. Gnomes, it seemed, were very easily offended. As he got up, Girvan noticed him stirring and closed his fingers around the mushrooms as if to hide them from view. Perhaps he was embarrassed that years of practice resulted in the power of mushroom picking, Brendon thought, but then reminded himself that it was certainly more than he could do.

Picking up the shillelagh he walked over to the stream to get a drink. The stream was clean and pure . . . and very cold, so much so that it was necessary to drink in short sips in order to avoid a “brain freeze,” something he had learned a little too late the night before. Setting his shillelagh down, he used both hands to brace himself so that he could sip directly from the stream, since his hands were fairly dirty and he didn’t like the idea of drinking out of them. His thirst was nearly slated when he noticed a soft green light glowing at his side. He turned to see the shaft of the shillelagh pulsing rapidly. It had never done that for him before, and he couldn't imagine what it meant now.

Confused, he leaned back over the water to finish his drink when he heard a loud hissing sound from behind him. Slowly turning his head, he saw a large black and orange snake, mouth open, fangs glistening as venom dripped along the sharp pearly daggers. It crouched, poised to strike, and Brendon froze. The shillelagh was at his side, but he doubted he could bring it up and swing it before the snake bit him. Fear and doubt overcame him and inwardly he screamed to move or do something, but he could not. Just then, the snake launched itself at Brendon, who shut his eyes and yelled.

Two things happened almost at the same moment; first, the serpent stopped in mid-strike, suspended as if held by invisible ropes, and then it shuttered and writhed in the air until finally collapsing to the ground in a twisted heap of smoldering black and orange scales.

Astonished, Brendon looked around to find Scioldmed grasping the air with his hands and looking equally as shocked as Brendon. The old leprechaun relaxed and looked at Brendon with surprise, and a little excitement. "What just happened?" he asked.

"You saved me with some awesome 'mind trick' of yours. That was so cool! Thank you for saving my life, I'm really sorry about what I said yesterday." He looked at the serpent, twisted and broken on the ground before him. It was several feet long, and had a large diamond-shaped head much like a cobra he had once seen on television, except for the odd coloring. His heart pounded with adrenaline, fear mixed with amazement. After a moment he got up and ran over to where Girvan had been practicing and told him what had happened. Scioldmed just stared at Brendon as he left. In moments Risteard returned from scouting ahead and, noticing the look of bewilderment on Scioldmed's face and the dead snake lying near the stream, asked him what had happened.

"Such power . . . and with his voice alone," explained Scioldmed looking at the snake. "I had merely held th' creature in place to prevent him from harming our young… Druidae—but then his voice—'twas beautiful and terrible all at once. It crushed th' life out o' th' serpent while burning it from within," he paused and then turned to face Risteard. "He has no idea of what he has done, and what more, he has no idea of what he is capable of doing."

"All th' more reason to find Bidzil quickly. Then we can return him to th' tutelage of Mr. Dabir," responded Risteard. They walked back to camp and prepared themselves for the day's trek, while Brendon continued to describe Scioldmed's heroism to Girvan. In short time they were packed and on their way northward.

Eight

At first Conall was slightly offended when Quinlan had offered to carry both of their gear packs, but after an hour of running, he was grateful that he had not let pride get the better of him. Unlike the other groups, Conall, Quinlan, and Kiwidinok were not hampered by having to pick their trails through the dense forest. Instead they followed the wide path that led back to the outpost the gnomes had attacked the day prior. They were far enough away that stealth was not a major concern, but speed was imperative.

As Quinlan explained before they left, they needed to reach the slaves and their captors before they entered into the territory belonging to the Sphinx Dynasty. Once there, the captives would not stand a chance of escaping from the army of sagittaries that guard the realm. Conall still looked uncertain about what they were but Quinlan, noticing his confusion, explained that a sphinx was part lion, part human. A sagittary was like a sphinx, only instead of just a human head, a sagittary had a human torso and arms as well as the body of a lion. It reminded Conall of a centaur he had seen in a movie, only with claws instead of hooves. A shaman, a gnome, and a boy would be mere annoyances to a powerful adversary like that.

After another hour of running they stopped for a brief moment to rest and eat some dried fruit. Conall had never been much of a runner, but his dad had made him run with Brendon every day this past summer in order to stay in shape and prepare him for basketball season. It was also safer to have them run together.

Conall had hated it, but now he was thankful that he had spent so much time training—he would not have been able to keep up otherwise, and they needed him to identify his parents. He would not let them down.

Kiwidinok bent down to the earth and closed his eyes, employing his ability to reach out and locate life forms. A moment later he opened them and looked at Quinlan. "There are no life forms large enough to be human or naga for several miles. We are safe to continue running," he stated.

Quinlan shrugged on the gear packs and helped Conall to his feet. Reluctantly he complied and began to run again. The key was to concentrate on something else in order not to feel the fatigue and boredom. He decided to think about Kiwidinok and his ability to change forms. At first, he had been frightened to see a bear emerging from his room back home, but now it was just plain awesome. As he ran he wondered how Kiwidinok did it, and if it was something that could be learned. Conall decided he would ask him about it when they had a chance to talk. For now, he just focused on getting closer to his parents, one step at a time.

***

Throughout the rest of the day the small group ran, taking breaks when they could. The dark pine forest they had first entered was now a mixture of broad leafy trees as well as pines and shrub. They varied in height and were not nearly as tall as the redwood giants, but they were still quite dense and without the path they would not have been able to move so quickly.

By nightfall Conall's legs were so sore they felt numb, and his feet had blisters. He sat by a large rock a short way off the path they had been running on while Kiwidinok scouted the outpost a few leagues ahead. Quinlan gathered pine needles together in order to create some ground cover to soften the earth underneath them, and to insulate them from the chill of nightfall.

Quinlan was not the biggest of the gnomes he met that day, but he certainly seemed the most fit. Though smaller in features, he was muscular and lithe. He wore less armor than the other gnomes had, dressed only in a leather tunic, with a black metal band of chainmail that circled his neck and shoulders. His arms were bare, and his leather breeches were tucked neatly into his boots. He carried a small knife and a strange spear with a half-moon blade on one end, and a conical greenish gray stone on the butt. Conall had watched him spin his half-moon spear during the skirmish, and marveled at the speed and athleticism of this diminutive warrior. Quinlan noticed him staring and looked at him directly.

"I like your spear," Conall said somewhat sheepishly, "It's cool."

Quinlan glanced at the half moon spear with a bewildered expression on his face. "I don't see that its temperature is any colder than that o' another weapon."

Conall smiled, recognizing his use of slang as a language gaffe. "I meant to say that it is very . . . inspiring to watch you use it."

"Perhaps I could teach you to use it, sometime," he said, and then went about the business of re-packing the gear in case they needed to move out at a moment's notice. Conall thought to himself that if they were not in a dangerous world, chasing dangerous people to rescue his parents, this would be an awesome adventure. Way better than a video game, only with a lot more permanent results.

Conall tucked his hands underneath his arms and brought his knees up to his chest. The pine needles were poking him through his shirt, but they did seem to block the chill from the wet forest floor beneath them. Noticing his posture, Quinlan removed a tunic from his pack and draped it over Conall's shoulders.

"It is too small to wear, but it will help keep you warm. I would build a fire, but it be not wise to advertise our location," he explained kindly. Conall nodded but was already drifting to sleep despite the chill.

Sometime in the middle of the night, or perhaps early the next morning, Kiwidinok returned to the camp, out of breath and pointing back the way he came. Conall was asleep but stirred when he heard the old man's voice. "The barge just left, there were people on it, but it is too dark to make out faces, even if I could get you close enough to the outpost to spot them. I followed them for a few miles to make sure they had prisoners. It is a slow-moving barge, however, and we should be able to catch up. The river curves and doubles around on itself, from what I could see from the air, so we may even be able to get ahead of them. But first I need to rest." He sat down on a pile of pine needles and took a sip of water from the water pouch Quinlan offered him.

"Forgive me, shaman . . ." began Quinlan.

"Kiwi," interrupted Kiwidinok.

"Er . . . Kiwi," he continued, "But how can we manage to keep up with th‘ flow o' th‘ river. We would have to run without stopping. And th‘ boy, forgive me Conall, th‘ boy is just not able to do so. I am not sure I am able to do so."

"You are right. What we need is a horse," said Kiwidinok as he winked at Conall. A smile crept over Conall's face, not only because he understood Kiwi's plan, but also because he knew he would not have to run any longer.

***

The morning passed quickly into the afternoon, and this part of the forest was much warmer than the day before. The heat wasn't the only thing that changed; Conall now rethought his previous excitement about riding on horseback instead of running. His backside was painfully sore, and his legs hurt from trying to keep himself upright on Kiwidinok's equine form. Quinlan, who sometimes rode, sometimes ran ahead, seemed not to be phased in the least.

From time to time they stopped to allow Kiwidinok to switch forms and search the forest for the presence of the barge and its passengers. The river snaked around various bends in the Talamh Glas Woods, and in order to stay fairly close, they had needed to leave the path that followed alongside and meet up with it again as it swung lazily around various hills and valleys. It took time to pick their way around the undergrowth, but several game trails leading to the water's edge had proved valuable.

From Kiwidinok's last reading, it seemed the barge was making its way towards the edge of the woods, beyond which Kiwidinok could not see. He had seemed puzzled at that lack of life forms, and on this leg of the journey had galloped at a much faster pace, adding to the discomfort in Conall's thighs and rump.

For the past hour, the hunting party had continued without stopping for food or even water, pressing onward in an effort to overtake the barge. It was just before evening when they finally caught sight of it, tied to a dock at the end of a short pier. Soldiers in armor were milling around, while the tattooed men watched over the captives. Just beyond the dock the landscape changed dramatically. As if nature had suddenly given up, withered, and died, the forest abruptly ended, and a vast barren landscape began.

" th' Wastes of Magadesh. This is where th' Sphinx Dynasty begins. We would be wise to turn back, th' sagittaries kill those who trespass on their lands," said Quinlan in a fearful tone.

"Not without looking for my parents," Conall seethed. He had come all this way, they could at the very least try and take a look. Even if they could not be freed, knowing they were alive would be better than nothing. Perhaps there would be a way to free them in the future. But the first step was finding them, he thought to himself.

"Forgive me, young boy, but yer parents are lost," Quinlan stated matter-of-factly. "'Twas a fool's quest to begin with. Had we o'ertaken th' barge in th' forest, maybe we could have been successful. But this is th' port of Ramsebo, and there are saggitary guards watching th' river and th' border for intruders. We would not make it out alive. At best, we would be captured and taken along with th' other captives. At worst, we would be eaten."

Normally the prospect of being eaten would tend to detour a young boy, but in this instance, it did little to sway Conall from his mission. He felt his temper rising even though he knew he could do nothing against this trained warrior. "Fine, coward, you stay here while Kiwi and I go and see if they are here!"

Quinlan bristled at the word coward, and his face darkened with fury and contempt. But before he could respond Kiwidinok took Conall by the arm and started down the trail towards the port, "It is not wise to alienate our friends, young Conall. Keep your tongue in check."

They moved slowly and deliberately towards the small port city. "City" was a misnomer as it was mostly a collection of small buildings in and around the dock, most likely used for storage and other supplies. There was no market, no livestock, no crops. It appeared as though it were abandoned, but for the activity near the dock.

The buildings were meager in size and architecture, with wide spaces in between, so it would not offer much in the way of concealment. Having left the tree-line, they were now squatting behind some scrub brush, still several yards away from the water and the barge. Conall tried to make out the figures on the barge, but was still too far to see individual faces. They had to find a way to get closer.

Inching their way towards the nearest of the outbuildings, they arrived just as the sun began to set. The evening shadows would help conceal their arrival, so long as they kept the sun behind them and stayed low to the ground. The glare of the sun would prevent the soldiers from spotting them, and they tried to not stand high enough to cast much of a shadow as they moved quickly towards the embankment below the pier. From there Conall would have a good view of the occupants of the barge and they would know once and for all if his parents were on board.

Although nightfall brought cooler temperatures, the heat of the day had baked the soil around the pier into shards of clay as the water evaporated and left the hardened silt behind. Twice Conall slipped and nearly slid into the water, which surely would have alerted the guards. If not for Kiwidinok's quick action in catching him both times, they would have been discovered.

After laboring slowly and carefully they finally found themselves under the pier looking towards the dock that extended a few yards out into the river. It was dusk now, and the guards would have a difficult time seeing them hiding below the pier, but Conall would also have difficulty seeing the captives. He strained his eyes to catch a glimpse of the poor souls tied and bound on the deck of the barge. None of them seemed familiar—clothes, hair—nothing that would give the impression that these were his parents.

He looked for a long while, making sure to inspect every one of the captives. No, these were not his parents. A mixture of relief and newly discovered fear overcame him. If his parents weren't here, where were they? With that Kush or Kish guy Cian had mentioned? Were they still alive? How would they ever find them? Conall was overcome by emotion and stifled a sob in an effort not to cry out loud. Instead he emitted a sort of gasp that caused the soldiers on deck to start and look in his direction.

They remained perfectly still in an effort to not be spotted, but almost immediately the snake-like eyes of the guards landed on him and a commotion began as soldiers and guards alike tried to jump from the barge to the dock in an effort to capture this new quarry. They hurried back the way they came, forgoing the need for stealth and focusing on their escape. Behind him he heard a splash as guards jumped from the pier into the water and began to run towards them.

The ground continued to give way as Conall ran up the embankment and towards the forest. He used his hands to get a grip and heave himself up onto the path, Kiwidinok close behind him. Standing up he turned to run towards the spot where they left Quinlan when an enormous shape vaulted in front of him and he heard a deafening roar. He fell to the earth and looked to find the source of his challenge.

What he saw shocked him more than anything he had yet seen; there in front of him stood a man, only where his legs should have been the body of a powerful lion pawed at the earth. The creature held a large triton and a round buckler shield, and its fierce gaze told Conall he knew how to use them. It sneered as Kiwidinok ran at him, but his cold, calculating eyes never left Conall.

Kiwidinok shifted to the form of the Kodiak bear Conall had seen the day before, but halted his approach when he saw the point of the triton hovering inches above Conall's chest. Kiwidinok shifted again and the sagittary growled at him through gritted teeth. The guards from the barge caught up with the fugitives and bound them with cords.

It was all Conall's fault, he thought, if he had just been quiet they would not have noticed. And now Quinlan was right, they were as good as dead—either to be eaten, or sold as slaves. Conall didn't try to hold back his emotions now, and he cried out for help as tears flowed freely in between his breathless sobs. But no help came, and in this forsaken land, it never would . . .

Nine

Donovan Baird had always been the quietest of the Baird boys. He wasn't shy, not by any stretch of the imagination, but he wasn't talkative, unless you brought up the subject of football. His friends' parents would often jest that when giving him rides home they at first thought he couldn't speak, until somebody mentioned a game or statistic having to do with football, then you couldn't get him to shut up.

Although he had a lot of sports games for his gaming console, the one that got the most use was college football. And turning nine next summer, he would finally be able to join the pee-wee football league his brother Conall once played in. He couldn't wait to put on pads and push people around, his young bravado telling him he would be the greatest receiver of all time.

That bravado was absent here, in this strange place, with people he barely knew or didn't know at all. With his parents lost, Donovan felt alone and wondered if he would ever see his home again. Suddenly, football wasn't so important.

Cian Torin organized the group into three parties, one to scout ahead and one to act as the rear-guard, preventing any attack from enemies who might try and follow. The middle party contained himself, Mr. Dabir and Cian Torin. Mr. Dabir no longer carried that strange stick of his, having given it to Brendon. What did he say about it belonging to Grandpa Baird? Donovan couldn't remember, there was a lot he was still trying to figure out, so instead he concentrated on putting one foot in front of the other.

Cian Torin was a commanding figure. Though gruff in voice, he seemed kind-hearted and wise. His men were devoted to him, and his orders were carried out without question. He had a bulbous nose, but his beard and mustache were so thick it didn't seem out of place on his small head. He had blonde curls held in place by a bronze circlet that must have served as some sort of crown, as it had no defensive purpose and no other warrior in the party wore one. His dark leather armor had metal caps covering the shoulders, and black metal plates sewn into the leather covering his torso. His powerful arms were bare to the leather braces and gauntleted hands. He was otherwise covered in the same dark leather and carried his buckler shield in one hand, and a massive mace in the other. The mace had a ring of greenish gray stone around the end of the club, and Mr. Dabir kept eyeing it curiously.

Around mid-day they came to a stream, not quite big enough to require a boat, but deep, wide, and swift enough to make crossing difficult. Donovan sat down as the gnomes worked on creating a make-shift rope bridge. Cian Torin explained that the bridges made by the aesir were either in disrepair or were watched by patrols of Naga soldiers. A quick rope bridge would get them across and avoid a much longer hike down river to find an easier place to ford the stream. Donovan took the opportunity to eat a few pieces of dried fruit and drink some water while resting his feet.

One of the gnomes took a rope that was attached to a sort of bolo—three stones tied in leather—and threw it around a low hanging branch. He tied the other end off and pulled himself hand over hand across the gully. On the other side he began to unpack other ropes in his satchel. In short order two ropes were fastened to a tree on either side of the stream. The bottom rope was fairly thick for stepping, and the higher rope would provide the balance.

The gnomes sprinted across effortlessly, but then came Mr. Dabir. Taking off his tweed vest (why he still kept it Donovan did not know), and handing it to Cian Torin, he took the rope by both hands and slowly inched his way across the stream. Donovan could tell he was putting on a brave face, but his shaking hands and legs belied his calm appearance. He was quite a sight in his blue oxford and suit pants, his bow tie disheveled to one side, his thick mustache, short cropped beard, and bald head glistening with sweat. As his left foot reached the wet grass on the far bank, Mr. Dabir let out a breath and a look of relief washed over his face. Donovan decided that Mr. Dabir must not know how to swim, otherwise he would not have been so afraid.

"'Tis your turn, lad," said Cian Torin as he offered to help Donovan to his feet. Placing his right foot of the rope, he lifted his left foot off the ground. Immediately the rope began to sway back and forth, and Donovan gripped the upper rope with all his might in order not to fall off. The gnomes had made it look a lot easier than it was. As he shuffled his feet forward both ropes began to sway.

"Don't hang on to th' upper cord . . . put your weight on th' rope below you and use th' upper cord as balance," called out Cian Torin over the noise of the water below. Testing this technique, Donovan found that the ropes would not sway as much if he put his weight on the lower rope and just balanced against the higher one. After a few more steps he began to get a little more comfortable and looked up, away from his feet. By keeping his focus on the far embankment, he could keep his movements steady and calm.

At that moment out of the corner of his eye he thought he saw a beautiful white horse. He turned to look at the place where the horse should have been, and his foot slipped. Hanging onto the guide rope with his right hand he carefully placed his foot back on the heavier lower rope and swayed his body upright. He carefully began to cross again, wondering to himself where the horse had come from and where it had gone. After a few more steps—which seemed like an eternity—he finished crossing the stream.

Behind him Cian Torin vaulted onto the rope and, with a spryness that defied his larger frame, nimbly walked across the expanse.

"We nearly lost you young one," Cian said with a somber tone. "Why did you take your concentration off th' task?"

"I thought I saw something. A white horse," responded Donovan.

A hushed whisper and a look of fright appeared on the face of many gnome hunters. Cian Torin looked at the boy then glanced up river at the place Donovan had indicated.

"Listen to me boy. There are spirits in this land who would do you harm, just because it is their nature. When you are near water, do not be fooled by a Nykr or any of th' Nøkker for that matter."

Mr. Dabir was puzzled by this comment. "I'm not sure I am familiar with these terms," he said.

"A Nykr is a river horse, though like all Nøkker 'tis only a water spirit, not a real horse. They delight in leading people to their deaths by drowning. They then steal th' life essence from their victims. Very nasty business, th' Nøkker," explained Cian Torin.

As Cian Torin finished his warning the gnomes pulled at a thin cord that was tied with a series of bends and bights in what one gnome referred to as a “Highwayman’s Hitch” and the ropes on the far side went slack. They reeled them in and within moments no evidence was left of their crossing. With that, the party moved on, towards the setting sun.

Although the temperature here was colder than it had been at home, the dense forest prevented any breeze from cooling their skin as they walked. Donovan began to feel tired and a bit dizzy. When was the last time he had anything to drink? He was definitely thirsty, and decided to step off the path and catch up to Mr. Dabir and ask him about getting something to drink. The leaves and branches were thick on this game trail and he ducked under a branch just as his foot caught a root. He spun and rolled down a hill, as everything went black around him.

***

Donovan awoke to the sounds of a crackling fire. The smell of the firewood mingled with a savory aroma of food made his mouth water. Looking around and feeling a little disoriented he tried to remember how it was he had arrived at the clearing he was lying in. He remembered walking all afternoon through the woods, but he could not remember this clearing or anything that led up to it.

Noticing his movement Mr. Dabir arose from his seat by the fire and walked over to where Donovan was lying. He sat down again slowly, an indication of soreness and discomfort from the days march.

“How do you feel, Donovan?” he asked. “Do you remember what happened to you?”

Donovan looked sheepishly at the ground, trying to remember.

“It’s OK. You pushed yourself hard today, too hard. A little heat exhaustion, I imagine. When you fainted, you fell down a ravine, scratching your face and bumping your head. Cian Torin himself carried you for the last few hours of the day until we arrived at camp. We were worried that you may have broken something, but your limbs seem to be alright. I am glad to see you're awake. Would you like something to eat?"

Donovan nodded his head, which made him feel a bit queasy, but his stomach was growling, and he knew he needed to eat to have energy. One of the gnomes brought over a bowl of soup and a spoon. It smelled delicious.

"Rabbit stew," said Mr. Dabir, "I think you'll find it tastes a lot like chicken. But then again, most things do," he smiled.

Donovan gulped down the stew and then, without wanting to, drifted off to sleep again.

***

The next morning the air was brisk, and the camp fire was reduced to a few glowing embers. The gnomes busied themselves in preparations to leave, and Donovan sat on a fallen tree eating dried meat and drinking a warm apple cider. He felt a little better, although the bump on his head was a little larger, and his body felt as though he had been tackled by the entire Michigan State defensive line. He felt a little embarrassed about having fainted the day prior, but the gnomes seemed to pay him little attention.

Cian Torin walked into the clearing and announced that it was time to go. Donovan stood and was about to throw his excess cider into the fire when a gnome hunter stopped him. "It will make too much steam and smoke. Easy to see from a distance. Better to bury it." Then he took a scoop of dirt and threw it on the fire. Others helped and soon the fire was smothered without creating billows of smoke that might have alerted the enemy.

They began to move again towards the west; at least Donovan assumed it was the west. Maybe the sun rose and set differently here, but Donovan figured west was a good enough description as any. After a while the soreness in his legs began to work itself out, and he found himself keeping a fairly good pace with Mr. Dabir and Cian Torin. Once again, the other gnomes had been assigned the vanguard and rearguard duties as the day before, and so it was just the three of them trudging along together.

The march seemed a little easier today, and Donovan thought he knew why. It felt as though they were walking downhill, rather than on flat terrain. The lush forest surrounded them as before, but it was a little less dense here. From time to time he thought he saw more signs of life—a squirrel here and there, other animals making sounds in the distance. It was . . . peaceful.

"We are entering lands not regularly patrolled by th' Naga," Cian Torin announced. "We will shortly meet up with th' other two parties for a midday meal and then travel together from that point on." Then, as if noticing Donovan's expression on seeing more wildlife, he explained, "The Naga frighten most creatures away, much as a poisonous snake is avoided. But this land is protected by gnomes and members of He-lush-Ka's tribe of Saami. th' forest knows and respects us, for we know and respect th' forest."

Within a few hours they reached a large stump of what was once a tree of great dimensions. Here they found the group that had scouted ahead preparing a small meal for lunch. Donovan was grateful for the rest and once again devoured his food in minutes.

"I think I'm beginning to like rabbit," he said cheerfully. The gnomes exchanged glances with one another, smiling as they did so. One of them looked at Cian Torin who nodded, and then turned to Donovan. "They didn't find a rabbit," he said, "This is squirrel."

"Still tastes like chicken to me," said Mr. Dabir, as he reached for the cooking pot to ladle out more stew.

***

Mr. Dabir was engaged in conversation with Cian Torin for the bulk of the afternoon trek, and so Donovan was left to himself as he made his way down the path. The gnome hunters alongside him were also quiet, and although they were in a safer part of the forest, they remained vigilant, their eyes darting all around them.

Before long the air began to change a little. Donovan thought he smelled something familiar, and when he heard the cries of gulls and waves crashing against the shore, he knew they were nearing a large body of water. An hour or so later and the trees cleared enough to offer a glimpse of the horizon. Below him was a vast sea, stretching as far as the eye could see. Having grown up on the shores of Lake Michigan, Donovan felt like this was a taste of home, and his pace quickened as he realized they were heading for the beach.

The party arrived at the shore just as the sun began to set. The gnomes chose to set up camp just inside the tree-line to provide shelter from the night breezes, and to cover the glow of the fire.

"How much farther until we meet up with He-lush-Ka?" asked Mr. Dabir.

"We will arrive tomorrow after midday. We follow the coast until we reach his camp. It will take longer for us to travel on th' coarse sand, but the bulk of th' peninsula is made up of rocks, fallen trees, and crushed shells, so th' sand is preferable," responded Cian Torin.

"How many people does he have with him?" Donovan found himself asking.

"We can't say for sure. Although we maintain a friendly relationship with th' Saami, we seldom visit. Our home is in th' foothills north of Talamh Glas. It is a march of at least three or four days north of our present location. We have traded information with scouts from time to time, shared supplies now and again, but more details we do not have. We are not even sure we will be welcome in his camp, since you are strangers to them. But we shall see," explained Cian Torin.

They continued to travel into the early evening. Walking together in one group created more noise than before, but apparently stealth was no longer an issue. Cian Torin explained that the Saami would know of their arrival regardless of how quiet they proceeded, and since they came as allies, it was best not to appear as though being secretive in their passing. A few of the gnome hunters threw out lines into the dark waters near the camp site they had selected that evening, while others searched for beach wood to burn for dinner and for warmth. They chose to have a somewhat larger fire this evening, and the smell of cooked fish made Donovan's stomach grumble again.

The fish was boney, but delicious, and Donovan had several helpings. He had never been one to like anything more than fish sticks back home, but he was so hungry that everything seemed to taste better here. His mother had accused him of being a picky eater, but she would not say so now. Donovan thought about his mother and hoped she was eating something good as well. He curled himself up and, despite the incessant call of the birds hovering in the night winds nearby, fell asleep rather quickly.

***

The next morning, they had left without preparing a breakfast. Donovan was handed some dried fruit and some fresh water as they began to make their way down to the beach and along the shore. There is a part of a beach where the sand is just wet enough to offer support and traction, but not so wet as to sink into it. It was this section of the beach in which the party tried to maintain as its path. They walked now in single file, so as not to crowd one another, and Cian Torin took the lead. To his right Donovan saw that most of the peninsula was indeed barren, consisting of deadwood and shells, and the occasional large boulder. It would have been much slower had they tried to walk through that debris.

After a few hours there began to be signs of wildlife, prints in the sand, the chittering of squirrels, and birds calling to one another. Reeds and other grasses were more abundant here and small shrub trees dotted the interior of the narrow strip of land. At one point, Donovan thought he saw a large animal behind some fallen branches. It looked like a coyote or a fox. But when he looked again he saw nothing. As they continued he thought he felt more and more eyes upon him, but he still did not locate anything bigger than a dragonfly (which continued to annoy him by flying in front of his eyes every so often).

Distracted thus, he jumped in surprise when a branch snapped a few feet from where he was walking, and Donovan looked up just in time to see a tail flash behind a boulder. He was about to comment on it when one of the hunters shushed him. "We see them. th' shaman have found us."

Ten

Conall woke up as the sun crested the hills and low-lying mountains to the east. He saw that he was bound and gagged, as was Kiwidinok, and tied to a post in the center of the barge with the other captives.

Kiwidinok had not moved since they tied him up last night, and Conall wondered if he was still alive, given the severe beating he'd received from the saggitary guards the night before. Closer examination showed him to be breathing, only they were slow and shallow breaths. One of the feathers had been yanked from his ear and was dangling by the thread of skin that was still intact.

In all the torture, Kiwidinok had not told them anything, and had not used his shift magic to leave, fearing they would kill Conall if he did so. Conall knew he was to blame, and he felt guilty and helpless. They shouldn't have tried to get close to the barge, but then what if his parents had been on it? He would never have forgiven himself if he had not at least tried. However now they were both captives, and there was no help coming. At least not from Quinlan.

He couldn't blame him, Quinlan had cautioned against it, and Conall had ignored the advice. If Quinlan had come with them, he would have been caught as well. At least now there was someone to tell his brothers what had happened to him. He would either be eaten or enslaved. Frankly, he wasn't sure which one he preferred.

The Naga soldiers and tattooed guards were now joined by two sagittaries. There had been a brief interchange at the dock before departing, and Conall was not able to overhear, but it seemed the sagittary and the Naga soldiers were at odds over what to do with Conall and Kiwidinok. After Kiwidinok was beaten and dumped on the deck of the barge, the sagittary who captured them shouted something to the others on shore and another joined him on deck. He seemed to be the leader.

Conall was unsure why he was not able to understand the saggitary, since the shillelagh had allowed him to communicate with the gnomes and understand the Naga. Perhaps it wasn't a language, after all it did sound more like a series of growls and grunts to Conall, and as such may not be considered a language.

Conall turned to get a glance at the leader from behind. Two sets of massive lion paws gripped the deck while his tail swished back and forth. As if noticing his gaze, the sagittary turned to look at him with a grizzled face, that of a man, only more fierce and intense, short tan fur surrounded his chin and neck, much like a mane. Conall looked away, feeling ashamed as he did so. He was justifiably afraid, but still wished he could summon the courage to look that sagittary defiantly in the eye, just as Kiwidinok had done the night before.

Kiwidinok stirred and tried to raise himself up and off the deck. He was still too weak to do so, but eventually he managed to get himself into a sitting position. He didn't look at Conall just yet, and Conall wasn't sure he wanted him to. He felt so terribly guilty!

Conall turned his attention to his captors once again. The Naga soldiers were dressed like the ones he had seen on the island, a strange sort of armor that looked like overlapping scales with bits of metal plates and fastenings. The helmets looked something like that of a Japanese samurai, only they did not have masks. They were conical and pointed and didn't have horns or ornamentation like the helmets he had seen at the Museum of Natural History on a field trip last year.

The tattooed men who guarded the captives were completely different, and it was obvious they were subservient to the soldiers. Their skin, which at first looked as though painted, was heavily tattooed and they were naked except for a loin cloth each wore. They seemed to have no hierarchy amongst themselves, and communicated very little. They only carried a spear and a short knife, while the Naga soldiers hefted a polearm and a long, curved sword on their backs.

However, the most formidable of his adversaries was still the sagittary. They each had a breastplate on their torso, but wore no other armor. The larger of the two, the one that had captured him, carried a steel three-pronged triton and a small round shield. The other had no shield but carried two strange pieces of metal that had a spike on both ends, and a small curved blade around the knuckles of the hilt connecting the spikes. There was a small hook on the blade just before the spike. The entire weapon looked as though it was meant to slice and tear at its opponent. Conall had no wish to see it in action.

The day wore on and the captives were not given anything to eat or drink. The sun had risen high in the sky and in the heat of the day Conall found it was difficult to breathe with the gag in his mouth. He looked over at Kiwidinok again, but he had not budged since sitting upright. His wounds appeared to have stopped bleeding and started to heal. His breathing was also more regular and much deeper than before. Conall felt a little better, but was glad he did not have to look him in the eyes just yet.

He tried instead to make eye contact with the other prisoners. They seemed to be human, like himself, but were mostly adults.

Five or six, he remembered from the night before. They were wearing dirty tunics and leather slippers, and looked as though they were used to this treatment. When he had tried to get their attention, they had just turned the other way. Apparently, they had given up hope as well. Conall wondered if they were from Faer Ri or if they were from his world, but with the gag in his mouth he could not ask them.

The barge moved fairly swiftly down the river. Conall began to notice that the western side of the river was void of vegetation and it seemed as though the sand dunes went on as far as the eye could see. The eastern side of the boat was not so barren. There was an occasional scrub tree or smattering of tall grass. The mountains that could be seen in the morning were lost in the haze and the heat of the day, but as dusk approached he was able to make out their shapes again.

The barge did not stop for nightfall, but continued on under a moonlit sky. He and the other captives had not eaten or drank all day, and he was feeling very weak. Kiwidinok still had not awoken, and as the cool air of night crept over the dunes across the deck, Conall huddled close within himself and gave into sleep.

***

There was movement near his face, but he had a hard time opening his eyes as the bright sun was facing him as it rose the next morning. Rubbing the sleep from his eyes, his wrists still bound, he squinted and made out the forms of the tattooed men bringing water and what looked like a piece of stale bread to each of the captives. When they approached him they removed the gag, and stood over him while he ate. The bread was more like an old biscuit, and made his mouth even drier, but he was too hungry to stop. His palate began to hurt since his saliva could not break down the food. He drank more water and did his best to gulp down the bites he had taken. In a few moments, he was done, and they gagged him once again.

They moved on to the next person behind him and Conall looked over at Kiwidinok. Had he eaten? Had he awoken? Conall could not tell, but it did seem he was breathing normally and his cuts and bruises from that first night looked to be healing quite nicely; in fact, you could barely make some of them out at all. Conall remembered the Saami ability of healing and wondered if the shaman was employing that magic to restore himself. Knowing that his friend's health was improving caused him to feel a little better, but now he wished Kiwidinok would awaken. Feeling alone and helpless, he would rather face guilt than continue wondering if his friend was truly alright, and if Conall was forgiven.

The day wore on and the sagittary gave occasional orders to the Naga soldiers, who complied, if not willingly, quietly. But the glances they gave one another told Conall that there was no love lost between them. Conall looked out again at the scenery, or lack thereof, in this dry and desolate land. Desert, as far as the eye could see. Both sides of the river now proved to be a barren wasteland, and Conall wondered what sort of creature would want to live in this environment. Fatigue and the heat of the day worked on Conall's resolve to stay awake, and he eventually fell asleep again.

He awoke at dusk and looked up to see Kiwidinok staring at him. He seemed as though he had healed a great deal, and his ear had even closed over and healed the tear of the feathered earing, enveloping the rawhide and repairing it to its former state. A feeling of relief came over him and Conall thought he could see Kiwidinok smile under his gag. Conall wanted to apologize, and his eyes pleaded with Kiwidinok to forgive him, but a furtive glance from his friend towards the front of the barge caused Conall to turn and look in the same direction.

It was a city—a MASSIVE city. It seemed to reach from the desert floor and climbed high into the sky. Smoke rose from chimneys and candlelight filled windows. The streets appeared to be crowded with multitudes of people making their way from one location to another. There was an ornate look to the city that made it appear as though carved out of living stone. Its buildings were all the same desert-sand and earth hues, and there was little variety from one building to the next; except at the top. Here there was color and variation. Dark green palms and other tropical plants surrounded the rooftop and the walls were white with gold trim. It appeared to be a palace of sorts, with green gardens in and around the structure.

Conall looked back at Kiwidinok. Would they stop here, or move on to another destination? As if in answer to his question the barge began to turn ever so slightly towards the city. Maneuvering around a bend in the river, the barge entered into a small bay. Two things immediately caught Conall's attention. First, the city was much bigger than he had at first thought. They had only seen the upper portion of it and now the immense base was visible as they approached a set of docks where many other barges had been tied. Second, there were rows and rows of pyramids dotting the land around the city, dwarfed in contrast to the massive mountain metropolis that consumed the landscape.

The river widened in front of the docks and the barge was able to be prodded slowly to the pier. In a moment he was being lifted and hoisted to the edge of the barge and dropped onto the pier. Conall thought he was to be separated from Kiwidinok and began to panic, but then Kiwidinok was helped up and walked over to the pier as well. Thc larger sagittary barked an order to the smaller one and they were coaxed onto their feet with the sharp blades the other wielded. Walking away from the barge, Conall looked over his shoulder to see the Naga pushing away from the dock and steering the barge back down river. Looking into the eyes of his former captors, he saw relief mixed with a little anger. Obviously, they disagreed about the fate of their newest prisoners.

"Welcome to Ba'asada, slaves!" shouted the smaller sagittary in a mocking tone as it menacingly raised its weapons. Well, that answers a few questions, Conall thought as he made his way towards the city gates. For one, they did speak a more articulate language apart from guttural grunts and growls, which he was able to understand. Secondly, he was to be a slave, rather than an entrée. Both realizations brought relief to the young twelve-year-old.

The enormous doors of the gateway into Ba'asada looked as though it had not been in use for some time. In fact, they were partially buried by sand and debris. Built of sturdy oak and reinforced with iron hinges and overlapping bands, it may have been an integral part of the city's defenses once. But now it only served as ornamentation. Curiously, it was mostly humans who walked in and out of the gates, and through the streets. Two sagittary guards stood watch at the gate, but could not have closed the gate should they have wanted to, and they did little to control the flow of pedestrians through the aperture.

It was obvious they were ceremonial at best. Upon entering the city Conall and Kiwidinok were taken to the left, up a rampart and around the interior walls. As they walked the street gradually rose higher and higher. After a long time passed they came to a familiar view, the harbor from where they had just come. Conall realized that the street wound itself around the city and each concentric ring was a level higher. He was again surprised to see very few sagittary inhabiting the lower rings of the city. The traffic was mostly comprised of humans, and the occasional tattooed Naga. Not even in the shops and other opened doors did he spot anyone like his captors.

He wondered where they were going, and how much longer they would have to walk. He had very little energy and was feeling faint with hunger and thirst. At this rate it would take a long time to get to the top, if that was the destination.

He soon realized it was not. After completing the circuit one more time, the larger sagittary continued up the path while the smaller one with the curved blades unlocked a rusty metal door, ushering them into the small opening and down a dark corridor while he closed and locked the door behind him.

The light from a torch in a sconce at the entrance was barely enough to make out the steps at the end of the hall that led down into another corridor, but not of cut stone, rather of hollowed-out rock. They continued down this tunnel until it opened into a vast chamber lit by many torches. Here the sounds of screams and suffering from the denizens of this dark dwelling sucked any thought of freedom and happiness from the soul. Conall had seen enough movies to recognize a dungeon when he saw one.

A shirtless, round-bellied man, human by the look of him and only wearing a long leather skirt and a leather harness, walked towards Kiwidinok and Conall while eyeing them up and down. His eyes were white, having seen too little sun for too many years, and his face and scalp showed signs of disease and infestation.

"Where do you want these, Sharedzia?" he asked in a dry whisper, reminiscent of someone suffering from an allergy attack.

"The youngling is to be a gift for his majesty. The old man will compete in the arena. Keep them together, and kill the young one should the old man try to escape," said the saggitary in a deep and powerful voice.

"Feed them, clothe them, and tend to their wounds," he continued, "They serve no good if they are dead. Set watch over them." And with that he left Kiwidinok and Conall with the prison steward and returned down the tunnel from which they had emerged.

The heavyset man scratched his splotched belly and looked again at the captives. "Why would he want to give *you* to his. . .exaltedness," he wheezed looking at Conall, "and how does he expect an old man like you to survive for more than a minute in the arena?" he queried indicating Kiwidinok.

Conall and Kiwidinok just stared back at him. Then Kiwidinok pointed to the gag in his mouth and shrugged his shoulders.The prison steward called to some of his men to come and untie their new "guests" and to remove their gags.

"Where were you taken?" he asked in that breathless voice of his. Not wishing to share too much information, Kiwidinok quickly blurted out that they had been taken at the edge of the forest. He looked at Conall to keep silent about revealing any more. The steward eyed them suspiciously and then scoffed.

"We've never had anyone escape, can't imagine. . . what you two could possibly do to change that, but we will. . . be watching still the same," he said between labored breaths. Then turning to the two guards who approached he said, "Put them in with the traitor, it is a clean enough cell, and. . . fetch them some water and something to eat." And with that the jailor waved his hands and lumbered back into the light of a cave he had emerged from.

The two guards, also human, directed their prisoners to the indicated cell. The cell was fairly large and had straw strewn about the floor. Unfortunately, the smell of waste was still quite pungent. If this was a "clean" cell, Conall was hoping he would never have to see a dirty one. As his eyes adjusted to the even dimmer light of the jail cell, Conall made out two other shapes. One looked like a sagittary, only it was chained and had a burlap bag covering its head and face. The other was a human, who stirred as they entered. Another guard brought a bucket with a ladle in it as well as some more of those hard biscuits they had eaten the day before. The door of the cell was locked behind them and the sentries returned to their posts.

"Home, sweet home," remarked Kiwidinok sardonically.

As they turned back around to look for a place to sit that wasn't covered in waste or filth, the man in the cell sat up and looked them up and down.

"What's your name?" he asked in what sounded like an English accent. He stood up, and Conall noticed that his torn clothes looked like they had once served as some sort of uniform. Noticing the scrutinizing glance from Conall he smiled.

"Judging by your clothes you're not from around here neither," he said as he extended his hand. "My name's Ganju."

Eleven

At first Conall didn't accept the hand offered to him. He was wary of the man, but not because of the way he had addressed them, it was his demeanor. His eyes were wild, and he was giggling at some secret joke. His hair was unkempt, his clothes disheveled, and he had a nervous twitch in his left eye. He seemed a bit, well, loopy. Ganju smiled wider and stretched out his hand even further.

"I haven't had anyone to talk to in weeks—nobody here speaks English, except for you. But the Warden understood you. I can't get 'im to say 'boo' to me. Just as well, he's a bit on the grumpy side if you know what I mean," said Ganju in a giddy, off-handed way. Kiwidinok stepped between the two of them and took his hand.

"We are grateful to make your acquaintance, Ganju," he said softly, a hint of sadness in his voice, "My young friend and I are tired and would like to rest. Where do you suggest we lie down?"

"Just about anywhere's as good as the next, although they don't like when we get too close to that bloke," said Ganju, gesturing at the hooded saggitary. "Not sure what he's done, but they barely give him enough food to get by." Ganju pointed a jittery hand at the empty bowls next to their fellow prisoner.

Conall looked at the corner of the cell where the sagittary was chained to the wall. His fur around the back pair of legs was a mixture of matted straw and dried blood from the iron shackles that had obviously been digging into him for some time just above the paws. Then he noticed that the human arms were also chained to the wall, which would allow some movement but not enough to lie down or remove the hood. There were cuts and scrapes all over his hide, and the human torso was bruised and stained with blood and dirt. This creature had once been very powerfully built, but his muscles had atrophied, his skin tight around his emaciated form. He appeared to be a mere shadow of his former self. What would have been his crime to receive such a brutal punishment?

Kiwidinok took a seat on a pile of straw that appeared to be dry and motioned for Conall to join him. They ate their bread quietly; washing the bitter, dry morsels down with the stale water they had been provided. Conall was so hungry he didn't care, and Kiwidinok, seeing his hunger, offered him some of his bread. Conall declined and Kiwidinok offered it instead to Ganju who gobbled it down without even so much as a 'thank you'.

Conall looked around again at the cell and through the bars into the center of the chamber. There seemed to be several tiers of cells surrounding the cavern, perhaps four or five levels, all opening towards the middle of the dungeon. Fires burning from the cavern floor and a few scattered torches were the source of the dim light that helped Conall make out his surroundings. They were on the third level, with two floors above and what looked like two floors below—his view was cut off by the ramps that circled in front of the cells and allowed access above and below.

The wailing of other captives began to worry him, and his emotions came to the surface in the form of tears. Kiwidinok put his arms around him and did his best to comfort him. This caused him to cry out loud for a few minutes, but then slowly his sobs turned to sniffles, and then erratic breathing. Kiwidinok just patted his back and reassured him that all would be well. He didn't believe him, of course, but he let himself relax and drifted off to sleep.

***

The sound of rustling keys and iron grating on iron woke Conall with a start. He blinked the sleep out of his eyes and pulled the loose pieces of straw from his red cheek that had been pressed against the floor. Two guards, dressed in red tunics with a black sun on their chest, eyed them as they opened the door to the cell. One of the guards entered and tossed bundles of rags in front of Conall and Kiwidinok, while another brought dishes filled with a dark steaming liquid for the three human captives. The hooded sagittary moved its head in the direction of the sound but the guards didn't even acknowledge him.

"Eat quickly, get dressed, and we will return for you in a few moments," said one of the guards. He was human, by the looks of him, but based on Ganju's reaction he was speaking a language other than English. The magic of the shillelagh must be permanent for whomever it is invoked, figured Conall.

The guards left, shutting and locking the cell door is they did. Ganju began to devour the contents of the bowl, but Conall took one whiff and decided he could not stomach it. Kiwidinok tasted a portion of the black liquid, shrugged his shoulders and began to eat.

Looking around the cell, Conall noticed that the guards had not brought any food for the poor creature in the corner. Summoning courage, he stood and walked with his bowl over to the chained prisoner. Kiwidinok and Ganju didn't notice him get up, so it wasn't until he was standing in front of the manacled beast that they realized his intent.

"Conall! Do not approach him!" cried Kiwidinok, a look of fear in his eyes. He jumped to his feet but at that moment the chained sagittary reached out and grabbed Conall's arm. Kiwidinok started to lunge towards them when he noticed Conall showed no fear—he heard, or rather "felt" the mind of the savage that held him and in an instant, he knew he would be safe and that he would not be harmed.

"It's OK, Kiwi, he's not going to hurt me," he said with conviction. With his free hand, he cautiously reached out and took hold of the hood. He raised it slowly up and then off the head of the poor, beaten creature. The face, human as with the others, had been battered and bruised beyond recognition, disfigured with malice from cruel torturers. However, it was his eyes that drew Conall's attention—they pleaded for mercy. Conall brought the bowl close to his mouth and offered a drink. He tried to swallow, but coughed it back up. Conall tried again, and this time the sagittary gulped down a small portion of the bowl's contents.

Kiwidinok walked slowly over to Conall, his eyes fixed on the chained sagittary and the grip he had on Conall's arm. "Conall," he said quietly, "while I applaud your charity, I am not pleased with your tendency to put yourself in harm's way. This creature is chained for a reason. We don't know if he is dangerous or if he is even sane. The abuse suffered here can affect the mind in ways you cannot imagine. Ganju over there is barely keeping it together. You could have been killed."

The sagittary coughed again, and turned his eyes on Kiwidinok as a coarse whisper escaped his lips, "Would . . . never . . . harm the child." His eyes fluttered a moment before they closed. He released his grip on Conall and leaned against the wall. Conall replaced the hood carefully so as not turn hurt him, and returned to the other side of the cell before the guards could return.

Examining the bundle of clothes their captors left behind, he discovered a black tunic with the emblem of a crimson sun, a dagger plunged through the middle, embroidered into the center of the garment. It was roughly his size, so he put it on over his t-shirt and jeans. Kiwidinok gathered up the rest of the bundle and found another tunic and a belt. He removed his flannel shirt and put the tunic on, gathering it around the waste with the belt. It was designed to cover the knees, but he kept his jeans and boots on just the same. This tunic was once white, but had no embellishment whatsoever, and various rips and tears in the fabric had been stitched up. Although relatively clean, dark stains around the stitching revealed this to have been worn by someone who had been injured and lost blood.

A few moments later the guards returned. Opening the door, they pulled Conall and Kiwidinok out onto the ramp and locked the door to the cell. Then the bigger of the two pulled out a club and shoved it into Kiwidinok's back. He was an ugly brute, unshaven and uncomely. Remains of the dark stew that had been served for breakfast could be seen in his beard and on his shirt. "Move slave," he said as the started down the ramp. Conall began to follow, but the other guard with the long nose and wideset eyes grabbed his tunic and spun him around. "We go this way, slave," he said without malice. They began to move up the ramp towards an opening above.

He passed several cells as the ramp rose higher and higher in a concentric circle until they entered a tunnel that led to a stairwell. Steps, carved into stone, and worn smooth by years of use, took them higher still into the mountain. Conall began to breath heavy but the jailor would not let him rest. His heart felt as though it would pound out of his chest, and his ears were starting to fill with pressure. After what seemed like an eternity they finally emerged into the bright sunlight. Conall blinked back tears as the sun burned eyes that had become accustomed to the darkness of their cell. Gradually he was able to squint and see his surroundings. He was at the top of the mountain he had seen from the barge. Looking down he saw the city spread out below him leading to the docks. One could see for miles from this vantage point, and Conall peered into the distance, tracing the river northward, hoping that somewhere out there his brothers were safe.

The guard closed and locked the door to the stairwell and turned Conall away from the view of the harbor and towards the palace. It was breathtakingly beautiful. In stark contrast to the dry, dusty landscape around the city, this oasis on top of the mountain was truly a garden in the desert. Trees and flowers surrounded the outer walls, while the sound of fountains and birds chirping came from within the green curtain of foliage that filled the palace grounds.

Conall was prodded towards the main entrance, two large wooden doors painted red and covered with black iron studs. At their approach, a small door opened in the middle of the right gate. From it came two guards, similar in dress to the man who escorted him. They nodded, but made no other effort to communicate, nor did they even look at Conall. He felt invisible. Upon reaching the door, which was not as small as he had first thought, a saggitary sentry peered down at them before moving aside to allow entrance.

Once inside, Conall was astonished by the transformation from the barren desert that dominated the landscape into this lush oasis on the top of the city. First, he noticed the air temperature was markedly cooler, as the shade from the trees and water cascading from dozens of fountains provided a more comfortable climate in the courtyard.

Each fountain stood about eight feet from the surface of the water, the contents gushing forth in a torrent of refreshing spray arching and falling into a large reflecting pool that stretched from one end of the compound to the other. Verdant palms lined either side of the pool with large crimson flowers exploding from vibrant green bushes swaying slowly underneath the towering trunks. At the far end of the enclosure a sweeping banyan tree stretched its protruding roots and branches in an effort to embrace the bright white walls of an ornate palace located behind it.

Surrounding the gardens stood arched verandas with marble flooring. Occasionally a door would open and a servant, wearing the same black tunic as Conall, would emerge carrying a tray or some other object. As Conall and his escort reached the far end of the reflection pool they veered to the right and entered another door with a patchwork of iron framing bolted into the thick wood.

Upon entering the vestibule, Conall was once again impressed by the beauty and ornamentation of the walls and windows. Every inch of the inner walls had been carved into a decorative design, and mosaic tiles covered the floors. Here too were fountains, only smaller and carefully placed in small round pools.

There were many humans walking from one part of the palace to another, either dressed in the red tunic of the guards, or in a black tunic like the one he wore. The sentries watched them all closely, yet they seemed not to notice one another, or if they acknowledged each other, it was a curt nod—nothing more. It was eerily quiet.

The inner courtyard was rather expansive, and it took them a few minutes to cross it and enter a third set of doors, this time guarded by humans in red tunics. Here the thick walls kept the air cool and damp, and after a few twists and turns through service hallways they emerged from the palace into an atrium surrounded by tall marble slabs and white pillars. Here the atmosphere differed greatly from the outer courtyard, not only from the lack of vegetation, but also due to the noise and chaos coming from the center of the arena.

Armed men were fighting one another in a large stone pit, the size of a swimming pool, while others yelled from the sides of the pit—a series of steps leading from the main floor. Stone columns surrounded the lower level of the palace where a few sagittaries watched the blood sport from the shadows. Above the first floor was another set of columns, but they were more spaced out, and appeared vacant save for a golden dais, strewn about with red and black pillows, servants bustling around carrying platters and pitchers. In the midst of them the body of an enormous lion lounged on the pillows, a huge human head protruding where the lion's head would have been.

This creature was not like the sagittary, as it was much larger and had no human torso. The human head was massive with dark curly hair braided, tucked neatly under a golden crown, and a well-groomed obsidian beard neatly falling in a trickle of ringlets that flowed from his chin to his broad feline chest. His piercing yellow eyes were heavily lidded and shrouded in black kohl; his skin shone like melted gold. His tail flounced back and forth in a lazy, melancholic fashion.

Noticing Conall's reaction, the guard immediately stood in front of him and commanded in a hushed tone, "DO NOT make eye contact with His Royal Majesty, under penalty of death." He turned again and led Conall down through an adjacent hallway and up a set of stairs. At the top of the stairs Conall saw a multitude of servants moving quickly and quietly to and from the dais. His guard took him to a corner of the room where they waited to be noticed.

Conall tried to take stock of the scene before him. Below, out of site from where he waited, some sort of gladiatorial combat was taking place. Before him was a golden dais full of red and black pillows trimmed with gold embroidery with geometrical patterns and intricate tassels. From this vantage point Conall could see the entirety of the lion-man, His Royal Majesty, as the guard put it. Draped across his haunches was a golden chain of filigrees worked in with precious metals.

Men and women dressed in black tunics, some wearing black head scarves, were serving this magnificent being his food, while a smattering of guards and sagittary were scattered around the palace viewing room. So far Conall had seen a great deal more humans than sagittary, and therefore hoped to blend in and keep himself from being noticed. At some point Kiwidinok would figure out a way to escape and they could return to his brothers. In the meantime, he would "keep it together" as Kiwidinok had put it.

After some time, a portly man dressed in a red tunic, cleaner and more ornate than the others, looked up and noticed them. With his eyes downcast he whispered in the ear of the large human head of the king. The king nodded, and the man hurried over to them.

"His Royal Highness, Keeper of the Stone, wishes to inspect his newest slave," he said with a superior air.

The embroidery on his tunic was made of golden threads, and black beads had been woven in to add dimension to the design of the black sun. His voice was shrill and sounded disproportionate to his girth. But there was also malevolence in his eyes that was unmistakable to Conall and he quickly obeyed.

Twelve

For the past few days, Scioldmed was doing his best to keep Girvan away from Brendon. Since the morning of the snake encounter, Brendon had not had a chance to speak with or even sit near Girvan. It was as if Scioldmed was preventing his pupil from having any contact with the young Druidae.

The trail had become more difficult as it wound towards the mountain range in the distance, and at one point Brendon had offered a hand to Girvan to climb up a large boulder. Scioldmed had inserted himself between them and insisted on helping the young leprechaun himself. Furthermore, when they stopped for meals, Scioldmed kept Girvan occupied so that he would not have time to spend with Brendon. He obviously had an agenda and "Keeping Brendon away from Girvan" was item number one!

Somehow Brendon had offended Scioldmed but he didn't understand how. Had he not been grateful for being saved? Brendon had tried a number of times to thank him for coming to his rescue, but the old leprechaun just stared at him and waved him away nervously as he went about his tasks.

When Brendon asked Risteard about it, the stoic warrior simply said, " th' ways of leprechauns are a mystery to me," and left it at that. But there was a definite change in the way all of the gnomes were treating Brendon and it all stemmed from something that happened on the morning that snake almost bit him. Needless to say, it was a quiet journey. Risteard hardly spoke as it was, and now that Brendon had been ostracized by the other members of the party, he pretty much had himself to talk to.

The forest was still dense, and the canopy let in very little light, but the ground had changed from a soft loam to a rocky terrain. Outcroppings of limestone, worn away by time and water, were covered with thick moss and small ferns, which made keeping one's footing difficult in the early hours after the morning dew. Adding to their plight, there were dells and overhangs that were deceiving, and often they had to retrace their steps as they came to a dead end.

For Brendon it was nearly impossible to make out the time of day or the direction they were traveling. Contrary to what he had heard about moss, it actually grew on all sides of the tree. It seemed to Brendon that they were in a labyrinth of stone and wood, with trickles of water seeping from fissures in the jagged rock walls. However, the absence of light and the dark green of the forest floor didn't present a gloomy atmosphere; rather it was peaceful and serene. The sounds of woodland animals were clear in the distance, and Brendon felt as though he *belonged* here.

It had been several days since they had first arrived in this world. Brendon missed his parents terribly, and was worried for his brothers. Donovan should be safe, he thought, but what of Conall? He was a little headstrong, and that could get him into trouble. At least Kiwidinok was with him, and that man had shown himself more than capable of protecting his wards. *Who knows*, he thought, *maybe they have already located mom and dad. Maybe they are on their way back to the encampment of He-lush-Ka by now*.

Of course, that wasn't the only thing to worry about. They couldn't just walk back to the island, stroll up to the realmbridge and say, "Excuse me creepy snake-like people, thank you for your hospitality, but we'd like to go home now." One problem at a time, he thought. And the current problem was getting Girvan to talk to him. He decided that later that night he would wait for Scioldmed to fall asleep and then sneak over to Girvan to find out what was wrong.

They decided to make camp under an outcropping that had vines and moss fastened to the top of the opening and dangling nearly to the ground, effectively blocking the light from the campfire so as not attract any unwanted visitors. Risteard began to search for dry wood in order to make the fire. It would not be easy as this area was very moist and there was a great deal of water emerging from fissures in the rock face that seeped down to the forest floor and wound its way into creeks and streams which all led, assumedly, towards the large lake they had seen on his first day. The prolific ferns that covered the forest floor also hid much of the fallen branches under a sea of green, but Risteard was capable and soon found enough wood to feed the flame.

They had eaten mostly dried rations up to this point, but Risteard had spotted a grouse earlier that afternoon and Scioldmed had held it in place while he ran to it and captured it. As it sat on the makeshift spit, it smelled like roast chicken, and with the wild potatoes Girvan had located and placed near the fire, it would be his first hot meal since arriving in this world. His palate had become bored with eating the equivalent of beef jerky and fruit snacks for the past several days and he could hardly wait. The first thing he wanted to do when he got home would be to take a hot shower—rinsing off in cold streams and re-wearing his dirty track uniform was becoming unbearable (maybe that's why they were avoiding him). But the second thing he would do is ask his mom to order a pizza. Oh, what he wouldn't give for a deep dish right now.

Conversation was again limited as they ate, but Brendon didn't care. He was so very hungry. After gulping down his meal he volunteered to help wash out some of the cookware by collecting some water from the nearby rock face. He heated it and then, having watched the others, took a rock and scoured the pan and plates clean.

As he walked back to the enclosure he thought he felt someone looking at him from behind a copse of trees. He stared at it for a long time, squinting in the dark to try and make out a form or shape other than a tree. Seeing nothing but a large boulder, he continued walking towards the hollowed-out rock face where the fire was now starting to die down. He parted the hanging moss and found everyone wrapped in woolen blankets lying on the beds of ferns Girvan and Scioldmed had gathered.

Brendon looked at the pile of fern leaves left for him and arranged it so that his blanket would not become too wet from the water that covered the floor of the cave. He feigned a breathing pattern that resembled that of sleep, and squinted just a little to spy on Scioldmed through his eyelashes. The old gnome had not been asleep and was staring at him. Brendon did his best not to react and simply kept up his ruse. Eventually Scioldmed, satisfied that Brendon was sleeping, turned over and within moments was breathing deeply and soundly.

Brendon waited for a while—a long while. He almost fell asleep while waiting, but as the night wore on, a crack from something in the fire got his attention. He sat up and looked around. Everyone was still. Risteard had said they would not need to stand watch this far north, as the Naga did not venture into Fenian Chase. Yet he still wanted to hide the campfire.

Brendon dismissed the idea and crawled slowly over to where Girvan lay. He gently tapped him on the shoulder, and Girvan stirred. Putting his fingers against his lips, Brendon motioned for Girvan to follow him outside. Girvan peered at his mentor, and a look of concern and indecision crossed his face. Brendon pleaded with his eyes, and reluctantly Girvan followed him.

After they had moved several feet away from the encampment, Brendon turned and waiting for the slighter and stealthier form of Girvan to arrive. He dove right into his questions. "What's going on? Why is Scioldmed not allowing us to talk? What did I do wrong?" He whispered.

Girvan looked back at the camp. He shifted his weight from one foot to another, and then answered.

"You have a powerful magic. You can affect things with yer voice alone, whether you will it o' not. The great Bards of th' ælfen people spent years mastering their voices and learning th' words of power and th' songs and harmonics that allowed them to work together to create wondrous feats. You are Druidae, true, but to have th' power you exhibited at th' river th' other day at yer age. Scioldmed thinks that maybe it is Wild Magic. A magic that canna' be controlled, or at least should not be. 'Tis. . . unnatural."

Confused, Brendon tried to think of a response. Nothing came to him. He had no idea what Girvan was talking about.

"What magic by the river?" he asked.

"Scioldmed told me he had held th' snake in place, so that you could get away. It was you that twisted it, snapped its back, and scorched it from within," Girvan admitted slowly. He turned to look again in the direction of camp.

“I didn’t do or say anything,” Brendon exclaimed in a harsh whisper. “I just, well. . . sort of panicked and screamed in fear. I didn’t ‘will’ the snake to be mangled. It just happened.”

“Which is why you are dangerous,” came a reply from the darkness. Scioldmed stepped out from behind some trees. “I am to protect Girvan as well as teach him. I can’t take a chance that yer inexperience, or lack of judgment might harm Cian Torin’s son, and th‘ future leprechaun of th‘ clan. I do not believe in your aelfen prophecies, and I do not approve of us visiting some wild wielder of magic. But I obey my chief, and his will is that we escort you there safely. Once that is done, we will quickly return to Vloorhaven Glen and be rid of all this nonsense.”

He took Girvan by the arm and ushered him back to the campsite. Brendon was confused, and a little angry. He hadn’t wanted to come here, and it was not his fault that things were happening that he could not explain. After some time had passed, and he felt a little more in control of his emotions, he trudged back to the camp and wrapped himself in his wool blanket, fatigue overcoming his anger and resentment as he drifted off to sleep.

***

The sun was approaching mid-day as its rays pierced through the heavy green canopy of the forest, lighting the floor with a dazzling display of shifting and shimmering beams, the trees gently swaying in the breeze. It was still warm, but a cool wind brought a hint of the changing of the seasons, and in time those rich green leaves would turn red, brown, and yellow before relenting to the inevitable end of their cycle, falling gracefully to the ground.

But the tranquil beauty was lost on Brendon and the others, as they picked their way through the dells and ravines. Brendon had a sullen expression, which he wore in anger at the things said about him the night before. Girvan looked sad and a little bit guilty, while Scioldmed defiantly placed himself between Brendon and the others. Risteard, of course, wore no expression, and seemed indifferent to the moods of the company that followed him down into a hollow full of boulders, ferns, and fallen trees.

The clearing was spacious, the trees were spread far apart along the banks of a ravine that led to a formidable hill located at the end of the glade. The side of the hill facing them had been carved away over the years by erosion, the elements leaving a jagged wall of rock with fissures striating in all directions. Massive boulders and giant sequoias, once proud monarchs of the forest, littered the hollow which seemed to be another "dead end".

Brendon was about to ask when they could stop for lunch, but Risteard turned and put his fingers to his lips. As he stopped walking he motioned everyone to do the same. They crouched down almost in unison and began searching their surroundings for whatever it was that had alarmed Risteard. Brendon peered up at the tall trees that dotted the forest floor, but didn't see anything.

Several moments went by and nothing happened. Brendon began to stand up and was yanked back to the ground by Risteard just as a boulder swooshed by them where Brendon's head would have been. It smashed into a tree, splintering the wood and chipping off a piece of the rock. Spinning around they looked into the direction the boulder had come. Again, there was nothing. Brendon stared at the massive trunk of a fallen tree and a group of irregularly shaped boulders that sat in front of it. Was there someone behind the boulders?

As he watched, one of the boulders began to move slowly, as if it were being rolled off a ledge. Then, as he watched intently two eyes snapped open and the boulder *stood* up and began rushing towards them, moss and leaves falling from the figure as it approached.

Brendon, still crouching, didn't move, but Risteard jumped up to protect him in what assuredly would be a hopeless endeavor against the charging wall of stone and wood sinew. The hulking creature hurled itself at them with a long tree branch in hand. It roared as it hefted the makeshift club over its head and swung it down on Risteard. But Cian Torin's champion deftly leapt aside at the last moment and pulled his knives from their sheaths.

With a whirl of those strange green stone blades he launched himself towards the creature and neatly sliced the back hamstring—or would have had there been flesh to cut. The knife scraped against the earthen slab with a grating screech, causing no apparent damage. Without missing a beat, Risteard stabbed upward with his other blade towards the lower back of the beast. Again, no affect as his blade was turned aside by the rigidity of its skin.

The monstrosity of earth and stone ignored the attacks and instead lifted its branch to swing at Brendon, but before it could finish the blow Scioldmed grabbed Brendon's arm, the world around him blurred for a moment—and he appeared at the other side of the clearing.

He looked at Sciolmed and Girvan. "What just happen—" he began.

"Shhh. th' huldretrow seems bent on destroying you, so best to keep yer voice down," Scioldmed said quietly. He motioned for Brendon and Girvan to hide behind some fallen trees while he moved closer to where the beast and Risteard were exchanging blows.

Exchanging was not the best word—the huldretrow's branch had failed to connect with its target, and Risteard was doing no damage to his assailant. The attacker was close to nine feet tall, three times the size of Risteard, and as wide as two men. It wore a leather belt attached to a leather kilt, with a thick harness strapped across its torso. Its hands and feet were bare, but did not seem bothered by the rough terrain. Although it maintained aspects of a human visage, its hair was like dark moss draped from the crown of its skull to the shoulders, its skin a mottled gray with flecks of flint and rough sandy patches. Arms the size of tree trunks swung wildly as powerful legs churned the earth where it fought to gain purchase and chase down the nimble gnome. But the eyes, perhaps they were the most intimidating of all. An ominous hatred filled those black orbs as they threatened to undo any who would cross its path. Such fury was foreign to Brendon, and he wondered if they would survive this onslaught.

Scioldmed moved towards the creature and concentrated on a small boulder. It rose off the ground and sped towards the huldretrow who by now had realized that its prey had managed to escape. It turned to see the boulder moving rapidly towards its head and swung the large branch at the projectile. There was a loud crack as pieces of stone flew across the clearing, and the branch split neatly in half. Meanwhile Risteard had used the distraction to climb a nearby tree and now leaped onto the back of the huldretrow, thrusting his blades into the creatures back as he did so. But to no avail; once again they scraped harmlessly across the impenetrable surface and Risteard slid to the ground.

"Yer blades will not work; they clearly canna' pierce its skin!" shouted Scioldmed in exasperation. "Here, use these," he ordered as he took from his pouch two small clear stones. Risteard ran to

Scioldmed just as the pursuing creature reached them. Grabbing the stones, he dove aside as the huldretrow swung the back of its hand towards the two. Scioldmed was not as lucky, and his body was lifted off the ground and flung several feet before falling in a crumpled heap.

Risteard ran up the embankment of the ravine and stopped to adjust his daggers. He placed one stone in each of the hollow circles at the pommel of the blades, just below the hilt. Instantly his knives began to glow with a white-hot brilliance, taking on the aspect of the clear stones the blades became almost translucent, rather than the original greenish hue. He turned to face the huldretrow, who had paused and now looked as though it might be having second thoughts.

Then, as if triggered by a memory, the creature lurched to its side and ran towards the group of boulders near the location in which it had been hiding when the party first approached the clearing. Fearing the worse for Scioldmed, and unsure of the outcome of this engagement, Risteard launched himself towards the lumbering beast, intending to use his newly enchanted weapons to slay this menace once and for all.

The huldretrow reached the grouping and from behind the boulders pulled out a smooth wooden shaft that began to emit a green glow the moment he touched it. It reminded Brendon of the walking stick that belonged to Mr. Dabir, or rather, to himself, as Mr. Dabir had intimated. Risteard reached the monster as it turned and he plunged one of the blades into the huldretrow's forearm. The clear blade cut true, and the beast howled with pain and rage, pulling its arm free as Risteard rolled and resumed a guarded stance.

Then, oddly, its demeanor changed. The beast stood up straight and stopped its animal-like posture and growling. It spun the polished shaft around its back and over its head, showing great skill and prowess. Lowering the staff and pointing the end at Risteard, it spoke.

"You may gather your wounded and leave. Do not press further," it bellowed with a powerful grating sound from deep within its chest.

"We're looking for somebody called Bidzil," Brendon called from his hiding place. Risteard shot an angry glare at him, shifted his stance and focused again on the huldretrow, ready to pounce at any moment.

"There is no one by that name here," came the deep, gravelly voice. "You are mistaken."

"Then where might one find him?" asked Risteard, circling around the creature who was trying to keep an eye on both members of the party.

"One does not find him if he does not wish to be found. Those he finds often do not survive the encounter. Return from whence you came, and count yourself lucky," responded the huldretrow. With that he swung his staff again and planted it in the earth in front of Risteard, who flinched and squinted slightly as dirt and debris sprayed across his boots from where the staff had struck the ground.

"I know that look," said Girvan quietly, "He's not going to back down."

At that moment Risteard spun himself to the ground and then twisted his body up into the air kicking at the staff and bringing his blades to bear on the torso of the huldretrow. But the powerful brute neatly stepped aside, and brought his staff down on the back of Risteard, knocking him to the ground. Undeterred by the assault, Risteard rolled onto his back, flipped himself off the ground, and flung a knife before his feet had landed. The huldretrow moved to block the thrown blade with the staff, but did not see the other blade spinning towards his thigh. The first blade was slapped aside just as the other sunk into the stone-like flesh just below the leather kilt. He bellowed in rage and swung the staff at Risteard who leaped aside.

Again, and again the huldretrow struck the ground with its staff as Risteard dodged and ducked and barely escaped each and every bone-crushing swat, the huldretrow slowly advancing on his position. The skill with which the attacker wielded his staff was nothing like the bellowing, branch-swinging brute that had first accosted them. Were it not for the dexterity of Risteard, he would have met his demise with any one of those powerful blows.

Brendon glanced at Scioldmed who had not moved since the huldretrow had flung him aside. Risteard dodged another swing of the staff and his eyes landed on the blade that had been knocked aside. He feigned to his left and then sprinted to his right, intent on arming himself again, but the huldretrow was not fooled and Risteard was tripped up by the end of the staff, falling into a pile of dead branches. The creature swung his staff around again and raised it high over its head to deliver a final strike.

"Do something," Brendon shouted to Girvan, as the two of them looked on helplessly.

"You should have left when I gave you the chance," said the huldretrow menacingly, as it dispensed a killing blow upon Risteard.

Brendon had been paralyzed with fear, but at this moment a rage burned within him and he felt a fire kindled deep inside his soul.

"NOOOOOOOOO!" he yelled. The staff stopped inches from Risteard's torso and began to swirl first with green and then black tendrils of light before shaking violently in the troll's hands, followed by a deafening *BOOM* that knocked everyone to the ground, the staff flying from the would-be executioner's grip and landing in a pool of water at the base of the rock face. The shock wave shook the nearby trees causing a shower of leaves to fall all around the hollow.

The huldretrow looked at Brendon with fear and trepidation.

"How . . .", the grizzly visage of the huldretrow was awash in bewilderment.

Brendon still felt the power coursing through his body and, clenching his fists, he looked at the creature. An irrational feeling of hate and anger welled within him, and for a moment he thought he might be able to cause the huldretrow to shake as well. Before he could act on his instinct he heard voices--soft, sweet, subtle, distant and familiar. His anger and rage subsided almost instantly, and he felt a peace come over him. The voices grew stronger and he glanced towards Girvan who had heard them too and was looking for the source as well.

From the mouth of a fissure at the far end of the clearing where the limestone rose high from the forest floor, an old man appeared, singing a tune that seemed to harmonize with itself, as though many people were singing at once. Brendon could not make out the words, soft as it was, but he knew right away they had nothing to fear. An overwhelming sense of . . . oneness filled the void left by the torrents of rage that had been expelled.

As the figure approached he ended his song, and looked up with a wink and a smile.

"I understand you are looking for me," he said wryly.

Thirteen

As the newcomer, who appeared to be an elderly man in a grey cloak, pivoted on his back heel and returned towards the rock wall at the back of the hollow, the huldretrow retrieved its staff from the water and moved to follow. Upon reaching the wall, the old man looked back and winked before stepping to his left and *into the wall.* Brendon gaped for a moment and then watched the huldretrow repeat the same the action. A cave. That must be how the creature had appeared so suddenly. Brendon turned to look at his companions. Girvan had helped Scioldmed to his feet and Risteard looked at them as if questioning what to do next. Scioldmed nodded and Risteard began walking towards the hidden cave. Brendon, curious to know what sort of man this Bidzil was, ran to catch up.

Stepping into the small opening, Brendon discovered it was not a cave, rather a narrow channel that cut through the rocky hillside. Looking up he saw that the walls, at least thirty feet high, narrowed at the top and vegetation covered the opening. The angle of the fissure, the thick tree roots and dense foliage made this dell very hard to spot up close, much less from a distance. The floor of the channel was gritty, black sand, and Brendon noticed the impressions of footsteps made by the old man and his companion. Risteard brushed past him while observing his surroundings and took the lead, with Brendon following, Scioldmed and Girvan bringing up the rear.

The path wound back and forth, and Brendon worried that this may actually be a trap, but eventually the channel opened into a small box canyon shaped like an egg. The walls were very high, forty or fifty feet, sheer and smooth. As with the channel, several trees hung over the opening all around the circumference of the canyon. They did not completely obscure the sky above, however, and a shaft of sunlight filtered through the opening and rested gently on a small pool of water located near the center of the field.

To the left there was a cottage, neat and sturdy at first glance, and built of stone and timber. But closer inspection proved his first impression to be incorrect. The cottage did not seem to have been built, rather it appeared as if it had *grown* into existence. The stones themselves were very nearly identical in shape and size, but had no chisel marks on them, rather they seemed to have been formed into round disks. Furthermore, they were not stacked nor were they attached with cement—they were instead being held in place by the trunks and branches of several oak saplings surrounding the structure. The oak trees wove in and around the stones layer upon layer until they reached the eaves of the cottage and then spread outward a few feet and ended in a series of knotted bulbs.

The roof of the cottage was comprised of flat slate tiles that had been placed in an overlapping fashion supported by the limbs of a great blackthorn tree that stood at the end of the home where a fireplace might have been. The branches not covering the cottage spread away from and above the home, reaching towards the open sky and further sheltering the quaint cottage below. Around the structure were small gardens broken up by flowerbeds and pathways. It was beautiful--as if Mother Nature herself lived here.

Surveying the rest of the canyon, which widened to the right and stretched out another hundred feet or so, Brendon saw a gateway comprised of three enormous slabs of limestone, two ten-foot pieces serving as jambs with a four-foot lintel resting atop, leading into the hillside. The strange man and the huldretrow had stopped up ahead and were speaking softly to one another. The beast eyed Brendon as he entered, and then snorted in derision as he turned and headed towards the stone portal.

"Friends, come," said their elderly host. "Let us get to know one another. Fearghas is tending to some matters for me, but he has graciously offered his home for us to share a meal together," he said motioning to the neatly appointed dwelling. Curious, thought Brendon. He assumed that the monstrous huldretrow would live in the carved-out hole in the hillside, but instead they made their way through the gardens and towards the door of the cottage. It appeared much bigger now that they were standing next to it, and the gnomes marveled at the intricate woodwork.

"Impressive, yes?" asked the old man. "The huldrefolk have many skills, and many only remember their work with ore and gems. But to watch a huldretrow create a dwelling is truly a sight to behold." His voice was soft and clear, with no hint of malice or misgiving.

The old man opened the door and bid them enter. There was one room in the cottage, containing a large bed (again the wood seemed to have grown into the shape of a bed), a basin for water, and a pot belly stove where small tendrils of smoke drifted up from white coals and ash through a metal chimney that climbed along the wall before exiting the side of the building through an aperture a few feet below the ceiling. The only furniture not "attached" to the floor was a table and two chairs.

"Forgive me--we do not receive many visitors. Why don't you sit here, young man?" he said to Brendon indicating one of the chairs, "And your friends can have a seat over there," motioning to the bed, which was really more of a wide bench.

Brendon looked at Risteard who nodded as he hopped up onto the wooden platform. Girvan followed and finally Scioldmed, who seemed bitter at having been offered a seat at "the kid's table". Brendon turned his attention back to their host who sat down gingerly in the other chair. He was dressed in a loose-fitting tunic, gray and a little worn, but clean and embellished with green embroidery around the sleeve cuffs and neck. His light brown pants were tucked into a pair of well-made brown leather boots. He had no beard, but his white mustache drooped down past his lips and disappeared under his long hair, which was held in place by a leather cord. Brendon took the seat that was proffered him.

"Fearghas will bring us something to eat in a moment or so," he stated offhandedly, and turned his clear blue eyes on Brendon, looking deep into his eyes as if measuring him somehow. "Well, how can I help you?"

"You think we would eat anything made by a huldretrow?" spat Scioldmed.

"Have you known many of the huldrefolk?" asked the old man. Scioldmed just scowled and looked away.

"Apparently not, for they are *wonderful* cooks! Again, please forgive Fearghas, as he was only protecting our home," he said politely. Then, eyeing Brendon, "Besides, I was talking to the young man here. What do you want to know, young Druidae?"

Brendon was taken aback by the title. How did this man know who he was, or at least who he was supposed to be? "Are you . . . we're . . . looking for *Bidzil*," said Brendon, timidly, "Is that you?"

"I have been known by many names over the years. But yes, Bidzil is what the gnomes call me. The firbolg used to know me as

'Amrhán Gabha', the huldrefolk call me 'Syngeskaper', and the Naga frighten their children with tales of the 'Mauta Dilara'. It has been a long time since any have called me by my true name, which is of little consequence as I have little use for it these days. Fearghas simply calls me 'Grandfather', although it is quite evident we are not related. You may call me what you wish, and I will answer."

Brendon stared at the old man as he spoke. Whispers and echoes seemed to emanate from his mouth, but the others seemed not to notice, and Brendon shook his head as if to clear out the voices. At first, they were indistinct, but just as the old man finished, Brendon thought he heard a name.

"Something troubling you?" asked Bidzil, a wry smile on his face.

"Er . . . no, just . . . I thought about a name I heard once, that's all," replied Brendon.

"And what name was that?" inquired Bidzil.

"Caedmon Anluan?" he asked. An audible gasp from Scioldmed suggested he had said something wrong, but the ancient host just smiled.

"Where have you heard this name?" he gently inquired.

Mr. Dabir had mentioned that name, but Brendon didn't remember what he had said—so much had happened since—so he simply shrugged his shoulders. The old man, whose face was etched with deep lines where wrinkles had become a permanent fixture, continued to stare at Brendon with those clear blue eyes.

At length, he shifted his gaze to Scioldmed. "What can you tell our young friend about Caedmon Anluan?" he asked. Scioldmed shifted in his seat, debating on whether he should speak or not, and, finally relented.

“Th‘ early histories of th‘ aesir have been mostly forgotten by the gnomes, but many centuries ago our people and th‘ aesir had commerce with one another. In those days our leprechauns were sent to study with th‘ children of the Chaldees, Saami, and Druidae. They were allowed to learn a discipline, but never reached th‘ level o’ magi, shaman, nor bard. Nevertheless, they became disciplined in th‘ art o’ magic, and were a great boon to our people.

“In th‘ days before the Naga Invasion, a High Bard was chosen from among th‘ Druidae and tasked with th‘ protection o’ th‘ aelfen race. Caedmon Anluon was considerably more talented than th‘ other bards o’ that time. He accepted the task o’ protecting his people and took this roll seriously. And so, it was when Naga scouts entered th‘ aelfen lands, Caedmon chose to capture and question them, rather than turn them away. They told him of their emperor and his vast army, defying anyone to challenge their might. Some say Caedmon could have sued for peace. But, this was not the path he chose. He prepared an army o’ magi, shaman, and bards and left for th‘ heart o’ th‘ Naganese empire. Such power had never before been seen by th‘ Naga, and Caedmon was great and terrible in his destruction of the Naga homeland.”

The room was quiet. Scioldmed looked a little uncomfortable. He continued his story.

“When they returned to Aelfhiem they found th‘ city had been attacked by an army o’ Naga, who had ventured northward by ship. There were many who had been taken captive, others had fled into th‘ woods, but th‘ dead outnumbered them both. Caedmon had taken his best warriors with him, leaving the city nearly defenseless. The Naga army had retreated for th‘ time being, but he knew they would be back. Caedmon left the city and withdrew to th' mountains, having blamed himself for th' loss o' so many o' his people.

"Th' surviving aesir met as a council once again, to determine their fate. Their allies to th' north, th' firbolg, were enmeshed in a war with th' huldrefolk of Drukkars Moor, while th' sagittaries in th' south had been silent, not returning their missives. th' gnomes, o' course, would help them, but they had nowhere to go, and could not fight off an enemy indefinitely.

"Preparations to leave th' city began, and scouts were sent to determine a safe passage through th' mountains north of th' firbolg kingdom. And then one day Caedmon returned. He had discovered a way to hide th' city by means of a realmbridge. He had somehow gained an understanding of a stronger, wilder magic previously unknown to th' aesir. Throughout th' winter months they prepared th' realmbridge, finishing it just before th' return of th' Naga army in th' Spring.

"A large group of their strongest warriors had ventured to th' mainland to guard th' exodus and to protect th' city while th' magic was enacted. th' magic would cause th' city and all who lived therein to shift from one reality to another, hiding them from th' Naga without th' need for bloodshed. Only those who knew th' secret would know how to find th' portal. The last of th' warriors would then enter once th' city had been hidden. Several shaman and magi volunteered, but it was Caedmon who insisted on leading th' rear guard, sending his bards to help th' shaman elders with th' realmbridge.

"Caedmon and those with him harried and harassed th' Naga as they marched through Talamh Glas. Having bought their people th' time they needed, th' group of warriors returned to th' island in order to join them. But Caedmon noticed that something had gone wrong. th‘ city was still visible, but th‘ people had all vanished. He could no longer feel them anywhere on Faer Ri. Yet before he could do anything to repair what had happened, the Naga invaded, eventually capturing th‘ realmbridge along with th‘ city as its defenders escaped.

“Th‘ remaining aesir quarreled and in time the Chaldees retreated west into th‘ skerries, while the Saami banded together and moved from location to location, continuing to watch for th‘ return of their loved ones, while fighting th‘ Naga when they could.

“Many gnomes had been in th‘ city with the aesir when th‘ magic went awry, but there were many that remained hidden in th‘ Fells to th‘ north. Caedmon did what he could for th‘ gnomes who were left behind, eventually using his magic to protect those that remained from being discovered. He was both revered and feared among my people. We were grateful for his watchful eye, but his demeanor changed drastically. He was sullen and melancholic, regretting what he had done to his people. Years later th‘ Naga began to use the realmbridge to harvest slaves from another world. Unable to forgive himself for his failure, he eventually wandered away from th‘ gnomes, never to return. Many generations have passed since his death, but his name is still remembered in my homeland.”

Scioldmed, who had stood dramatically towards the end of the account sat down once again and looked at the man sitting across from Brendon. Bidzil’s countenance had become clouded, and his eyes distant. Again, there was silence for the space of several minutes.

Brendon jumped as the door opened abruptly, and Fearghas brought in a tray laden with fresh bread, strawberries, walnuts and tankards of water. He placed it on the table, but seeing the expression in the eyes of his master he shot a glance at the visitors and stood again to his full, menacing height. The old man shook himself out of his thoughts, and smiled a weak smile.

"Thank you, Fearghas, this will do quite nicely," he said with a relaxed air.

"Is there anything else I can do for you, Grandfather?" he asked. The old man shook his head. With a disapproving look at the newcomers, Fearghas left the room, but did not fully close the door. Bidzil looked again at Brendon.

"Tell me how you came by that name?" he asked again.

Deciding to tell the truth, regardless of the consequences, Brendon said, "Well, Mr. Dabir—he's my friend—he told me that my walking stick, er . . . shillelagh used to belong to him."

"Anything else?" inquired Bidzil admiring the shillelagh.

"And. . . " continued Brendon, "I heard it in my head." Another gasp from Scioldmed, but it was the change in the countenance of the old man that drew Brendon's attention—the oppressive spirit seemed to lift and a light returned to his eyes. He stood up, quicker than Brendon would have expected, and moved towards the door.

"Friends, I regret that I cannot join you for mid-day meal, I have something that needs my attention. Please eat and relax. I know you have not concluded your business with me, but it will have to wait." He moved to the door and opened it. Brendon was not surprised to see Fearghas standing in the garden a few feet away from the door. The man smiled at Brendon, and then, before closing the door he popped his head back in.

"Thank you, leprechaun, for your historical account of the departure of the aesir, albeit slightly inaccurate and absent of some rather pertinent details." And with that he closed the door, a look of indignation on Scioldmed's face causing Brendon to smile as he picked up a strawberry and popped it into his mouth.

Fourteen

All was quiet, except for the rhythmic crashing of the waves against the shore. Long tufts of sand reeds danced in the light breeze, while the warm glow of the setting sun painted the clouds with splashes of red and orange. But the peaceful vista went unappreciated by those gathered at the seaside that evening. The men were somber and silent as they carried their fallen comrade to the funerary pyre built upon a small boat that sat half beached.

Donovan looked into the faces of those in the procession. These were a hardened people, a proud people. They had known grief and pain, and yet this loss had affected them greatly. There were many more women than men standing or sitting along the beach, and while the men kept a resolute demeanor, the women quietly showed their emotion through tears and the occasional stifled sob.

When they arrived that morning, He-lush-Ka had barely acknowledged Cian Torin, but not out of disrespect. The man they had lost was the chief's only son, and the grief-stricken leader was unable to offer more than a nod before turning away at the sight of the newcomers. Years of struggle had taken its toll on the band of fighters, and only twenty or so men remained, most of them elderly. With the loss of the chief's son, hope had also vanished.

They had been offered food and blankets, as well as a place to sleep. Cian Torin explained that they would join the camp in mourning and discuss their purpose for coming the following day.

Donovan had been offered a change of clothes—a pair of tanned leather breeches and a loose-fitting blue tunic. He was glad because his clothes from home were soiled and torn. He kept his shoes—they would fit better than the leather boots he had been offered, but he would definitely need to wash his socks.

Once dressed, he explored the campsite. It was very much like being on a movie set. The homes were round and small, made of sapling trees that had been bent and tied together, with the walls made of animal-skins and bark. Mr. Dabir called these "wickiups". They had a low entrance, but once inside you could stand to full height. There was no furniture inside, but they had pelts and blankets laid on the ground for comfort when sleeping or sitting.

There were also a couple of structures that looked more permanent, with a platform above the ground and a patchwork of broad leaves for the roof. These he called "chickees," and it is here where they had been taken to eat and refresh themselves. They were larger, and several tables and benches had been placed in them.

Later in the afternoon, the tribe had come together to reminisce about Kenoa-lush-Ka, his exploits and his humorous stories. It was here that healing took place, as they remembered him for who he was. They were dressed in loose fitting tunics of blue, and red, and some green. The men wore leather breeches while the women wore brown skirts with a black threaded embroidery on the hem. Almost all of them wore beaded necklaces of varying materials including bone and wood. Each was different and unique to the person bearing the adornment.

The chief, however, did not wear a necklace. Over his tunic he wore a breastplate of beads and woven leather, and feathers had been sown into the leather adding tufts of color here and there. It was some sort of ceremonial clothing, as it seemed to serve no protective purpose. The chief himself looked like he had been carved out of wood, his hard face etched with lines brought about by age, sun, and the weather from countless years living in the wild. He appeared to be wise and strong. But his eyes were empty, and Cian Torin had commented that he seemed a hollow shell of his former self.

Finally, as the sun neared its final moments of life that day, the condolers bore the deceased to the shoreline. He was covered in a ceremonial shroud and placed on the boat. He-lush-Ka said a few words and then placed a torch under the kindling of the pyre as the boat was set adrift. The sea carried the vessel away as the flames engulfed the body. Then, as if by some signal, He-lush-Ka and the other men of the camp gave a series of loud whoops until one by one they died down. In silence, the camp walked back to their homes, Donovan following Mr. Dabir and his group into their wickiup. Mr. Dabir showed him a space to lie down and handed him a blanket. Curling up on the floor of soft pelts, Donovan swiftly succumbed to slumber.

***

Donovan awoke to the sounds of a heated discussion outside his wickiup. Having slept in his clothes, he quickly put on his shoes and stepped into the light outside the dwelling. There Cian Torin and Mr. Dabir were trying to explain something to He-lush-Ka, but the chieftain's eyes held a cold unwelcome stare. As Donovan approached, they stopped talking and turned towards him. At first nobody said anything, but then Mr. Dabir bent down in order to be at eye level with Donovan. That was never a good sign.

"Donny," he said softly, "They have not seen your parents. In fact, they have not seen anyone outside of their own people, save for the Naga troops that came through the area earlier in the week. And he has not heard of anyone being taken recently. It seems that he and his people have been weakened over the years, and they no longer have sufficient numbers of fighters or shaman to contend with the enemy."

Donovan thought for a moment, then, in a quiet voice he asked, "What does that mean? Now what do we do?"

The hopelessness in his voice must have softened the heart of He-lush-Ka, who for a moment seemed as though he might speak. His eyes searched for something in Donovan, but did not seem to find what they looked for. He turned his head and instead looked down the path towards the beach.

It was Cian Torin who finally broke the silence. "We will take you to Vloorhaven Glen with us, and await th' results of your brothers' quests. We will stay here for one more night in case Quinlan returns, but then we have to leave. He-lush-Ka and his people have been discovered, and it is only a matter of time until a larger force is sent to *exterminate them*," he said, turning towards the chief as he emphasized the last few words. Donovan felt as though he was missing something, and the look on his face signaled as much. Mr. Dabir stepped forward.

"We were just speaking with He-lush-Ka about the fate of the Saami in Faer Ri, suggesting that they move their camp, northward towards the firbolg lands, where the Naga are not likely to go because of the colder climate. He says he and his men are prepared to die to protect their homes. He will not relocate his people, nor will he help us to find your parents. He is ready to accept death," explained Mr. Dabir.

He-lush-Ka had been watching Donovan's expression as Mr. Dabir explained. For his part, Donovan didn't know what to think. He mostly was worried about his parents, but at the same time he felt a deep sadness for the people that had been so hospitable to him the day before.

"You mean they are all going to die?" he asked.

"If they stay here they will," piped in Cian Torin, "At least going north with us there is a chance."

At this point He-lush-Ka shimmered and changed form to a large grey wolf. Just as he did so, Donovan thought he saw something—it seemed to be tendrils of greenish blue threads that arose from the ground just before the chief shifted. The wolf eyed him quizzically, and then loped away down the path away from the group. Cian Torin threw up his hands in disgust and called for his men.

After giving them directions to gather more supplies, and to prepare to leave the next morning, he looked at Mr. Dabir and said, "We will have to leave th' area, for our own safety. If 'th others come here looking for us, they will also be in danger. If I knew how many lives had been lost over th' past few months, I would have never suggested He-lush-Ka's camp in th' first place.

If I divide my men and try to send word to th' others, they run the risk of being captured and killed as well. I know this isn't what you want to hear, Farzan, but it is my only choice. If He-lush-Ka and his people survive th' next battle, they will tell out friends where we have gone.

If not, we will have to rely on their skill to track us and follow us home. I trust my son will be able to discern a trap. If he doesn't feel it is safe to come here, he will go home to find us there. Risteard will be heading there as well when they conclude their business with Bidzil. That's th' best I can do. I am sure Conall is safe in Quinlan's and Kiwidinok's care." With that he walked off to help with preparations for the next day.

Mr. Dabir turned towards Donovan, "It will be OK. Perhaps your parents are safe and on their way back as we speak. Kiwi is as lucky as they come; he is probably with your parents right now and bringing them to us."

"But Cian Torin said this place is dangerous," said Donovan, his lower lip beginning to quiver.

"Not for a crafty old badger like Kiwi. He'll keep them all safe. Don't you worry one bit," Mr. Dabir smiled and turned Donovan towards a chickee that held a table with smoked meats and fresh fruit. Donovan was hungry, and he hurried towards breakfast, as Mr. Dabir's smiled faded.

***

He-lush-Ka padded slowly towards the beach where he had honored his son, Kenoa. He had intended to spend the time in solace, but his mind was racing as he thought about the young boy he had just met. There was something special about him, and not just his potential as a Druidae. It seemed as though the boy could see his shift before he had finished thinking about it. As though he could predict that it would happen. He had looked at the ground just before He-lush-Ka had shimmered into the wolf. What did he see? How had he known? The old chieftain could not dismiss the idea, no matter how he tried. The boy was *special*. He-lush-Ka looked once more at the shoreline, then changed into a swallow and flew back towards the village to keep an eye on the boy.

***

Donovan had spent the rest of the day watching the Saami tribe go about their business. Not all of them were shaman. Those that were, men and women, seemed to use their ability openly and without giving any notice to those around them. An ox that had been pulling a cart of wood shifted into a man who then took the wood and stacked it neatly beside a clay oven. A raven flew from branch to branch of a high tree dropping nuts to the ground, where, as a woman, she gathered them up in a basket. Each time Donovan watched and with each change he saw those same tendrils, only different numbers of strands and shades of green accompanied the changes. Occasionally he felt as though he were being watched himself, but when he looked around, he saw no one.

And so it was until night began to fall and the tribe gathered for an evening meal. There was still a somber atmosphere, but Cian Torin's men were talkative, as they shared stories and discussed the best routes for returning to their home. It would take another three days to get there, depending on the pace. At that last thought, Donovan felt sheepish. He knew they could move faster without Mr. Dabir and himself. He knew he was a burden, and wondered just how much Cian Torin would accommodate them before deciding that they were better off without them.

He-lush-Ka had spoken little during the meal. Donovan looked at him several times only to see him staring back. Donovan would look away but out of the corner of his eye he could see the chief had not. This happened a number of times until he thought he heard his name being called.

"Donovan," said one of Cian's men, "What would you be?"

"Sorry? I wasn't listening," he replied.

"If you could only change into one animal, what would it be?" repeated the gnome.

Donovan thought about it for a moment. He liked all sorts of animals. They had owned a rabbit and a guinea pig, but he had always wanted a dog. But would he want to be a dog? No, maybe something fierce, like a mountain lion, or a bear. Before he could decide, someone else was answering and Donovan had been skipped. He looked around the table and over to where He-lush-Ka was sitting, only to find the chief had left the table at some point.

Soon the dinner had concluded, stories had been shared, and the men of Cian Torin's company were heading to their wickiups to get some sleep. Donovan was tired as well, and knew that a long day of marching awaited them. He curled up into a tight ball and covered himself with the blanket. Although the days were warm, the breeze at night cooled things off quite a bit. As he lay there he kept thinking of his answer…what would be his animal of choice? Soon his eyelids began to become heavy and he drifted off to sleep, thinking of his childhood pets.

***

"Where is he?!" a voice called out just outside the wickiup.

Donovan stirred and stretched his arms and legs. He opened one eye and then closed it again. More shouting and voices from outside the wickiup as a commotion was going on. He flipped onto his stomach and stretched again. He sat on his back legs and twitched his whiskers a bit to get his bearing. He sensed he should move to the side of the wickiup—whiskers?!

He looked down his nose to see whiskers sticking out on either side of his bright pink nose. He looked down at his. . . paws?! His heart began to race as he hopped out of the pile of furs and blankets in which he had been sleeping. Was he. . . no way. He was a *rabbit*!

A little excited, and then a little afraid, he didn't know what to do. First, he wriggled his nose, and then he shook his bushy tail. How had this happened? His emotions vacillated from exhilaration to dread. How had he managed to do this? How high can he jump? Would he be able to change back? How fast is he know? What would he have to eat? What if someone tried to eat him?

The voices were growing louder when the bark was pulled back off the doorway to reveal Cian Torin, Mr. Dabir, and He-lush-Ka. They looked enormous! Donovan began to back away into the furs and bedding when something peculiar happened. . . He-lush-Ka smiled. Donovan stopped and looked right at him. Did he recognize Donovan? His question was answered by another surprise—laughter. The chief was actually laughing. The other men looked at him in confusion, but he just pointed at Donovan and said, "Shaman!"

Fifteen

Brendon could not believe what he was seeing. A tree was literally growing right in front of him at an amazing rate. He watched as the writhing roots twisted into the soil, digging deeper and deeper, while the trunk grew new bark, shed it and then grew new bark again as the diameter of the tree increased. The branches swayed this way and that struggling to reach the sky as leaves sprouted from buds to grow full size, fall and then be replaced by another growth.

Bidzil was humming, a smile on his face as he willed the tree to grow. His countenance had been nothing but cheerful these past few days, as though he had no cares in the world.

After that first afternoon, the party had been treated with the utmost of respect, and even Fearghas who, as it turned out, was only part huldretrow, did his best to make them feel welcome. Brendon noticed that Fearghas watched him a lot, as if measuring him up, but never treated him with any sort of mistrust.

They had each been given a comfortable bed hand-crafted by Fearghas who was quite skilled at carpentry, and a set of table and chairs to fit their needs. An awning was constructed in the glade to offer shade and prevent the dew from dampening the inhabitants therein. Brendon had wanted to witness the huldretrow use his magic, and was a bit disappointed when the accommodations were built using an assortment of tools stored in the large cave.

Fearghas was also an accomplished gardener, judging by the rows of vegetables and herbs that grew alongside the perimeter of the cottage. Brendon noticed that Fearghas sang to the plants as he watered and tended to them. Though his voice was rough and low, there was a sweetness to it that belied his haggard appearance. He was wholly unlike the ferocious beast they had met in the hollow that fateful morning.

For the last two days Brendon had felt a great peace come over him. Although Bidzil had told them he did not know of the whereabouts of the Baird parents, he had agreed to help them, and had said he would do everything in his power to locate them. It made Brendon feel a little better, but not any less anxious to find them. Still, he felt as though he was where he was meant to be, and trusted Bidzil at his word.

On their first day in the glade, Bidzil had showed them his home, which turned out to be the cave they had first assumed belonged to Fearghas. The entryway consisted of two slabs of stone standing on end and narrowing just a little where they are met by a third slab which served as a lintel. Above the lintel a proliferous tree root system served as the roof. Inside the entrance, the roots were thick and tangled as they grew down the sides of the earthen walls and into the floor. As one entered the cavern it became increasingly cooler and somewhat tighter until it opened up into a large chamber. Here there were bowls of dried fruit and meat and other food stores.

Bidzil had walked them through the chamber and into another that served as a kitchen with a brick oven that vented out through a chimney in the rock. Just beyond that room was the final portion of the dwelling, containing a large chest and a bed that had been woven from hundreds of small branches.

These caves had no stalactites or stalagmites, leading Brendon to believe that they were not formed naturally. As a young boy, he thought it would be pretty awesome to live in a cave.

Owing to the friendly treatment of the party by their hosts, ample food and comfortable shelter, everyone had felt more relaxed and safe.

Everyone except for Scioldmed who was sure they were in great danger. This in turn caused him to continually badger and annoy Risteard who patiently endured the incessant rantings of the elder leprechaun. The crux of the protest was the need to leave and return to Vloorhaven Glen. But Risteard had given his word to Bidzil that they would allow him to work with Brendon for a few days before moving on. To make matters even more contentious, Bidzil and Fearghas intended to accompany them on the journey. Girvan had quickly supported the idea which vexed Scioldmed to no end.

Bidzil finished the tune he was humming, and the tree shuddered once more before resting in place. In a matter of minutes, it had grown from a seed to full maturity, and blossoms were beginning to form. It was an apple tree and the bees were already making their way to the fragrant flowers to pollinate them. Bidzil had explained that he wanted to store some dried apples before they left, and that it would take a few days to do so. Little did they realize that he had meant to start from scratch!

"Brendon," Bidzil said as he sat down on one of the boulders nearby, "What do you know of that shillelagh you hold?" he questioned, looking down at the gnarled wooden cane lying next to Brendon. He had a soothing voice, and when he spoke the words fell softly on the ears of those who listened.

"Not much, just that it was my grandfather's and that he had wanted us to have it. Also, that it was made by Caedmon Anluan," answered Brendon.

"Well yes, it was made by Caedmon Anluan. It was taken from a blackthorn tree," he pointed to the tree that grew beside Fearghas' cottage, "In fact that is the very tree right there. A branch that was shaped around a long piece of Neim Stone that had been embedded therein. Many ancient songs have been sung to this branch, imbuing it with tremendous power. It is, perhaps, the most valued of artifacts from his day. To see it safe and in the hands of a Druidae brings me joy," he said with a bit of reverence.

"Neim Stones are not that uncommon, wild magicker." Scioldmed had walked up from behind and inserted himself into the conversation. "Most of our warriors use them on their weapons to ensure th'blades stay sharp and th' wood does not break."

"Yes, I noticed their use. I also noticed the clear labradorite gems of Findias your companion inserted into the hilt of his blades. That is a nice bit of wild magic you discovered," said Bidzil with a hint of amusement.

"IT. IS. NOT. WILD MAGIC!" bellowed Scioldmed, "It is ancient lore handed down to us for generations. Th ' Findias stones have been used to cut and shape Neim Stone, and so a natural adaption when fighting an enemy whose armor or *skin* is hardened!"

He was livid and turning himself about as he huffed away in a cloud of gall.

"You seem to know how to upset him," said Brendon.

"Yes, and isn't it fun?" replied Bidzil. "Well, as I was saying, this is quite a precious artifact. Fearghas is perhaps the only one that has anything similar to yours, and his is not nearly as old nor as powerful. In the hands of a practiced Druidae, that shillelagh can increase power twenty-fold."

"Twenty-fold—what does that mean?" queried Brendon.

"That means it makes the user twenty times stronger than he would be without using it. It means he would be able to do more than twenty Druidae could do. That is, of course, if he is trained. A very special artifact indeed," concluded Bidzil.

Brendon looked at the knurled, serpentine piece of wood. It was a dark midnight black, with sharp bumps covering every inch of it, except for the handle which had a big rounded knot where a person would grip it if used as a cane. The other end was smooth and just the right size to be gripped by two hands. The knot was heavy enough to be wielded as a club if used as a weapon. He remembered the few times he had seen it in operation, how it had glowed green.

"I saw it turn green a few times, when Mr. Dabir was fighting the reapers and again when we were able to understand the gnomes speaking," he mentioned.

"That is the Neim shard that is inside, along with the magic infused with it. Allow me to show you something," Bidzil said as he extended his hands.

Brendon offered him the shillelagh and Bidzil walked over to a clearing in the glade. He pulled a seed from his pouch and placed it in the soil. Holding the Shillelagh, he struck the ground as he began to hum. The ground exploded as a fully formed tree burst from the area where the seed had been planted, showering the area in dirt. The flowers on the newly formed apple tree bloomed, collapsed, and then grew into apples. Bidzil stopped mere seconds after he began, and opened his eyes.

"Hmmm. Yes, I had forgotten how that felt," he said reverently as he turned and walked back to an astonished Brendon. "Perhaps it's time we see what you can do with this." He offered the shillelagh to Brendon who slowly reached out to accept it. As he did he felt energy surging through the shaft of the artifact, slowly diminishing as it exchanged hands.

"How do I use it? What should I do?" he asked.

"Something small to begin with. You see, almost all Druidae have a link to the magic, it is their natural tendency to perform magic that leads them to that discipline. In reality, any of the aesir can learn magic. For some it is just easier, more natural. The easiest to learn is the Saami discipline, to become a shaman. It takes some practice, but you can learn if you try.

The Chaldees are more studious, and to follow that discipline you really have to apply yourself. It takes many years to become a magi, but any of the aesir could do it with time and effort. Being Druidae is different. You have to have natural talent as well as practice. It is something you are born with. That is why there are so few of them. I think for now you should focus on ripening the fruit of this new tree," answered Bidzil.

"Start with imagining in your mind what you want to happen. Hold tight to the shaft of the Shillelagh so as to draw strength from it," he continued.

Brendon imagined the apple being formed and growing. He held the shaft tightly and closed his eyes.

"Now add a song, or if you are shy you can try humming. It focuses the mind and harmonizes ourselves with nature," offered Bidzil.

Brendon hummed quietly but felt foolish when nothing happened. He tried for a short while before eventually giving up.

"It didn't work. I don't think I'm a natural," he said dejectedly.

"Not so. I saw what you did to Fearghas' staff in the dell; you prevented your friend from being killed as you shouted out. That was Druidae magic that I sensed. Give it time, you are still young," said Bidzil encouragingly. "Now let's get something to eat. I'm famished!"

***

Scioldmed watched from his vantage point behind one of the boulders in the glade. He saw the attempt to teach the young boy, and was relieved when nothing happened. Perhaps he misjudged the situation. . . perhaps he need not worry after all.

As Bidzil and Brendon walked away, he approached the tree to examine it closely. The flowers were still in bloom, bees lofting from one to another, collecting pollen as they went. Nothing had changed. Scioldmed turned and started back towards Bidzil's cave to join the others when he heard a rush of wind behind him. He turned again towards the tree to see the branches laden down with apples—more apples than an apple tree would normally produce.

As he watched the apples began to rot and fall from the tree in large numbers, until they all sat on the ground shriveled and dry. The tree branches were all twisted and bent, from the excessive weight of the fruit, and the tree tilted to one side before falling to the ground. Before his eyes the tree dissolved and decayed back into the ground. There was nothing left. No fruit, no leaves, nothing. With a hint of satisfaction Scioldmed confirmed his fears about the young Druidae! He *was* dangerous!

***

The mood at dinner that night was subdued. Brendon didn't care for the vegetables they were eating, and was still feeling sorry for himself for not being able to perform any magic that afternoon. Bidzil was eating heartily, as was Girvan and Risteard (who rarely spoke anyway). Scioldmed was eying Bredon warily, and Fearghas was eyeing Scioldmed. It made for an awkward meal, although nobody seemed to notice.

"I think we need to leave tomorrow," blurted out Scioldmed after a while. "You have a tree of ripened fruit, and I think you can prepare that for drying tonight. I would even help." At this last remark everyone stopped what they were doing and looked at Scioldmed.

"I'm. . . I'm . . . just trying to be helpful," he stammered. Again, more stares. Girvan's mouth opened and food fell from his mouth onto the plate.

"That is. . . anything is better than just sitting around," Scioldmed continued. "Cian Torin will be worried and . . . and th' boy's parents might have already been found. We should stop lollygagging and leave in th' morning," he said matter-of-factly.

Risteard seemed to be considering this newest complaint more seriously than the previous requests. But before he could say anything, Bidzil surprised everyone by saying, "Agreed. Fearghas, let's plan on leaving at daylight."

Risteard nodded while Scioldmed did his best to conceal a smile. They finished dinner much as they had begun— in silence. Afterwards the gnomes went about packing their things while Fearghas began preparing food and travel equipment for Bidzil and himself.

Bidzil took notice that Brendon was not engaged and invited him to get something out of the cave. It was much cooler in there than outside, even with the cook fires left to burn themselves out. Bidzil made his way to the back of the system where the bed and trunk had been. He opened the trunk and rummaged about for a bit before taking out a green tunic and some dark brown canvas pants. He offered them to Brendon and then rummaged some more before finding a pair of leather boots. Brendon looked at himself and his clothes. The track suit had been stained to the point of not being recognizable. Although he tried to wash the dirt and grime out of them, they were still soiled and torn. A moment later Bidzil found a few more items of clothing, including undergarments and such. Primitive compared to what he was wearing, but it seemed more durable.

"I will leave so you can change. I know you may want to hold on to these items from your world, clothes and such, but you will be less conspicuous and better prepared for the elements wearing these. Especially where we are going," he said.

Brendon thought for a moment. "How is it you have clothing my size?" he asked.

Bidzil was walking towards the exit when he stopped and looked back. "They belonged to someone I knew," he replied,

Brendon looked at the clothes he had been given. Deciding it was better to change after all, and grateful for something clean to wear, he nodded and began taking off his shoes. Bidzil left the room and walked through the kitchen and storage cavern and then out into the glade. The sun had set, and a slight breeze stirred the leaves causing the branches that hung over the perimeter of the canyon to sway this way and that. Bidzil's smile was gone and a tear slowly trickled down his weathered face into the folds of his cloak. Footsteps marked the sound of someone approaching.

"Is everything ok, Grandfather?" asked Fearghas, tenderness and concern in his gravelly voice.

"Yes Fearghas. I was just thinking about my son."

Sixteen

The Saami were busying themselves with loading carts and dismantling their wickiups. As they peeled back the bark and animal skins the slender saplings that had been tied together at the top were revealed. They created the domed roof and the leather thongs were untied so the small trees were shaken loose from one another allowing them to straighten themselves.

The leafy roofs of the chickees were broken and scattered, while the timbers were dissembled to be taken to the beach and cast into the water as driftwood. In a matter of hours, the camp looked as though it were again a pristine wilderness, except for the carts and people gathering the last of their belongings.

Cian Torin was still amazed by the change of heart He-lush-Ka had undergone. One moment he was pushing them out, willing to lose his life against all reason. The next morning, after Donovan's strange experience, he decided to pack everything up and go with the gnomes.

At least part way. They were heading towards the Dearmed Skerries, islands that lay west of the Fells of Beag Cairdeas and the gnomes of Vloorhaven Glen. They would share a path for the first three days before parting ways. Cian Torin was glad to know they would be heading towards a safer location, even though his people would now be the only ones patrolling these woods against the Naga.

It had been nearly three-hundred years since the Naga invaded the Woods of Talamh Glas, and Cian Torin's great-great-great grandfather had fought with the aesir in that final war, just before the fall of Aelfheim and the departure of their aelfin neighbors.

Caedmon Anluan himself had given much praise to the gnome-hunters for their effort on that day. Some of the gnomes, including many of the clan leprechauns, had also crossed over via the realmbridge, fearing the Naga would conquer the lands north of Talamh Glas. But as it turned out the Naga would not do more than harass the borders of the gnome lands, the climate being too inhospitable for settling in the area. Their giant lizards and drakes could not be coaxed to venture into the colder regions of the north, and their fear of the firbolgs was also a deterrent.

For their part, the Saami and their shamans had been unwilling to give up their lands, moving camp from one location to another. Hiding, fighting, and doing their best to hinder the Naga slave-trade as it developed over the years—the Naga had discovered a way to use the realmbridge to cull inhabitants from another world.

After a while, the Saami realized that the slaves being taken were actually descendants of the aesir who had crossed over. Only something was different; time was moving at a much faster rate in their new world, roughly sixteen years would pass there during one cycle of seasons here in Faer Ri. At first only clothes had changed; then it became the language and even their appearance. Eventually the gnomes agreed to work with the Saami to rescue as many as they could, but they were severely outnumbered.

Cian Torin had yet to disclose much of this information with Mr. Dabir, and struggled to justify his choice to withhold the knowledge that even if the newcomers could return, they would find their home world very different from when they left it. And yet, if they truly were meant to usher in a new era of magic then perhaps they would abandon their wish to return. However, considering the impetus to find their parents and leave that was abundantly evident in the boys, he doubted that would be the case. How would they react upon hearing that they might never be able to go back? And could the prophecy still be come to pass given that young Donovan had shaman-shifted in his sleep that morning?

***

Donovan didn't know what to say. For that matter, he didn't know what to think. It had taken the better part of the morning for him to change back into his own form. He-lush-Ka had tried to explain as best he could; teaching him about the shaman shift magic, but it didn't help. It wasn't until the chief had shifted into and out of the rabbit form several times that Donovan finally memorized the tendrils with their shape and number. Then he imagined those same tendrils coming from the ground and into his body. There was no pain or discomfort, just a bit disorienting at first. Once he resumed human form the chief encouraged him to try some other forms, specifically animals that he knew well. The better one knew and understood a species, the easier it was to shift.

Donovan had been reluctant at first, but also a little excited. He had tried a dog, a cat, and even a mouse. They had all been easy once he knew what to look for. He-lush-Ka would demonstrate a few times, and then Donovan would copy it. The chief was elated, explaining that not only was he very young, but his gift of seeing the tendrils was not typical. Most shaman would spend years learning and watching the animals, imitating them, their actions, and learning as much as they could. Then, after much practice, they could assume the form. Donovan, however, was able to master an animal after mere moments, and He-lush-Ka was reticent to leave his side.

The camp had been packed up, and they were awaiting the last of the scouts to return before setting out. Donovan sat next to Mr. Dabir, who also seemed a bit at a loss for words. They had been sitting on the back of a cart for the past half an hour, watching silently as the others went about their preparations.

"I'm sorry, Mr. Dabir," Donovan finally said.

"For what, Donny?" he replied.

"You know. For being a shaman, instead of a Druidae bard. I mean, I didn't try to do it, and I'm sorry if it messes things up," Donovan said with a remorseful tone.

"There is no reason to apologize. I am the one who is sorry for making you feel as though you had to be something you are not. It is very exciting to see you embrace the shift magic, especially so young. I am just curious how you are able to do it, as it is unlike anything I have ever heard of. These tendrils you are seeing are not recorded in anything I have ever read. That's all. Besides, maybe your brothers will be able to perform as a bard, and that would still launch a return of the Druidae practice," said Mr. Dabir.

As they finished their conversation, an older man walked up to them and introduced himself. "Hello, I am Dak-ro-Nee. I will be conveying you this morning, if you are ready," he announced. And with a nod from Mr. Dabir he walked towards the front of the cart and picked up a yoke, placing it on his shoulders before shifting into a large horse. With a lurch the cart began to move forward as other men and women moved towards their carts to follow suit. The gnomes trotted out in front of the procession, leaving a few to follow as rearguard, and the company began their trek.

High above, a black raven circled the carts as they left the camp. After a few more sweeps of the area it dove and banked in their direction before pulling up and, with a shimmer of green, became He-lush-Ka.

“We should be safe for the next day or so. The gnome scouts encountered nothing in their search of the beach, and I can detect no movement in the trees on the far side of the inlet,” he said confidently as he walked alongside the cart. “Perhaps young Donovan would like to accompany me on my next search. A raven is a simple form to adopt. . .” he suggested.

Donovan began to scoot forward on the bench in order to leap off when Mr. Dabir reached out and steadied him. “I think not, he is yet new to this and I worry for his safety,” he interjected. Donovan looked at Mr. Dabir with a hint of pain, but realized that he was right in not rushing things. He-lush-Ka looked a little dejected, but instead changed the topic.

“You know, instead of living with the gnomes, you can always come with us. We are your own people, after all. I could teach you much more than shifting into animal forms. I could show you how to heal wounds, cure the sick, and become one with nature. You would be an adopted son of the tribe,” he said enthusiastically.

“But I already have parents,” said Donovan, “We aren’t living with the gnomes, just waiting until my brothers come back with my mom and dad. All that stuff sounds really cool, but I just want to go home.”

“Bah!” responded He-lush-Ka “Your parents are most likely lost to us for good—slaves in some remote location or worse, they are dead. You should accept their fate and yours. Become a shaman and avenge them!”

Donovan's face went white and then red with embarrassment. He hid his face in his arms, not wishing for the others to see the tears that had sprung up.

"Now see here," began Mr. Dabir, "You have no business speaking to the boy in this way!"

"He should accept that this is his fate! Your desire to placate him and insist on the possibility of finding his parents is crueler than any of the words I have shared. I have given him a chance for a better life, while you offer hope and put your faith in a prophecy that will never come to be!" yelled the indignant chief.

"What's all this now?" Cian Torin had ran up from behind and inserted himself between the cart and He-lush-Ka.

"I am simply explaining that false hopes and false prophesies lead to more pain and suffering," He-lush-Ka explained in a low and steady voice, his eyes never wavering from Mr. Dabir, as though seeing him as a threat.

"Well, I for one choose to have faith in things to come. Hope, no matter how small, is a far stronger motivator than acceptance of one's fate, friend chief," said Cian Torin diplomatically. He-lush-Ka looked away, as if weighing this statement. Then, abruptly, he shifted into a raven and flew away.

Mr. Dabir put his arm around Donovan, and did his best to console him. "Donny, I believe your parents are alive. And I believe we will find them. Don't give up, and don't lose hope."

"I won't, Mr. Dabir," said Donovan after a while. But it was hard to get out. And getting harder to believe it was true.

***

The second day of their journey was uneventful. He-lush-Ka had kept to himself, rarely speaking with anyone, including his own people. Cian Torin and his men spent most of the day cutting down overgrowth on the trail, as well as removing falling timbers. This path had once been used by the aesir, and at one time may have been heavily traveled, but now it was in a state of disuse, and the company found it difficult to keep the carts moving at the same pace as the first day.

At lunch there was discussion regarding options should they run into obstacles too difficult to remove. Cian Torin regretted not having Scioldmed with him, he would be useful in removing things too heavy for this small band of hunters. The Shaman who was hauling the carts in the morning traded with those who had been resting, and the caravan continued throughout the afternoon.

It was just before dusk when He-lush-Ka returned to the company and announced the trail would not be passable the following day as a pass between two hills had been filled in with debris from years of neglect and storms. They would have to travel on foot for the rest of the journey.

Immediately the Saami stopped and broke down for camp, while a few dissembled the carts in order to create litters in which to carry the essential materials for homes, as well as clothing and food supplies. Feeding a village was not easy, and they could not count on foraging and hunting to sustain themselves this close to winter in the skerries. The elders of the tribe met that night to discuss their options while Cian Torin and his men supped with Mr. Dabir and Donovan.

"I think they would best be served by coming with us, Cian. They could rest in Vloorhaven for a season and then venture out into the skerries in the Spring. It is bound to be a harsh winter, and with little to no food stored they are not likely to survive," commented Grunwill, a burly gnome with a mop of blonde curls tied in a top knot.

Cian Torin thought for a moment. "I agree, Grunwill. But I have offered many times and have been rejected. He-lush-Ka is a prideful man, and has not been at his best since the loss of his son.

Like you, I fear he will lead his people to their deaths, and yet they will not question his authority. Tomorrow will be our last day with them before they make for Domhain Bay. Perhaps I can reason with him one more time."

"I think reason has left him for the time. How will they even cross the waters to reach the Skerries?" asked Mr. Dabir.

"At the edge of the Talamh Glas where it meets the Fells of Beag Cairdeas there is a cool mountain stream that is host to many birch varieties. I have watched Saami strip a birch tree and build a canoe in a relatively short time. They will have the materials they need to get their people and supplies to the skerries. As we are nearing winter, the water will begin to get colder, but they should be able to arrive long before the ice flows prevent them from doing so," answered Cian Torin.

Donovan stopped listening as the men continued to discuss their route for the following morning and the day after. He glanced over to where the elders were speaking to one another, watching He-lush-Ka as he listened to their plans to bypass the road and carry provisions in litters. The chief glanced at him once or twice, but did not make any movement to engage.

That night they slept peacefully as the wind whistled through the forest canopy. The trees rustled softly as the leaves spun around, clinging to the branches as the breeze tried to pull them from their lofty perch. The travelers below had chosen not to set up tents or wickiups, but rather to leave them packed so as to have an earlier start the next day. Donovan watched the leaves whirl around in the air currents, the underside of the leaves a gray silver, and the upper side a dark green. They seemed to wave to him as they fluttered.

Above the trees, a starry sky spread out before him. The multitude of tiny lights helped to illuminate the campsite around him as the fires had been banked for the evening. Mr. Dabir was close by, already asleep and wrapped in his woolen blanket. Slowly Donovan drifted off to sleep himself.

***

He awoke to the sounds of a busy camp. The carts had been taken apart, and wheels and axles had been loaded onto shaman who had already assumed the shape of mules, while the rest of their gear had been placed on several litters carried by teams of Saami. After a quick bite to eat they began their trek for the day.

Just as He-lush-Ka had reported, the trail ended in rubble and debris after the first two hours. The company made their way around the base of the western-most hill and across the fields that lay between the cliffs on the west and the forest on the right. They stopped for lunch and re-assignment and distribution of supplies before moving on that afternoon.

By evening they left the dense forest and were approaching a much rockier terrain. The trees were more scattered here, spaced out in clumps rather than all together. The land continued to rise and just ahead of them small mounds gave way to larger hills. In the distance vast mountains loomed high in the sky, their sides draped in a white blanket, their peaks hidden in the clouds and mist. Donovan stopped to survey his surroundings. He had never seen mountains in real life, having grown up in Michigan. They were beautiful! Majestic and strong, these megaliths jutting up from the earth felt powerful to him.

Men and women walked by him as he stared. Mr. Dabir and Cian Torin came up from behind to soak up the view as well.

“Simply stunning,” said Mr. Dabir.

"Aye," agreed Cian Torin, "The Dreich Mountains. Some say no man can pass over them, they reach so high into the heavens as to prevent all from even daring to climb. At their base live the firbolg--a race of giant men with whom we no longer have contact."

Donovan wondered what constituted a giant to the gnomes who were only a few inches taller than he. But his thought was cut short as the company had moved beyond them and they hurried to catch up.

***

That evening the scouts had returned with a worrisome look. A patrol of Naga had passed close to where the company left the road earlier that morning. They spent most of the day following them to be sure they did not double back and discover the route the gnomes and Saami had taken. With about thirty soldiers, and fifteen of the tattooed spear wielders, the patrol would have been a close match to the strength of the camp. It was great fortune they had not been discovered.

No fires were built that night, and sentries formed a picket line far from the main body of the encampment. All were a little anxious as they ate, and He-lush-Ka informed them that they should retire early as they would move out before dawn. Many of the men and women slept with their weapons close at hand, if they slept at all.

Before daybreak, the Saami had reassembled their carts and distributed their supplies once again. Without more than a wave goodbye, they departed to the west leaving Cian Torin and his men to head northwards into the hill country.

The trek went a little faster now, without the burden of the litters slowing them down. The terrain was rugged, and the footing was such that Donovan spent most of his day looking at his feet to make sure he did not slip due to a misstep. The gnome-scouts came and went, assuring them all was well. As the sun reached its peak, they had covered a healthy distance, and stopped for a break.

Looking back the way they came, he saw the enormous forest of Talamh Glas covering the lands in the horizon; the lush greens blending together in a carpet of tree tops. The air here was much cooler, and wind pulled at their clothes as it wove through the hills and crags. Most of the trees he had seen that day were in small groves or clumps in the valleys between the rolling hills. But there was the occasional lone pine or two on the hilltops, standing firm against the buffets of the frigid blasts.

They continued until it grew dark. Although only a half-day's march from home, it was unsafe to travel the rocky terrain at night, so they decided to make camp and ate the last of their food stores.

They wondered aloud about the fate of the Saami, and hoped sincerely they made it to the coast in safety. It would take a few days to prepare the canoes, but they should be safe from the Naga if they avoid campfires. The gnomes had chosen not to warm themselves with a campfire, even being within the boundaries of their homeland. It was still warm enough for enemy patrols to venture into gnome territory; no need to put their party at risk.

As Donovan lay underneath the star filled sky, he wondered again about his brothers, how they were doing, if they had found his parents. He was weary from the day's march, and keeping his eyelids open had become cumbersome. It was only a matter of minutes before his fell asleep.

***

A hand slipped around his waist while another covered his mouth. Donovan kicked out but was lifted off the ground by a pair of strong arms. He wiggled, trying to cry out, but the grip on him only tightened as the figure walked slowly out of the campsite. Mr. Dabir and the others were still asleep, even though Donovan tried his best to scream. After a few steps the figure crouched and waited for a gnome sentry to walk by before it began to sprint from the camp.

Donovan tried to pull the hand from his mouth but the figure wrapped his arms around Donovan so that his arms were pinned to his side. Faster and faster his captor ran, farther and farther away from the camp. Donovan began to cry. He wasn't strong enough to break free, no matter how much he squirmed. His mind raced for an idea of how he could get away. He was too weak, too small. Then it occurred to him . . . maybe he wasn't small enough. He concentrated very carefully . . .

The man carrying the boy lurched forward as the weight he had been carrying disappeared, and he fell to his knees. He looked all around and could not see the boy anywhere. He opened his hand and planted his palm firmly on the ground. There just to his left he felt it—a small mouse. He turned and pounced on the mouse with a speed that belied his age. As he lifted the mouse to his face the animal squeaked once and tried to wriggle free, but He-lush-Ka kept his cupped hand firmly about the creature.

"It is alright. It is me, I am not going to hurt you," he said softly. There was a green shimmer and Donovan stood before him, the chief's cupped hands now on his shoulders.

"Why did you kidnap me?!" screamed Donovan.

"Shhhhh. I didn't kidnap you, I just needed to get you away to talk to you. I made a mistake saying what I did the other day, and I regret that I hurt your feelings. I think it is admirable that you want to find your parents, and I will hope for their safe return as well. But in the meantime, you could come with us. We could care for you and teach you so much more. And, when your parents are found, they can join us as well. The gnomes will know where we have gone. You see? Does this not sound like a better plan?" He-lush-Ka's expression belied his dispassionate tones, his face contorted with umbrage and fear. "Surely you must see this is a far better plan than living in a hole in the ground!" his face became darker, more twisted.

Donovan was getting scared. Changing into a mouse would not save him again. He had to think bigger. Stronger. But first he had to let He-lush-Ka think he had won him over.

"You know, that does sound better," he said, "And it would be nice to live with my own people for a time."

The chief's face softened a bit and he forced a smile. Taking Donovan by the wrist he stood up and turned around, putting more distance between the two and the gnome campsite.

"I believe it would be faster if we shifted into another form. Perhaps a dog like you did the other day," He-lush-Ka suggested.

Donovan nodded. "Good idea, or maybe something more sure-footed for the terrain," he thought for a moment, "Maybe a mountain goat?"

He-lush-Ka stopped and turned, his toothy smile visible in the dark, "That is an excellent idea. Let me show you." He shifted and became a mountain goat, with a long fur coat, and big round ridged horns.

"OK, now show me how to turn back," said Donovan, "I don't like changing unless I know how to turn back."

The goat nodded and shifted back into the chief. But as he began to stand up a shimmer of green in front of him told him he had underestimated the boy. Donovan-mountain goat charged the man as he shifted back into human form, and lowered his head into the chief's, sending him flying off his feet and rendering him unconscious. Donovan turned and sprinted up the hill. This form *was* perfect for the terrain and after a few minutes of running he was back in the camp.

As he entered he shifted into his natural form and the sentry called out for help. The men awoke as Donovan told them what had just happened. Cian Torin sent several hunters to where Donovan had said he left the chief, while Mr. Dabir and Cian Torin asked Donovan to share the full story. Cian Torin was amused by the cleverness of the boy, but Mr. Dabir was angry that he had almost lost his charge.

"I am so sorry, Donny," he said. "I should have known he would not give up so easily."

"It's ok, Mr. Dabir. You are doing everything you can, and I know it."

A few moments later the gnome hunters returned empty-handed. He-lush-Ka had escaped.

Seventeen

Kiwidinok dove to his left rolling quickly to his feet again as the jaws snapped shut, missing him by inches. He sprinted towards the far side of the arena and turned to face his opponent again. The creature, a bizarre amalgam of crocodile, lion, and hippo, turned as well, saliva dripping from its enormous toothy smile.

It had the wide hind legs of a hippopotamus allowing it to stand at full height (several feet taller than Kiwidinok), and the front paws were furry and clawed like a lion. But its head . . . that was the real menace. Five feet long and three feet wide; its maw brimming with razor-sharp teeth crowded together at crooked angles, the real monstrous fiend's real threat. Kiwidinok had seen the creature snap the arm off a man a few days prior, ending the fight with a gruesome feast. Judging by its ferocity, it was hungry again.

Kiwidinok noticed that although it could strike with speed and savagery, it was not a very nimble animal, and labored to move from one side of the area to another, unlike the giant boar he had faced in his first exhibition. That animal had been fast as well as dangerous, but not very clever and easy to overcome. After a few near misses, Kiwidinok had shifted into the form of a porcupine and handled the threat with a few well-placed barbs. The boar had refused to go near him after that and was taken away, presumably to be eaten.

They did not allow him a weapon, but instead encouraged him to use the shift magic to assume the life-forms needed to protect himself and survive the combat. As in the gladiatorial matches of Rome, the blood sport seemed to be a favored pastime of the saggitary, and wages were won and lost as men and creatures died for the entertainment of others.

The monster moved closer as Kiwidinok skirted the outer limits of the pit, amid the booing and jeering of the spectators. The arena was a large marble lined courtyard, about the size of two basketball courts end to end. The walls were roughly fifteen feet high, with a viewing area on all sides for the general public, and a balcony on which sat His Royal Majesty surrounded by a myriad of servants. Oval in shape, it was the largest of the three arenas.

The other two were small courtyards where hand to hand combat events were provided with or without weapons. Ganju had excelled in these arenas, his military training as a Gurkha making him a standout and favorite among the sagittary soldiers. In those arenas they did not fight to the death, as both combatants were considered skilled and deserving of honor. Kiwidinok had not been so fortunate, his hand to hand fighting consisting of a few bullies he had put up with in junior high. So, he was deemed expendable and forced to fight in the pit with whatever oddity they would put before him.

The creature had closed in and raised itself to its hind feet. Instead of a growl or roar, it emitted a strange hissing shriek that sounded like the worn-out brake pad on his old truck. It swung it claws wildly, but more for balance than as a form of attack. They were a diversion, their only useful purpose in the tearing of flesh once the victim was rendered immobile. No, he needed to focus on those rows of mangled teeth, dripping with thick saliva--no doubt a bacterial wonderland--as the beast swayed left and right waiting to strike with its massive weight and quick snap of its mandibles.

Kiwidinok feared that even a gash from those teeth would mean his demise, as the infection would render him weak and unable to fight. Whatever he did, he needed to stay away from that filthy gullet.

It happened between blinks, the enormous mouth gaped open and then shot forward, barreling down on him before he could move. With no time to avoid this attack, his mind raced to think of the animal with the thickest skin, a crocodile, elephant, then just as the jaws began to close he recalled an animal he had studied in school. . .

The crowd of onlookers watched with glee as the ammit lunged towards its next victim, the captured shaman who had so far been a disappointment in this match—running from the beast rather than fighting. A few would lose their bets, but most favored the ammit and looked forward to a grisly end. But just as the jaws of the wretched beast closed on the man a green shimmer of light surrounded him, and a massive creature appeared, the length of which spanned the width of the arena.

It was bluish gray, with smooth skin and an enormous head, a giant eye blinking slowly just to the side of its wide mouth. It had fins like a fish, but it also had a fluked tail, and was considerably larger than any fish the sagittaries had ever seen. The mouth opened slightly revealing long evenly spaced sharp teeth about the size of a man's forearm, and the spectators on the near side of the arena jumped back as a large hole in its head opened and sucked air with a loud rush of wind.

As the crowd gaped in astonishment, the ammit finally succeeded in unlocking its teeth from the thick blubbery skin. It tried over and over to bite the huge behemoth, but the enormity and thickness of the skin made the attacks fruitless. Even clawing at the skin had little to no effect, as no blood could be infected. The ammit, moved away and began to pace back and forth, hungry and confused.

Kiwidinok chuckled to himself. With a skin layer fourteen inches thick, the sperm whale was the best defense against this foe, which had "bitten off more than it could chew". Another chuckle. But he could not stay in this form long. The sun was already blistering his skin and his skeletal structure could not support this weight for very long out of water. Having spent his college years studying nearly every species from the animal kingdom in his pursuit of his degree in Biological Sciences, he had amassed a wide array of forms, and was respected by other shaman for his diversity in shift magic. Safe for the moment, he developed a strategy in which a particular series of animals could be used to tire out the ammit and allow Kiwidinok to find a weakness.

Kiwidinok first shifted into a rabbit and the audience moved closer to the edge of the area to watch, as the ammit stirred and began to give chase. It was a bit pathetic, actually, as Kiwidinok had to slow down from time to time to allow the creature to get closer, baiting it in an effort to keep it moving. With those slow hind legs, and the heat of the day, the ammit was tiring quickly. But this would not end the fight. As he kicked up his back paws to the left, causing the ammit to dive in that direction, Kiwidinok steered his furry little body to the right and continued to keep it at bay, all the while studying the creature. Its scaly crocodilian back and tail would protect it from above. The hind legs had the thick skin of a hippopotamus, and so were also not overly vulnerable.

The ammit dove towards him, flattening itself along the ground. Kiwidinok jumped straight up and then landed on the head of the beast. He skipped along the neck and down the back as the enraged creature turned and snapped at his tail, just missing him again. As it arose, the strained breathing told Kiwidinok that the time was near. He looked again and noticed the fur on the underside of the beast, the robust chest where the paws of a lion clawed at the earth trying to gain purchase. Here was the weakest part of the flesh, although defended by the snapping jaws.

He thought for a moment and looked around the arena. A banner of some sort hung from a pole near the gate he and the beast entered.

Then he remembered something he learned about alligators and crocodiles while interning as a marine biologist in Florida. As the ammit lunged at him again, mouth open, he shifted into a swallow (humorous choice, he thought to himself) and flew to the banner. He shifted again and became a raccoon, quickly untying the banner allowing it to fall to the sandy floor of the pit. The ammit began to amble over to where he was, so he waited, poised above on the pole. As it got closer he jumped to the ground and shifted into a kangaroo rat, grabbing the silken banner in his teeth. The ammit, seeing this, mustered its remaining strength to rise on its feet and plunged downward. Kiwidinok waited until the last moment before jumping straight into the air, high above the ammit as it snapped its powerful jaws around the flowing banner. At the apex of his jump, Kiwidinok shifted into a large silver back gorilla and fell on the back of the ammit, grabbing its snout, and wrapping the banner around and around until the prickly maw was contained in a silken web. Pushing himself off the beast, whose paws were not long enough to reach and remove the material, Kiwidinok considered how he would finish the ammit.

A clever tactic; in remembering that crocodiles and alligators had incredible jaw strength but lacked the converse muscles to open their mouth; he rendered the beast ineffectual. Exhausted, the creature collapsed on the ground and stared at its lost meal.

Looking at the poor beast, laboring to breath and remove the banner, Kiwidinok felt pity. There was no honor in killing it now, and so he shifted into his natural form and walked back towards the gate.

The crowd began to boo and sneer once again. Angry and disappointed for having lost wages on their bets--this shaman having proved himself more than a match in wit and ability--and even more upset for not having seen the death of one of the combatants. He ignored their protests and continued to wait at the gate, when out of nowhere a heavily built sagittary leaped from the gallery and landed in front of him. It was the same powerful adversary who had first captured him and Conall. The creature sneered and raised its trident striking Kiwidinok in the gut with the shaft before turning and thrusting its speared end into the ammit's chest with one smooth motion. A roar of approval from the crowd followed and he acknowledged their praise with a thin smile, the defeated creature hissing and closing its eyes for the last time.

***

Conall watched from behind the golden dais. He was unable to keep his attention on the fight, as his duties included carrying trays of assorted meats to and from the servants who in turn fed His Royal Majesty, Keeper of the Stone, Sehmak III. His Royal Majesty spoke to no others but Tilsave, Master of Slaves, the portly man in the ornately embroidered tunic he had met on his first trip to the palace. Tilsave was not overly harsh; in fact, the slaves were treated fairly, as long as they did not disobey. They were fed and clothed, and Conall had been treated well enough, other than living in a cell. It seemed to him, after several days of service in the palace, that the slaves were accustomed to their treatment, and unwilling to do anything to displease their master. Kiwidinok had determined that most of those that served had done so since they were young, having been born into captivity. Many lived in small dwellings in the palace, without the need for a lock and key as they were completely loyal. Therefore, having not known any other way of life than this, why would they assume there was anything better?

The crowd roared. Conall brought his attention back to the present. Each time Kiwidinok entered the arena, Conall was sure it would be the last, and with his demise, any chance of escape would be impossible. The applause died down and the spectators began to shuffle out of the viewing stands. If he was quick, he could catch a glimpse while His Royal Majesty was assisted in propping himself up off the pillows he had been lounging on.

He waited until eyes were turned away towards the dais and scooted himself forward to the edge of the balcony. There below, was some cross between an alligator and a lion perhaps, only the legs were gray and wrinkly looking. A trident was being pulled out by a large sagittary while Kiwidinok, doubled over, was being escorted back through the gate into the cell blocks below. *Relief.*

"Boy!?" it was Tilsave, "Be about your business at once!"

"Yes . . . Master Tilsave," Conall said between his teeth. It had been hard for him to take orders, but Kiwidinok had said this was the only way to bide time until he came up with a plan. Conall shuffled back to his place beside the dumbwaiter, where food from the kitchen was brought up to him to then be carried to the dais.

Dumb-waiter, he smirked, that fit his description as well. Seen and not heard.

Before long the enormous and lethargic form of His Royal Majesty lumbered past. Conall kept his eyes downcast, as he was taught, so he only saw the lower tip of the dark curly beard and ample paws of the sphinx, as Kiwidinok had referred to it.

A contingent of servants followed and shortly the door closed behind them. Conall looked up to see other servants in black tunics cleaning the area around the dais. He set down the empty tray he had been holding and fetched his own bucket of soapy water. His job was to mop the floor of the viewing area and return all dirty dishes and trays to the dumbwaiter back to the kitchen for cleaning.

It was not hard, and it gave him a chance to think. On his first day he had tried to talk to the others while they were cleaning, but they had been very reserved, and would only speak a few words at a time. Since they did not live in the cells below the palace, but instead in the palace itself, they feared that Conall must be some sort of criminal, and were wary of him whenever he approached them.

***

It was nightfall before Conall was escorted back to his cell. The rest of his day had been spent in menial tasks, fetching this and that, cleaning one thing or another, tiring but not dangerous. It was Kiwidinok who had it the worst. Ganju, who had become a favorite in the court, also put his life on the line several times during the week. As they finished the last turn of the staircase leading down into the damp dungeon, the sound of a man crying out in pain flooded the inner cavity of the prison chamber. Fearing for his friend, Conall sprinted past his escort and around the corner towards his cell. He ran into a group of sagittary who were exiting the cage, laughing with one another. The largest looked down at him and sneered as he shoved past Conall and down the ramp to the training grounds.

Spinning around, Conall dashed into the cell expecting to see Kiwidinok lying there, but instead he was alone. Alone except for the hooded sagittary, whose frame shuddered in the corner, chained to the same wall as he had been since before their arrival. Conall took pity on him, once again. He had taken to sharing his food with the fellow prisoner as often as he could, but could do nothing about the pain and discomfort the poor creature was suffering. Nor had Kiwidinok been able to heal him, explaining that he didn't know enough of the sagittary biology to be able to do so.

The guards brought him food and water, and closed the door to the cell. Kiwidinok and Ganju must be eating with the fighters that night, which had happened on occasion. Ganju's mental health had improved greatly with the ability to have conversations in his own language, as well as instructions translated for him by Kiwidinok. Having served as a soldier, he was fit and well-seasoned; unlike Kiwidinok, he was not likely to be killed in combat. In fact, the sagittary begrudgingly bet on him, as he had yet to be defeated, even though he was older than his opponents. A British military training, he had explained, and then saluted with a smile.

Conall looked over at the hooded prisoner again. He had been asked by Kiwidinok not to interact with it unless he was present, but the food was here and Conall didn't know how long he would have. He picked up the bowl of stew and piece of bread, and walked over to the far side of the cell. As he approached, the chained sagittary turned its head towards him. He was still a little afraid, wondering what had been done to merit such treatment. Slowly he removed the hood and realized immediately the source of the painful cry he had heard. The creature's face had been slashed at an angle from forehead to chin, the blood still running down his face and into his left eye and dripping from his lips. Brandon set down the food and grabbed the ladle out of the water bucket, walking back slowly so as not to spill any. He stretched as tall as he could and let the water pour down the face of the shackled prisoner, who shuddered in pain, but did not cry out. This he repeated several times until most of the excess blood had been washed away, the cut having sealed over for the moment.

"You . . ." gasped the sagittary, "take great risk in showing me kindness." They had never spoken in all the other times he shared his food. Either the creature was beginning to trust him more, or it felt less threatened when alone with Conall.

"I suppose so," responded Conall with some trepidation. "But I can't very well let you stand here while I sit there and eat"

"So, it is out of selfish desire for a comfortable meal," the sagittary said dryly. Conall didn't know what to think until a small smile appeared at the corners of the sagittary's mouth.

"Yes," he replied with a smirk, "I suppose it is." Conall relaxed a bit and took a piece of bread, proffering it to the captive. "My name is Conall. Conall Baird"

The sagittary did his best to swallow, "Ajeetabbas. But my friends call me Ajeet. Though I appear to have only one friend these days," he said graciously to Conall. They shared a few more bites of bread before starting on the stew. Conall had eaten some of the untouched food from the palace viewing room earlier that day, so he decided to give all the stew to his new friend.

“How long have you been a prisoner here,” Conall asked between spoonfuls, looking over his shoulder periodically checking for guards.

“I have been in captivity all of my life, as my father before me and his father before him. I do not know what my great grandfather did to anger His Royal Majesty, King Sehmak I, but we have been forever condemned for it.”

“And the chains? No food?” asked Conall, “Surely you haven't spent your entire life tied to a wall.”

“No, my friend, this I earned for wishing to marry above my station. My family has been allowed to marry, but only those of the lowest caste. I became enamored with the sister of Nakhoda, the captain of the Royal Guard. I believe it was he who captured you and your companion,” explained Ajeetabbas.

“And the cut on your face?” asked Conall.

“This I earned for not dying. A punishment, I am afraid, you may share if you continue to help.” Ajeetabbas shifted his weight in an effort to relieve pressure on one of the manacled legs, wincing as he did so. Conall looked down to see a fresh trickle of bright crimson blood weeping from the raw skin where it met the iron shackle. He felt indignant at the abusive treatment of a living creature, and wondered what kind of society could condone such behavior.

After another spoonful of stew, the bowl was empty, and with a final morsel swallowed, the bread was gone as well. Enough food to survive, but not enough to make one full. Conall gathered another ladle of water to quench the thirst of Ajeet. He thought for a moment, looking at the weakened lion man before him.

“Then you will just have to escape with us,” he announced.

Ajeetabbas growled within himself and it took Conall a moment to see it was laughter. “Escape?” he said incredulously. “From here? There is no escape. There has never been an escape. The sooner you accept that, the easier life will be.” He closed his eyes to rest, and Conall returned the hood carefully so as not to touch the red wound across Ajeet's face. They *would* escape, he told himself. And they would have to do it soon.

Eighteen

Brendon was exhausted. They had been hiking westward for nearly three days in the dense forest of Talamh Glas. After leaving Fennian Chase they crossed several streams and walked through a series of winding ravines before the ground rose slightly into the thick woods in which they traversed today.

Scioldmed and Girvan walked ahead with Risteard in the lead, while Fearghas brought up the rear, leaving Brendon with Bidzil in the center. Over the past few days he learned a great deal about the land and the climate, as well as the magic so abundant in this world—Faer Ri.

Brendon agreed this is where the phrase "Fairy Tales" came from, as Mr. Dabir suggested. . . Tales from Faer Ri, as it were. Bidzil delighted to know that their culture had been shared in the new world, and that it had a large effect with the children of his day.

"Tell me more of this Diz-Knee, and Moo-Vees," he had said, wondering how such curiosities could not be considered magical. In the end Brendon gave up and changed topics. And so, for hours on end they would chat about Faer Ri, and about his home in Michigan. It felt good to talk about his home, and his parents. Bidzil was a polite and eager listener, with lots of questions and such an expressive face. Brendon felt a kinship to him, like a member of the family.

Not so for Scioldmed. It was obvious that he was listening, but every day he seemed more and more apprehensive towards the old man, and even more so towards Brendon who had not spoken to

Girvan during the entire trip, his tutor still preventing such interaction. Risteard was, well, he was himself--aloof and unaffected by the feelings of anyone in the group. He simply focused on his charge of returning them safely to Cian Torin. The politics of the group was unimportant to him.

Fearghas was another matter altogether. He spoke openly with Brendon, in that deep, raspy voice. Brendon had not spent much time with him in the glade, but here in the woods he found himself staring at the large huldretrow and watching him move silently through the forest. It was as if he was a part of the woodland, nature incarnate. As he touched a tree, or moved through the brush, the leaves and branches seemed to part for him, as though allowing him to pass with their blessing. His skin, though gray and stone-like in appearance, was not as rough as he thought it would be—something he noticed when Fearghas lifted him over a fallen timber. His hair, which looked like dark moss and fibrous bark, would fly about in the wind when a breeze stirred the air. Like Brendon, Fearghas also carried his enchanted shaft, but it was longer, and smoother than the blackthorn walking stick Brendon was given.

He did not use it for any purpose other than walking, but Brendon remembered how fearsome he had been when they had first met. Somehow that image softened, and Fearghas seemed more benign, even softhearted, and in every way more human than monster.

They stopped for a short lunch that afternoon before turning north. Risteard explained that the next day and a half would be more rigorous as they would be gaining altitude and entering the hill country of the Fells of Beag Cairdas. They would also have to cross a river, rather than the small streams they had already encountered. This would involve either finding a boat (as close as Risteard came to telling a joke) or using a fjording place known to the gnomes.

The river, he explained, was a natural deterrent for the Naga, as it was a raging torrent of frigid glacier melt. It kept the eastern borders of the gnome lands free of Naga scouts. The companions would reach the river sometime the following morning, and after crossing their journey would be much safer.

Brendon began to notice a change in the landscape as the ferns and oaks gave way to pines and other evergreens. The ground here was firm and solid compared to the peat moss and loam they had been walking on for the last few days. Brendon began to use his shillelagh as a true walking stick in order to keep his balance at times.

Soon the day came to an end, and the party took shelter for the night under a series of large red-pines (Bidzil made a point to explain the unique characteristics of the red-pine, its ability to self-prune and its constant morphology, all lost on Brendon, though he listened politely). Once again, they ate small food stores with no fire. The gnomes took turns watching the camp that night, refusing the offer Bidzil made for Fearghas and himself to take a turn. Risteard seemed prepared to accept, but a glance from Scioldmed gave him pause, and with a roll of his eyes he politely turned down the offer. Brendon tucked himself into his blanket and quickly fell asleep.

***

There were voices, not too distant, but far enough away he could not make out what was being said. Brendon's eyes fluttered open and he rubbed the sleep from his eyes. Several yards from where he lay, a giant sat on a boulder under a large red pine. At least Brendon thought he was a giant. His height, while sitting, was higher than that of Bidzil who stood next to him, and his shoulders were the width of two men.

The man had fiery red hair and a shaggy beard to match. He was wearing armor plates and chain mail on his torso, with strips of thick studded leather that hung from a belt. Below the leather strips a patterned wool kilt covered his legs down to his knees, and large thick boots with plated greaves on his shins that matched the leather vambraces on his forearms. A massive bow straddled his lap as he spoke to Fearghas.

Fearghas was looking away into the forest, and Bidzil was doing his best to placate the stranger, who kept his eyes on the huldretrow as he spoke. Eventually, their business concluded, the large man stood up to full height, nearly a match for Fearghas in size and build. Fearghas turned, softened his expression, and clasped the man's extended hand. A look of sadness clouded the eyes of the stranger who then broke eye contact and looked towards Brendon. He squinted for a moment, then turned and bid farewell to Bidzil before running northward into the mist that gathered in and around the distant hills.

As Bidzil approached, Brendon couldn't contain his wonder. "Who was that? A giant?"

"That was Iomhair," answered Bidzil, "King Haral's 'First'. He is not a giant, he is a firbolg. And . . . he is a friend."

"Well?" interrupted Scioldmed, "What did he want?"

"That is Fearghas' business. You can ask him, if you like," responded Bidzil. Scioldmed looked at the huldretrow with a sour expression. Fearghas, ignored the fussy gnome and began to gather the gear together for departure. After a moment's hesitation Scioldmed harrumphed and trudged over to Girvan, barking orders for the young leprechaun to busy himself with packing. Despite himself, Brendon smiled. Bidzil smiled as well.

In short order they were off again, the morning dew making his breeches wet as they passed through meadows of high grass in between the clumps of brush and copses of trees. It was very picturesque, and Brendon enjoyed the slight breeze that cooled his skin as they marched along. They kept the same order as days before, with Fearghas in the rear, searching the horizons for any threat that might come their way. He was more than just protective of Bidzil, he revered him and was as loyal as a friend could be.

"Tell me about how you met Fearghas, Bidzil," he asked after a while.

"Oh, that is a very special story," replied the old man. "You see, Fearghas is one of a kind. You may recall me telling you that he is only part huldrefolk. He is also part firbolg."

"Why is that special?" Brendon asked.

Bidzil chuckled. "Well, to explain that I will have to deviate from my story. You see, huldrefolk are the among the oldest beings in Faer Ri. First came the dragons, then other magical creatures . . ."

"Dragons?! There really are dragons?!" interjected Brendon, his eyes wide with excitement.

"Well, there were. And I suppose they still exist. But let me finish please," he chided kindly. Brendon nodded.

"Where was I . . . yes, other magical creatures. And then the Living Stone--don't interrupt please--the Living Stone wished for someone to care for the land, to tend it and make it beautiful. So, it created the huldrefolk. They range in shape and size, but most are between ten and twenty feet tall. They are known to have strong magic, able to sing the elements from the earth. Very similar to what Druidae are able to do, and yet the magic is different. Huldrefolk are part of the earth, and when they sing they are putting a part of themselves in the magic of their creation. Druidae *command* the elements, huldrefolk *request*. That is the only way I can explain it.

"We call them huldrefolk because they are one with nature and blend in to the land around them. Their name means "hidden ones", and if they don't want to be seen, you won't see them. The term huldretrow is the singular form of huldrefolk and it means "one who is hidden and alone". It is often used incorrectly, assuming all huldrefolk spotted by themselves are solitary. But in the case of Fearghas it is apropos. But I am getting ahead of myself. Where was I? Oh yes, the huldrefolk are a noble people, but sadly they are a finite race. Do you know what that means?" Brendon shook his head.

Bidzil continued, "It means they can't procreate. You are blushing, so I think you know what *that* means. Anyway, the huldrefolk kept to themselves, peaceful and yet powerful. Next, the Living Stone created the firbolgs. Strong, long-lived, but not magical. They are a very hardy people, but sometimes their heads are as thick as their chests, and they are known for their tempers. They live in the foothills of the Dreich Mountains, and have lived there since their creation."

"What about the aesir and gnomes?" Brendon asked eagerly.

"They came later, but that is another story for another time. Now, the firbolg and the huldrefolk had no quarrel with each other. In fact, for many years they had open trade between the communities. That is until the loss of Griogairheim. In their pride the firbolg did not heed the warnings of the huldrefolk, and so it was when their chief city was lost in the Great Dreich Floods, they somehow blamed the huldrefolk for their misfortune, and every misfortune since. Interaction between the two races became forbidden, and they no longer traded goods nor services."

The party stopped for a moment while Risteard sprinted ahead to scout out the crossing point of the river. Brendon sat on a nearby outcropping, pulling a piece of wild sage and placing it to his nose. It was a fragrant and bitter smell, but it reminded him of Thanksgiving dinner for some reason. Bidzil chose to sit on the trunk of a fallen tree. Scioldmed and Girvan sat just ahead on a pile of rocks, close enough to hear the story without seeming interested.

Bidzil continued, "So time passed, and one day a firbolg woman came upon hard times and was found near death. A huldrefolk by the name of Fearleighis came across her and tended to her wounds. After caring for her for many months, he found himself fond of her. In time they fell in love, but neither the firbolgs nor the huldrefolk would accept them in their communities. They had a child, a miracle birth since no other huldrefolk had ever born offspring. The child took upon itself aspects of both his parents, and raising him made them happy. But eventually the mother would grow old and die. The father, in his grief, left the child in my care and chose the withering path."

"What is the withering path?" asked Brendon.

"Huldrefolk who give up on life eventually become still and solid, and become the land they protect. They simply wither away," answered Bidzil.

Risteard returned. "We are close. Just a few more leagues and we are there"

"We had best hurry," came a loud voice from behind. Fearghas was running towards them. "We have been discovered and are pursued by a Naga raiding party. Thirty or more soldiers," he said as he helped Bidzil on his feet.

They began to run in the direction Risteard indicated. Were it not for their agility, the gnomes would have been outpaced by the longer legged members of the party. But they seemed at home in this rocky terrain and it did little to slow them down as they picked their way through the crags. Before long they came to a large meadow that led downward towards the sound of water. They were nearing the fjord.

Risteard stopped abruptly and turned to the others. "If they see us crossing at the fjord, they will learn of it, which would endanger our people should they use the shallows to construct a bridge to span the gap. Scioldmed, could you use your magic to allow us across at another point?"

"I do not believe I can levitate all of us, no," responded the older leprechaun between breaths.

Bidzil looked ahead of him, and back the way they had come. "Take the boy and cross at the fjord. Fearghas and I will create a diversion and meet you two leagues north of here on the other side of the river," he said. Scioldmed looked as though he was about to protest, but the aelfin magic-user silenced him with a determined glance.

Risteard agreed that it was as sound a plan as any given the time they had to decide, and shouted for the gnomes and Brendon to follow him. Brendon ran to catch up, looking over his shoulder a few times to glimpse his Bidzil and Fearghas as they prepared to meet the enemy. Brendon hoped with all his heart they would be alright.

The fjord was indeed hidden from view. They had to use a switch back trail to reach the bottom of the ravine, walking thirty or so paces before turning and repeating the action. This occurred a number of times until they reached the water's edge. At this point, the river was wider and moved slowly, and Risteard assured him that it was much shallower than it seemed. Risteard told them to relax and wait until they could be sure the enemy had moved on. Brendon placed his foot in the rushing water he immediately felt a numbness from his ankle to his toes. He pulled his foot back out and looked questionably at his guide.

"I know 'tis cold, but this is th' only way. th' current is much stronger upstream and downstream, and that is what keeps th' Naga from crossing or building a bridge," explained Risteard sympathetically.

It was difficult to judge how much time had passed while they waited, unable to see the sun while they were down in the ravine. The rushing water made it impossible to hear anything that may be taking place in the meadow above. Brendon watched the water swirl around in little eddies, the occasional piece of wood drifting by slowly and deliberately, bobbing along without a care. Insects flew from branch to branch, many pestering the travelers by landing on faces and hands. A few lighted upon the water from time to time, occasionally to their demise as a trout would pluck them from the surface. Finally, after what seemed like an eternity, Risteard motioned for them to gather themselves and enter the water.

They made their way holding each other's hands to prevent anyone from slipping and being carried away, the river rocks slick with green algae. At the deepest point the water came up to their waist, and was bone-chilling. Brendon could no longer feel anything below his knees, but he kept moving forward, teeth chattering. On the far embankment, they rested a moment before climbing another switchback trail to reach the top of the ravine. Scrub trees and brush hid the trail from above and along the side, so the Naga would have had a difficult time find the fjord unless they had followed someone who knew the way. Catching his breath at the top of the climb, Brendon hoped again that all was well with Bidzil and Fearghas.

Before moving on, Risteard had them take off their wet clothes in order to dry off and avoid hypothermia. Brendon was a little bashful and changed behind a clump of tall grass. All he had in his leather sack was his old track suit, and so he donned it once again, wringing out the wet clothes he had been wearing and placing them in the sack. His shoes were still wet, and he knew he would get blisters if he wore them. Risteard took fabric bandages from his pack and wrapped them around everyone's feet. “Here, this will do until we can build a fire and allow our boots to dry out,” he said.

They proceeded northward in the direction Bidzil had suggested. After a couple of leagues, they found a copse of trees where they laid a small fire and proceeded to dry their clothes.

***

“You shared an awful lot about me today, Grandfather,” said Fearghas. They were waiting for the Naga soldiers to arrive so they could act as a diversion.

“No more than what was needed,” replied Bidzil. “Besides, he's family.”

A spear whizzed past them from their right, narrowly missing Fearghas.

“Ohh, you didn't see that one, did you my friend?!” said Bidzil with amusement.

Fearghas growled and turned towards the tattooed man who had been concealed in the tall grass. He charged him with his staff raised. The man stood up and his jaw dropped with fear as he turned to run but was rendered unconscious before he had taken his second step. Other Naga were coming from the east, these were soldiers in their armor-plated suits. Their leader rode a giant lizard whose tongue flicked this way and that as it ambled over the terrain towards Bidzil. Fearghas heard more movement and saw several of the tattooed warriors coming towards him through the tall grass. Time to move. He ran back towards Bidzil and shouted the need for haste. Bidzil smiled and gathered his robe as he ran after his hulking friend.

As they had planned, they made their way towards a stand of trees on the south end of the meadow, the tattooed warriors giving chase while the soldiers marched in formation behind their leader who turned and rode towards the wooded area. As soon as Bidzil passed the first few trees, he turned and put his hands on the ground.

“Are you ready my friend?” he asked.

Fearghas turned and placed his hands on the staff and planted it in the ground next to Bidzil. “We shall see, Grandfather.”

They began to sing. At first it was just their two voices, but then other voices could be heard. An exquisite melody, filled with power and layer upon layer of harmony. The ground began to tremble as the trees swayed to and fro. The tattooed Naga were about to enter the tree line when shoots began to sprout up beneath their feet, spiraling upward at an unnatural rate. They stepped back in awe as saplings formed fully grown trees right before their eyes. The music began to increase in intensity and the wall of trees grew thick, their branches and leaves obscuring the sun and creating a ring of wood around the grove of trees wherein Bidzil and Fearghas sang. The earth shook, steady but not violently. When the rumbling ceased a final creak of wood announced the end of the song.

***

The Naga captain sat astride his basilisk and waited for his lieutenant to report.

“It has been over an hour, Captain Upahasa, and none of the ska'utsa have returned,” the man stated in an anxious tone. “What are you orders?”

Upahasa thought about it for a moment. The tattooed ska'utsa were expendable, they always had been. They were from one of the primitive tribes on the outskirts of the empire, unlike he and his men who were born in the capital, groomed to be leaders. Losing a soldier was more serious, and involved explanations and letters to family members, not to mention a tarnished war record. He would have to rethink his plan of sending soldiers into the wooden barricade that had sprung up all around their prey. It was quite possible that he had lost all of the ska'utsa in his command by sending them into that ring of trees. A better plan, he thought, would be to flush them out.

“Burn it down,” he said in a cold, calculating voice. “Surround the ring and set fire to the wood. If the smoke and fire do not kill them, then we will as they attempt to escape the protection of the trees.”

“As you wish, my lord,” replied the lieutenant, who then barked out orders to the rest of the men. With a raiding party of forty soldiers and ten ska'utsa, he should not have had any trouble capturing these men. But they were no mere shaman—they were something more, and the gray one may be a firbolg judging by its size. Strange to see a firbolg this far south, especially given their mistrust for those not of their kind.

The men prepared bundles of wood and rags and doused them in pitch before arranging the brands at the base of the trees. As soon as everything was in place, they set fire to the bundles and stood back. Smoke began to wander in and out of the woods choking the soldiers and forcing them to step back. Soon the flames spread to the trees themselves. Upahasa smiled and watched as the blaze grew in intensity, imagining the fear and pain of those inside the inferno.

***

Bidzil and Fearghas watched from the safety of a small bluff some distance away. Bidzil frowned as he saw the fire spread, engulfing the trees and the sleeping ska'utsa inside. It had not been his intention to harm anyone. After they created the wall, he planted Jasminia Gargantua, a large vine that creates trumpet like flowers known to induce deep sleep. Then it was only a matter of sneaking out before the soldiers encircled the woods. Fearghas could blend in to his surrounding at will, but Bidzil had needed a little magic to keep himself from being spotted. It was a good plan; any who entered would be rendered asleep for as long as the vines produced pollen, perhaps for a day or two by his reckoning.

But he had not expected the leader of the Naga to stop sending his men into the grove. Nor did he expect the callous treatment of those who had entered—burning down the woods just to capture his prey, not knowing the fate of those already inside. They would not suffer, unable to rouse themselves from sleep, but they would not survive. It was deplorable.

“We must go, Grandfather,” said Fearghas.

Bidzil nodded and they set off northwards towards the mountains. They would cross the river at another location, north of the fjord, and then double back to find the gnomes and Brendon. He was grateful Brendon had not seen this. Sometimes even the best of plans can fall apart, as Bidzil knew all too well.

Nineteen

Ganju paced the cell floor, while Kiwidinok muscled down what passed for breakfast in the dungeon. They had been throwing out ideas to one another, discussing possible ways to escape. So far, nothing was sticking.

"E'en if we did get past th' palace guards," said Ganju in his imitation cockney accent, "'ow do we get outta th' city? We can't just wolk outta th' palace and stroll fru th' gates. Then there's th' matta' of transportation. How d' we trafel all the way back 'cross the desert? We don't haf' a raft. A bit pointless, innit?" concluded the old Gurkha. Kiwidinok smiled at the performance, but Conall didn't appreciate the candor, even delivered as it was in a playful manner.

"Kiwi could transform into a camel and carry us," piped up Conall. Kiwi snorted at that comment, immediately regretting it as he choked on the food in his mouth.

"No lad," Ganju resumed his normal voice, "even if he could carry us all that way, how would we find our way? And what would prevent the sagittaries from finding us?" asked Ganju. "Can't you turn into a sagittary, Kiwi?" He looked over at Ajeetabbas, hooded and unable to understand Ganju, he was only getting bits and pieces of the conversation. Kiwidinok followed his glance and shook his head.

"No, as I said before, any magical creature is simply not possible. I can't possess the magic it would take to maintain that form. It is hard to explain, but once we learn a form it is a part of us, our understanding. Magical creatures are outside the purview of our abilities since they were created by an entirely different magic than the one we use."

Conall thought for a moment. "OH! I saw this in a movie: We could pretend to be dead and when they put our bodies in a bag to take us to the cemetery, we escape!"

"Except they don't put bodies in bags to be buried," said Kiwidinok, "they feed them to the beasts they have caged down below. I watched them do it while training."

Conall thought some more. This was turning out to be impossible. There was no way to get the three of them, scratch that, four of them out of the prison without alerting the guards, and no way to get back to his brothers. He wondered how they were doing, if they were ok, and if they had found his parents yet. He sure missed them. It was easy to take your family for granted when they were all around you, but after being apart for, how long had it been now? At least a week or so had passed, he thought to himself. Long enough that he started to believe he would never see them again. Shaking his head, he tried to focus on the task at hand.

"We needed a distraction," the shaman said as he finished his meal. "Something to pull the focus of the palace guards away from our escape. Something that would take time to resolve," said Kiwidinok as he stood up slowly. His body was sore from the previous day's encounter with the ammit.

"Or maybe we need a hostage," said Ganju. Conall's eyes widened, as did the smile on his face. Ganju cocked his head to the side and looked quizzically at Kiwidinok. Kiwidinok simply shrugged his shoulders and looked back at Conall.

"Huddle up, guys!" he said, motioning them to move a little closer to hear his plan.

***

Everyone knew their part; they had reviewed the strategy many times over the last two days. Conall had to explain it three times, once for Ajeetabbas and twice for Ganju who kept interrupting and missing important details in doing so.

And so, it was then that Ganju, with the help of Kiwidinok as translator, began to plant the idea that fighting a sagittary would be a "better class of opponent. This he spread that around in the training grounds to the other combatants and gamblers who frequented the practices. Soon there was a buzz about the undefeated human and if he would really be fighting a sagittary. On the one side, sagittaries were supposed to be indomitable, but what if this human won? What would happen to the order and discipline if one of their own were to be defeated. And so it continued until Kiwidinok mentioned off hand that there was a weakened sagittary in the cells that could still be more than a match for this one human. The idea spread, the hubris of the sagittary spurning it on. If the human won, it was because his opponent was weak, and of a lower caste. If the sagittary won, it would ensure the belief that they were the supreme warrior race.

The idea had yet to be discussed with His Royal Majesty, fearing his condemnation of the idea. And it seemed that was the only stumbling block. Conall couldn't very well speak to the King, he wasn't even supposed to acknowledge him in any way. All he knew was they had to act fast, as Kiwidinok was going to be paired with a manticore in a few days, and there was no way of knowing if he could handle something so formidable.

His Royal Majesty lounged on the dais during another fight between a tattooed Naga prisoner and another slave. Each used a spear and they parried and stabbed with trained deftness. Neither was gaining on the other, and the crowd had almost dispersed. His

Royal Majesty yawned for the third time, and Conall looked over at Tilsave, who seemed nervous about the entertainment. Recognizing his chance, Conall motioned for him to come over to where he stood. At first Tilsave stood erect and looked down his nose at Conall, anger flashing in his eyes. But Conall just intensified his gesticulation with both hands, waving him over.

Tilsave looked at his master and then tip-toed over to Conall.

"What. Do. You. Want, *slave*?" he said articulating each word with emphasis on the 'slave'.

"Look, obviously this is boring. His Majesty looks like he is asleep. Do you want him to be upset with you for not procuring adequate entertainment?" asked Conall, focusing on the lines he had been rehearsing.

Tilsave thought a moment. "His *Royal* Majesty's entertainment is no concern of yours, and you would do well to mind your place before you wind up on the tray rather than serving it."

"Fine, I just thought you might want to know what the whole palace is talking about. The fight of the century, big stakes for those who wager," said Conall as her returned to his station by the dumbwaiter. The Master of Slaves looked left and right, and then followed Conall to his post.

"Big stakes, you say? Talk of the palace you say? Tell me more," whispered Tilsave.

***

By nightfall everything had fallen into place. Ganju was informed that he would be fighting a sagittary, and he had been given a trident in order to train that afternoon. Back in their cell they quietly celebrated their plan. Once the fight had begun, Kiwi would transform into a mouse and go up the stairs to join Conall on the balcony. That would put all four of them in the same part of the palace at the same time, allowing them to enact their plan. Conall was excited to finally be doing something, and hoped they could pull it off.

"Now remember, we will need to quiet the guards before we do anything else. There are usually only seven or eight of them, but the three of us . . . four of us . . . should be able to . . ." Kiwidinok trailed off as movement in the corridor indicated someone was coming. They spread out and sat down quietly as the keys to the cell door turned and Nakhoda, the sagittary who had brought them here, entered along with some of the sagittary in his command. They looked at Conall and the others as they walked in, but focused their attention on Ajeetabbas. Nakhoda stepped forward and removed the hood.

"Your time has come, to redeem yourself. You are to fight tomorrow, and so you will have a last meal," he said gritting his teeth.

"Last meal? We don't fight to the death in the fighting pit," said Ganju. Kiwidinok translated for him.

"Oh, that's right, you haven't heard the latest," Nakhoda said with disdain, "There is to be a mixed melee tomorrow. You three will fight each other. *And* the manticore!"

The sagittaries laughed as they unlocked the manacles and escorted the wounded Ajeetabbas out of the cell. The companions looked at one another, dejected and afraid. Ganju hit the wall with the palm of his hand before sliding down to his knees. Kiwidinok got up and walked over to him, placing a hand on the old warrior's shoulder.

"We will get through this, I promise," he said. But it wasn't convincing.

Conall turned his head as tears began to well up in his eyes. He had put such faith in this plan; he never doubted it would fail. Now his friends would be in the big arena, with hundreds of guards, and all eyes would be on them, including the manticore's.

***

Quinlan had debated going home many times. This was a "fool's errand", and he was a fool for trying to rescue the boy and the old shaman. But he thought about his father's promise, that they would protect the boys, and he knew he could not live honorably if he did not at least give it his best effort.

It had taken him several days to cover the distance from the outpost to the Royal City of Ba'asada. He had stayed close to the water and hid when barges floated by. He was surprised at how easy it had been to enter the city. Having watched people enter and exit all day, he realized that the guards were not even paying attention, and so he hid his half-moon spear with his leather armor and slipped his long knife into his belt before simply walking through the gate. His tunic was dusty and looked like everyone else. Scarf for his head, thanks to some drying laundry, and he was simply another child walking through the market. Much easier than he had expected.

What was hard was trying to find any sign of the two friends. Chances were they may not even be in the city, having been taken to the Naga homeland instead. Quinlan had decided he would spend one more day searching, walking through the markets and such, trying to find Conall and Kiwidinok. Beyond that he risked getting captured himself.

He had wondered if they were in the palace, but that seemed farfetched, and he had no wish to break into that stronghold. That is until he heard a rumor of a special event taking place. A sagittary would be fighting a human, a shaman, and a manticore. Could it be that Kiwidinok was the shaman referred to? He sighed to himself and trotted up the ramped pathway towards the palace to learn more.

***

The following morning the fighters were escorted down into the training grounds to warm up and eat a heartier breakfast. The area was an off shoot of the tunnel system that ran through the mountain, exiting below the palace plateau, but higher than the concentric rings of the main city. Ganju and Kiwidinok had originally proposed scaling the steep walls surrounding the enclosure and then climbing down the other side, but without the right equipment they would not be able to descend safely. Ganju had training, of course, and Kiwidinok could change into a bird and fly down. But that would leave Conall and Ajeet without an escape route.

The practice arena reeked of rotting flesh and soiled straw. Sawdust had been strewn about to soak up blood from training accidents, but it did little to mask the stench. They would not be fighting until noon, so in the meantime they would stretch and do what they could to keep themselves limber and stay hydrated. Ajeetabbas had not returned the night before, and the two men wondered if he would be fit enough to fight.

For his part, Conall was escorted back to the palace, but instead of the balcony, he was taken to the kitchens, one floor below. Even though he had given Tilsave a tip, it appeared as though he was to be demoted for speaking out of turn. So far, every aspect of their original plan had been foiled, and Conall blamed himself for suggesting the idea. Ganju was right, it was foolish to think they could escape. Why didn't he listen? His friends would likely not survive, and even if they did, only one of them would be allowed to leave the arena.

The scullery maids went about their business as he entered the kitchen and the door was closed behind him. It was a dark and foul-smelling room for a kitchen, and Conall fought back the urge to gag several times. Pots and pans hung from a steel rack above an open flame in the center of the room, an exhaust chute directly over the flame carrying the smoke and heat away. Along the left side of the chamber was a cutting board with various types of meat, and along the right platters and plates were being loaded with food ready to be served. A wide brick oven stretched across the far end of the room, with bakers hurrying to place loaves in the fiery furnace.

At that moment, a heavyset man with a white apron bellowed for him to hurry and carry raw meat from the salted barrels and place it on the counter for seasoning. He walked over to the barrels and looked in to see flies taking off and landing on the purple flesh. He glanced back at the man again who pointed once more to the barrel with his knife. He put his hands into the slimy, gritty mixture and pulled up a clump of meat to place on a tray. He then walked it over to the butcher who took the tray and gave him an empty one, motioning for him to repeat the act.

It was disgusting, handling raw and sometimes rotten meat. The butcher would carve the flesh that wasn't tainted or rotten, throw on some seasoning, and place it on a grill to sear in the juices before one of the cooks placed it neatly on a silver tray. The scullery maids then took the trays and loaded them on the dumbwaiter and, pulling the ropes quickly and evenly, raised the trays to the balcony above. The kitchen was unbearably hot, and Conall was dripping with sweat as he heard a knock at the door.

***

Kiwidinok and Ganju were escorted into the arena, where Ajeetabbas was already waiting for them. None of the combatants had been given a weapon, and the crowd showed their amusement, pointing and laughing at them in their realization that there would be no chance for survival. It was a "set up" and the betting houses were in on it, as evidenced by the ridiculous odds being offered from the vendors in the stands.

Directly above them a net had been placed across the top of the arena, ensuring they did not escape, and, they presumed, to prevent the manticore from flying out of the enclosure. They nodded to one another. It was obvious to their captors that they did not wish to fight each other, but given the ultimatum that only one would be allowed to leave, and that a dangerous beast would undoubtedly claim the life of one or more of them, instinct for survival would overrule their civility. At least that was what the betting houses were saying. The stands were full of sagittaries, with the occasional slave bringing them sustenance.

A thunderous roar came from the tunnel they had just left, and the three companions turned to watch the handlers bring out the caged manticore. It had the head and body of a lion, with wings like a bat, and a scorpion's tale. It was the size of two or three sagittaries, and took ten slaves to pull the cart out of the tunnel. The monstrous creature roared again swiping at the men pulling the cart. It didn't have enough room to fully open its wings, which caused it great irritation as it reared and pawed at the cage door. Its wings had tears and gashes in them, and a long, curved talon protruded from the joint at the end of each winged appendage. Its tail hovered like a cobra, venom dripping from the jagged stinger.

Truly this was an apex predator if ever there was one, thought Kiwidinok.

As soon as the slaves cleared the tunnel entrance, one of them took a hammer and knocked the iron pin out of the latch to open the gate while another prodded the creature from behind with a trident. The creature turned on the trident and the terrified man dropped it, running back down through the tunnel with the other slaves. The first man with the hammer turned to run as well but the manticore was too quick. It sprang from the cage with a fury and within the blink of an eye, pinned the unfortunate man to the ground. Raising its stinger above its target, it plunged the barb into the man's chest. The man gasped for a moment then went still. The manticore leaned down to eat its prey when it sensed other prey nearby. Orientating itself towards the three companions, it pawed the ground and stretched out its wings.

***

The scullery maid opened the door as a man, a short man, in a red tunic of the palace guard walked in and inspected the kitchen. The chief cook, noticing the intrusion, began to walk towards him in protest when the guard produced a knife from his belt and threw it pommel first at the cook, striking him in the head and rendering him unconscious. The butcher brandished his carving blade, but the guard was too quick, grabbing a handful of salt and tossing it into the man's eyes. Before the butcher could recover, he too was rendered unconscious by a blow to the head. The scullery maids screamed and ran from the room. It was only then that Conall recognized Quinlan as he turned and asked, "Where's Kiwi?"

***

Kiwidinok wasn't sure how much longer they could evade the manticore. His first thought was to pick something fast and agile.

Unlike the ammit, this beast would not tire easily. Also, the stinger was a good two feet long, so his whale tactic would not work again. Not to mention he had to look out for his companions, who could not use magic to avoid the creature's attacks. So far, they had spread out and did their best to distract and disorient the creature.

Ganju had picked up the hammer left by the fallen beast-keeper, but that was hardly a weapon against something so big. Ajeetabbas chose the abandoned trident, and seemed confident in wielding the weapon. Their best chance, it appeared, was to confuse the manticore, as it did not seem to possess a higher intelligence.

Each time the manticore looked away, Kiwidinok changed forms. When it would turn back and see a new form it paused to assess the new threat. It did not possess the reasoning needed to recognize that the new animal was the same person as the old animal, and so it kept looking for the other animals it knew it had seen. As it turned about Kiwidinok would change again, and it would respond with a roar, and then search for the last animal it had seen. He had been a Bengal tiger, a bear, a gorilla, and even a lion (that sparked a defiant roar that got the crowd cheering). When the manticore failed to look away, Ganju and Ajeetabbas would call out and get its attention. So far, the tactic had prevented it from attacking, but this would not last indefinitely.

Kiwidinok hoped poor Conall would not have to watch this, unsure of the outcome and doubting any sort of victory. At that moment a commotion on the royal balcony distracted him and he missed seeing the manticore turn towards him again. He spun around in time to see it spread its wings and glide towards him in one leap. He shimmered again and became an armadillo just as the outstretched claws raked across his chest. He flew like a beach ball across the arena, rolling and spinning around as the manticore leaped and pounced on him again, the sand of the arena floor spraying in clouds of dirt with every blow. Like slippery soap in a hot shower, the manticore fumbled again and Kiwidinok rolled away. Trying a new tactic, the savage creature brought its stinger down again and again, only to spin off the sides of the rolled-up rodent.

Ganju took this opportunity to call out to Ajeetabbas and he motioned for him to head towards the open cage. They ran inside and closed the gate, securing it with the iron peg.

"Kiwi will be a lot more effective if he doesn't have to worry about keeping us safe," said Ganju inspecting the cage. "If it can keep a manticore in, it can keep a manticore out," he explained. Not understanding anything the old man said, but not wishing to seem impolite, Ajeetabbas nodded his head before turning his attention back to Kiwidinok.

***

Quinlan and Conall pulled the rope of the dumbwaiter hand over hand until they reached the top of the shaft. After placing the ratchet pin in a locking position, Quinlan slowly slid the door open, just enough to see out but not be noticed. Peering into the chamber, Quinlan was surprised not to see any guards in their customary red tunics. But as he finished his survey of the room, his eyes were drawn to an enormous figure of a sphinx, lounging on a pile of black and red pillows atop a golden platform. The creature was magnificent, the rich amber hue of its thick fur shining in the sun. It wore a golden crown adorned with garnets and rubies, onyx and black sapphires. Covering its haunches and draped around its shoulders, finely intertwined silver and gold filigrees formed a mantel that glittered and created patterns of twinkling lights on the walls at thc back of the room as the light refracted from the miniscule surfaces. But all these trappings were nothing compared to the comeliness of the king's face. He had luxurious flowing hair and a long curly beard, each as dark as midnight, and kohl-lined, deep-set eyes that seemed to survey and cast judgement on all within view. There was a haughtiness about him, an air of feigned piety, and Quinlan felt justified in what he was about to do.

Opening the door a little wider, and carefully stepping out of the dumbwaiter, Conall grabbed a tray from the servant who held it while Quinlan pulled out his long knife and sprinted for the dais. Tilsave turned in time to see Conall shove the tray into his gut and then bring it up to his chin, knocking him off his feet. The other servants screamed and fled to the far side of the room, but at that moment the crowd was booing and jeering so loudly, nobody was paying attention to what was happening on the royal balcony.

Quinlan leaped onto the dais and mounted the back of the sphinx before it had even noticed what was taking place in the viewing room. Quinlan grabbed a handful of the black tendrils falling from the outthrust chin of the sphinx and placed his long knife to its throat.

"Say nothing if you value your life," the nimble warrior whispered.

Tilsave was on his hands and knees when he looked up to see His Royal Highness, Keeper of the Stone, straddled by a gnome, a blade to his throat. Seeing his master treated as such, he let out a gasp as his eyes rolled back in his head and he fainted.

With his friends safe, Kiwidinok began to experiment. He started with a springbok, which kept the manticore dancing, pouncing, missing and becoming more irate. Then he shimmered into a kangaroo, hopping this way and that. The manticore took to the air at this, and began to glide from one end of the arena to another, hoping to catch the kangaroo in mid stride. The more it missed, the more agitated it became. Kiwidinok had an idea. He simmered into a hawk and flew up and around the arena, just ahead of the manticore. Its paws and scorpion tail were useless, and he could not catch Kiwidinok. He had all but forgotten his other prey as he focused on this animal with many forms.

Then something out of the corner of his eye caught Kiwidinok's attention. Conall was waving to him and pointing at the golden dais where Quinlan *sat astride His Royal Majesty*! How in the world did Quinlan get here? And how did he find them? He banked left and then right as the manticore struggled to keep pace. An idea occurred to him, and he shimmered into a hummingbird and hovered in place just below the net. The manticore opened its mouth, sharp white fangs glistening in contrast to its black lips, and just as it was about to finally capture its quarry, the hummingbird flew straight up and through the netting, the manticore's jaws snapping shut in disappointment.

Landing on the ledge of the arena, Kiwidinok shimmered into a leopard and began to run around the wall of the enclosure where the netting was attached. Spectators began to yell and attempted to hit Kiwidinok with anything they could get their hands on; food, goblets, even a weapon or two.

He shifted again and became a cheetah, running faster and faster around the ring. The items being thrown now were mostly weapons, all of them missing as he raced around the top of the ledge. The manticore was enraged and struggled to reach for him, its paws and wings becoming entangled in the netting. Kiwidinok knew he could not keep up this pace for long, but for the moment the manticore was becoming more and more enmeshed in the net and gnawing at the lashings with its teeth. Below, Ajeetabbas and Ganju took advantage of the situation and left the protection of the cage in order to gather an additional trident and a shield that had been thrown, as well as a scimitar that had grazed the side of the manticore as it had missed Kiwidinok. Next, they both ran to the wall of the arena just below the royal balcony and waited, having an inkling of Kiwidinok's plan. All of the spectators were intensely focused on the struggle above them, and paid little heed to the forgotten combatants.

Nearly out of breath, Kiwidinok shifted into a finch, flitting over the raging manticore and flew higher and higher still, above the palace and into the clouds above. Then, in a large shimmer of green an enormous shape appeared in the sky. It plummeted towards the smaller manticore, who fearfully struggled to free its tangled self from the net.

The crowd was all but hushed as a large gray African elephant trumpeted down from the heavens and crashed into the manticore, tearing the net from its rigging and collapsing to the floor of the arena as a great barn owl emerged from a green flash of light and glided up and over to the cage, landing softly. The manticore lay in a heap under the net and broken rigging that had held it in place. Ganju grabbed at the netting—which had not only trapped a large number or spectators, but had also created a makeshift route to the balcony—and began to climb up to the royal viewing area, Ajeetabbas struggling to stay close behind him. But all eyes were on the scene of destruction they had just witnessed, staring in unbelief at what had just happened.

Seeing that his friends were all on the balcony, Kiwidinok launched himself into the sky and flew to Conall's side, shimmering once more into his human form. As he shifted he became aware of His Royal Majesty staring at him directly.

"Avert your eyes, and do not gaze upon His Royal Majesty, Keeper of the Stone!" a voice cried out to the multitudes, and all cast their eyes down at the ground.

"His Royal Majesty commands that all should remain present until he decides the fate of this extraordinary warrior," the voice continued. "Guards, keep the exit doors shut!"

Ganju, now dressed in a spare red tunic Quinlan had brought for Kiwidinok, held a scimitar to the back of Tilsave as he spoke; pushing it just enough to remind the portly Master of Slaves that he was serious in his threat. Quinlan, still mounted on His Royal Majesty like a cowboy on a wild bronco, was a sight to see, and Kiwidinok almost laughed out loud.

But they were not safe yet. Opening the door to the palace interior they made their way through the lush gardens and towering fountains towards the exit. As they went, Tilsave, escorted at sword point by Ganju and fed lines from Conall, reminded all to avert their eyes in the presence of the King. They reached the gates and he commanded they be opened, sending the guards ahead of him to clear a path and warn the people that His Royal Majesty wished to take a walk through his domain.

Kiwidinok shimmered into a lion, and Conall sat upon his haunches. Therefore, when they passed by the multitudes in the city, with their eyes downcast, all that would be seen were three sets of lion's paws and two sets of human feet. Unless they raised their heads to look, they would assume it was the king along with his personal guards, and Tilsave.

And so it was that Conall and his friends did indeed walk out of the city, unhindered, and unchallenged. They stopped to collect Quinlan's half-moon spear and armor before continuing on to His Royal Majesty's private barge. A crew of slaves had quickly been assembled on board and within moments they were rowing northward towards the outpost to survey His Majesty's Kingdom.

***

Nakhoda grew impatient. They had waited for nearly an hour. Finally, he moved to the exit.

"Open this door immediately!" he shouted.

"Not until His Royal Majesty orders it," came the reply.

"You fool, His Royal Majesty is not returning! Something has happened! As Captain of the Royal Guard, I command that you open this door, or I shall see you flogged!"

After a moment a locked clicked and the door swung open. Nakhoda called to his men who followed him, albeit hesitantly. They searched the palace and, finding nothing, made their way to the main gates. When they learned that His Royal Majesty had passed by, Nakhoda raised the alarm and summoned the full regiment of the Royal Guard.

"Fetch me a messenger bird and a scribe!" he bellowed to Sharedzia as he sprinted back to the palace.

Twenty

The wind had died down, and the oarsmen were struggling to maintain momentum against the current of the river. Even in shifts it was obvious they were nearly spent. The barge master, already suspicious of the situation (having asked why His Royal Majesty desired to survey his kingdom for the first time since he could remember) was questioning the need for the royal barge to travel at such a rate of speed.

Tilsave, with some persuasion by Ganju, threatened to reassign him to mucking out the stables of the royal menagerie should he continue to balk at the orders. This assuaged the curiosity of the barge master, but Conall knew the farce wouldn't last forever. Still, there was no vessel in the port of Ba'asada that could match them in speed, and they had a head start. The main concern was what to do when they reached the Ramsebo outpost, and how they would disembark without being discovered, not to mention what to do with their hostages.

The barge was very different than the Naga slave transport. For one, it used a team of oarsmen as well as a sail, rather than a tiller and punt system. It had an upper and lower deck, and sat lower in the water. There was also a cabin at the stern of the barge, ornately appointed with furnishings and a round bed for His Royal Majesty to lay upon. The scrollwork on the backs of the wooden chairs and table skirts depicted scenes of humans being captured in nets and put to work on the building of pyramids and other structures. Ganju and Kiwidinok stayed inside the cabin with their two captives, while Quinlan and Conall (dressed in the palace attire) conveyed messages for the barge master and crew in the galley. The two stood at the ship's bow this morning, searching for landmarks that might help them distinguish how close they may be to their destination.

"What are you thinking, Quinlan?" inquired Conall after a while.

"I'm thinking it would be wise to leave th' boat before we get to th' outpost. We could leave Tilsave and His Majesty tied and gagged in th' cabin, while we make our way inland. But I don't know th' terrain, and if we stay alongside th' river we risk being captured," responded Quinlan as he stared into the distance. "On th' other hand, if we take th' barge through Ramsebo and into Talamh Glas, we could increase th' distance between us and th' sagittaries and disembark without being seen. I know th' forest well enough to avoid th' Naga and any sagittaries they may try to follow. Problem is, how to get past th' outpost without raising alarm…" he trailed off.

The two continued to scan the horizon. Conall finally mustered the courage to say what had been on his mind since he first saw Quinlan in the kitchen of the royal palace.

"So, about the other day . . . I am sorry for calling you a coward. And I am sorry I did not listen to you when you said I should not go into the sagittary outpost to get a closer look at the slaves. And . . . I am really glad you came to rescue us," he admitted abashedly.

Quinlan turned to look at him. "Do not trouble yerself with such things. I understand how you felt, and I do not blame you for yer choice. Nor do I think Kiwi blames you for what happened. I am just grateful we had fortune on our side."

Conall nodded and looked off to his left. In the distance, he thought he saw the peaks of some mountains, blurred and indistinct by the heat of the sun beating down on the desert. As he watched them, the broiling haze of the desolate wasteland distorted their shapes making them appear very pointy and then flat. There were two, no three of them, all alone rising up from the sea of dunes in the arid wilderness. He was about to point them out to Quinlan when the barge master called out. Conall and Quinlan turned their attention back to the river ahead of them, and Quinlan muttered something under his breath.

"Come, we must ward th‘ others," he said and walked back to the cabin with Conall in tow.

***

Hazzar scratched his mane with his left hand, his right hand resting on the bow of the barge. The sand fleas were relentless this year, biting him all along his tan hide, his tail not sufficiently long enough to chase them away. Although older and fatter than the many of the soldiers in his command, he was known for his stern disposition, and his men were quick to obey him. The previous day, he received word through messenger-bird that the royal barge had been stolen, and that His Royal Majesty may very well be aboard, as a hostage.

Hazzar was instructed to make his way downstream with three barges and create a barricade to prevent them from reaching the outpost. His orders included boarding the barge with a squad of soldiers to ensure His Royal Majesty's safety, and hold prisoner any and all others on the barge until Nakhoda arrived to sort things out. He had never even seen His Royal Majesty from a distance, much less been in his presence, being from a lower caste than many of the sagittary in the Royal Guard. He worked diligently to become Outpost Commander, paying off the appropriate people along the way. He received combat training, and was a competent warrior, but that was not overly needed these days. Mostly he barked orders at his men and snarled at the Naga who used their outpost to resupply and launch their barges en route to their capital.

Nakhoda had recently visited the outpost on inspection, and Hazzar was reminded as to why he disliked the harsh Captain of the Royal Guard. Of course, it had to be the one time there was an attempted slave escape, for which he was reprimanded, and charged a mon th's wages. Nakhoda had caught the slaves himself, and reminded Hazzar that his position was contingent on his record, rather than his ability to bribe other officers. Hazzar had similarly reprimanded the men in his service, and collected his lost earnings from their wages. But he was not wont to repeat his failures when it came to matters involving Nakhoda, so he and his command staff set off that morning with three barges and twenty-one soldiers.

He squinted and placed his hand to his forehead to cover the sun's rays from his eyes. There, the distance he thought he could make out the mast of a ship. He bellowed orders to his men and to the other two barges. They maneuvered into position and dropped anchors. Punting the vessels so they came about stern-to-bow, they tied the barges together, barricading the river. Gathering their weapons, they waited for the Royal Barge to row towards them.

As the ship approached, the barge master called out to him. "This is His Royal Majesty's private barge. Make way or suffer his wrath."

"We have reason to believe His Majesty is in need of assistance," responded Hazzar.

This human was insolent speaking to him in this way, even if he was a lower caste of sagittary. "You will pull alongside us and prepare to be boarded, by order of the Captain of the Guard."

The barge master's face went white, and he immediately began to comply, shouting out orders to the galley crew. They pulled the oars and punted starboard side to maneuver the barge for boarding. As they did so, Hazzar growled and grunted the command for his men to board the ship. They leaped across the water and onto the deck, weapons drawn. While the other soldiers secured the galley, Hazzar strode over to the entrance of the cabin.

"Your Royal Highness?" he asked timidly after knocking lightly on the door. "Your Royal Majesty, Keeper of the Stone? Are you alright? May we enter?"

No reply. Looking back at his men, who either shrugged their shoulders or looked away, Hazzar decided he would get no support from them. He reached for the knob and opened the hatch. He peeked inside before taking a cautious step with his front paws through the entryway. It was dark, and it took a moment for his eyes to adjust, but as he stared straight ahead he suddenly became aware of two round eyes staring at him angrily. And just below the eyes a sharp, angular nose with a gag tied to a thickly-bearded mouth. Then the shape of an enormous lion became visible as Hazzar realized he had just been staring at His Royal Majesty face-to-face.

He quickly averted his eyes, a constant stream of apologies flowing from his mouth as he reached up to remove the gag and untie His Royal Majesty. One of his men entered the room and noticed the bound form of Tilsave who had also been gagged. As Hazzar untied the last knot, King Sehmak III brushed past him, his immense girth just squeezing through the doorway.

"FIND THEM!!!!!!" he roared as sagittary scrambled away from the enraged king, oarsmen striving with all their might to quell their curiosity and avert their eyes.

***

Conall and his friends climbed the embankment and began to head westward into the desert. Several hundred yards from the river came a loud roar, and assumed their ploy was discovered. They started to run, the smoldering sun quickly evaporating the moisture from their wet clothes and footprints, and erasing any evidence of their watery passing. They would not have much time before they were tracked, but Quinlan had suggested heading for the mountains Conall had seen from the barge. It was difficult to tell the distance, the heat playing tricks on their eyes, but if they could make it they might be able to hide from their pursuers.

Before long they had to slow their pace, the heat making breathing oppressive. They looked back once or twice, but the sun was still rising and looking eastward was next to impossible. They continued west towards the mountains, which now appeared like jagged teeth jutting up from the desert floor. They walked for more than an hour before realizing their destination was not a series of mountains, but pyramids laid out in a row.

There were at least three of them side by side stretching up from the landscape, the nearest sides awash with blazing sunlight, casting the opposite sides in shadow. The sun was arching towards its mid-day zenith, and the companions stopped to rest, looking behind them. They could see nothing, but chose not to rest for more than a few minutes, continuing on to the pyramids and what lay beneath.

As they neared the enormous structures, other features came into vicw. The ground wasn't level, it had uneven configurations of stone sitting at unnatural angles in the sand.

"What do you think they are?" asked Conall.

"I think this was once a city," replied Quinlan. "Buried here by decades of sandstorms." He walked around a small obelisk rising from the ground. "There is no knowing how deep th' sands run, or if it is safe. We should skirt th' city and move northward."

Ajeetabbas was walking between two pillars, his hands gently caressing the smooth cuts made into the capitals and cornices. His eyes went wide, "I think this may be one of the lost cities," he whispered. He bent low to stare at the frieze along the stone slab at the top of the column. Lions adorned the slab, carved from the rock with a precise and skilled hand. He admired the workmanship of the beautiful design before it dawned on him—this was the top of the column.

"My friends, I think it is good counsel that Quinlan offers. I believe we are walking on top of a city that may lie hundreds of feet below us. And this is some insignificant outpost. I think this may have been a Royal Residence at one time, judging by the workmanship. We should leave . . ."

Ajeetabbas paused as the ground below them shifted slightly. Everyone stopped and looked at him, but he was looking beyond them all at the massive wall of sand that was bearing down on them.

"Sandstorm! Hurry, we must get near to the pyramids and cover our eyes and mouths!" he cried.

They began to run towards the base of the pyramid when Ganju called out for help. They looked back to see him waist-deep in sand and sinking fast. Quinlan, who was nearer to him, grabbed his arm but had no leverage to prevent Ganju from sinking further. Kiwidinok shifted into a snake and slithered over to them before becoming himself again. He grabbed Ganju's other arm. Ajeetabbas and Conall stayed where they were, afraid to move, the sands swirling around their feet and in the air above them. With a shudder the ground shook and the entire party slid towards the center of a spinning pool of sand.

"I think the roof we are standing on is giving way!" called at Ajeetabbas. But it was lost in the noise of the approaching storm and the calls for help as they were sucked into the sink hole. They held their breath as the gritty earth swallowed them and pulled them into the darkness below.

***

Ganju coughed and sputtered, spitting sand from his mouth along with the others. He looked around at the spacious building into which they had fallen. The walls were a few stories high, and had once been covered in murals, but only parts of the paintings remained as large chunks of fresco had crumbled and fallen to the floor. A large mound of sand continued to grow as more poured in through a gap in the ceiling, a gap they had just fallen through. Ajeetabbas had walked over to a set of wide metal doors, testing to see if they would open, but time had rendered them useless, rusted shut. Conall and Kiwidinok sat on the floor, catching their breath while Quinlan made his way around the growing pile of sand to the other side of the chamber. Ganju, a sharp pain throbbing up his leg, walked gingerly towards a dark recess in the corner of the room. Here he found an alcove which led to a set of stairs leading downward.

Quinlan called out from the other side of the sand mound. "I see a window. We might be able to pry it open and make our way out," he yelled over the increasing wail of the sandstorm. "Only we will need a rope or something to reach it."

"I think I have found something too," shouted Ganju. "A set of stairs leading down. What do you think?"

Kiwidinok, acting as translator, called out to Ajeetabbas and Quinlan and told them Ganju had found something. Quinlan trotted around the mound of sand over to Ganju. "Let me check it out first," he said as he walked down into the shadowy depths of the stairway. Ganju, not understanding what he said, shrugged his shoulders and waited. Conall and Kiwidinok walked over, along with Ajeetabbas and peered into the depths. After a short wait, they heard a scraping sound and then the sputtering of something being ignited. The soft glow of a torch gradually illuminated the staircase as Quinlan bounded up the stairs.

"I don't know if it is a way out, but it is better than being buried by sand," he said gesturing at the mound that had now obscured the far side of the building. The others nodded approval and followed him down the stairs; Ganju following last, limping gingerly having twisted his ankle in the fall.

At the bottom of the stairs a stone corridor led them past several rooms, some with doors and some without. The rooms had not been disturbed and still contained furniture and other belongings of the previous inhabitants. Quinlan walked in front, with Ajeetabbas close behind, followed by Conall, then Kiwidinok. Ganju, still in the rear, did his best to keep up. He stopped to peer into a room, and thought he saw movement inside. Not wishing to know what he might have seen, he hurried as best he could to catch up to the group as they turned another corner into a longer, wider corridor.

The group traversed the tunnels for what seemed like a long time, passing several branches of smaller tunnels, but Quinlan and Ajeetabbas agreed the best bet was to follow this main tunnel to see where it led. The corridors were in good shape, the stonework even and tightfitting. Occasionally they would have to step over items that had been dropped or left behind, as if the inhabitants had left in a hurry, abandoning their possessions.

Eventually they came to a set of thick, iron-clad doors. Ajeetabbas and Kiwidinok pushed with all their might and eventually the door squealed as it creaked open just enough to let them pass. Inside was another cavernous room, empty save for a massive rectangular stone placed in the center of the floor. Quinlan found a few more torches near the entrance and lit them for the others. All along the walls they found more murals depicting sagittaries in various scenes. Some were harvesting crops, a beautiful city located in the background. Others were celebrating an event of some importance, while others showed sagittaries in mourning. Below the murals were pictographs, some carved, some painted, supposedly describing the paintings above. Curiously, there were no humans in the paintings, nor did they see a sphinx of any kind represented.

Quinlan walked the perimeter of the room, looking for an exit, while Kiwidinok examined the pictographs. Conall and Ganju walked towards Ajeetabbas who was standing next to the stone block, looking at the frieze on its base. He bent closer and his mouth fell open.

"This name. This is my *family* name," he said pointing at the writing inscribed in the stone. On the backside of the stone block Ganju raised his torch and climbed a set of stairs to a platform at the top. As he hefted the torch over the marble obelisk in front of him he saw a carved relief of a sagittary wearing a white tunic with a red sun painted on the chest. The sagittary was also wearing a golden crown with red and black jewels inset.

"I think you had better look at this," said Ganju, motioning for Ajeetabbas to join him. Although he did not understand the words, he recognized the gesture and crouched on his hind legs before springing up onto the platform, next to the marble obelisk. Immediately his eyes were drawn to the pictograph on the slab. There it was, a carved image of a sagittary wearing a similar crown to that of His Royal Majesty, only appropriately sized for a sagittary.

"I do not understand," said Ajeetabbas.

"I think I do." It was Kiwidinok, standing by the wall near the entrance. "I don't think your society has always been led by 'His Royal Majesty'. In fact, I don't think the sphinx race were the original leaders of any of the sagittary, if I understand these paintings correctly." He turned and brought the torch closer to the wall. There in bright colors was a throne where upon sat a regal sagittary with sagittary guards and younger members of what was presumably a royal family surrounding him. To one side sat a mangy form of a sphinx, dirty and almost obscured by the others. As Kiwidinok walked around the room, the murals and pictographs told a story, of sorts, and sagittary clearly were the dominant focus, the sphinx always in the background, at times in service, at times seemingly whispering in the ear of the king. Some areas were harder to make out, but it was obvious that the history portrayed did not evident signs of slavery or sphinx rule.

"It has all been a lie," whispered Ajeetabbas. "My family is not of a lower caste after all."

"What did he say?" asked Ganju.

Conall had forgotten for a moment that he could not understand Quinlan or Ajeet. “He said it has all been a lie,” he explained to Ganju. “His family is not of low birth. In fact, this city may have once belonged to his family.”

Quinlan returned from the far side of the chamber. “I found a way out,” he said panting. “There are some stairs that lead to a series of tunnels winding upward. I felt a breeze as I neared the highest one.” Ganju looked at Conall who translated for him.

“For now, let's rest. Ganju needs to get off his feet and we may as well wait out the storm. We are better off traveling by night anyway. Cooler and less likely to be spotted,” said Kiwidinok.

Lacking supplies and blankets, they had little in the way of comfort. Kiwidinok had managed to wrap some dried meats in some cheese cloth before leaving the boat, but Quinlan had exhausted his supply of food. They found a few more torches which they saved for later and gathered those that were lit into a pile for warmth. Conall closed his eyes as did Ganju and Kiwidinok. Quinlan went to explore the exit again, and Ajeetabbas used his torch to continue wandering the room, gleaning what he could from the series of carvings and paintings his ancestors had left.

***

Kiwidinok gently shook Conall's shoulder to wake him. Conall stretched, took the hand he was offered and stood up. The others were already moving towards the stairs Quinlan had indicated earlier that day. As they reached the top they turned to their left and walked up a long ramp that doubled back on itself and went the opposite way at an incline. After two more switch-backs they came to a large shaft. Here Quinlan stepped inside and walked slowly until he reached a dead end.

Bending down he lowered himself to the level below and then disappeared. A moment later he returned and beckoned them to follow. When Conall reached the ledge Kiwidinok helped lower him down to where the others waited. He looked past them and saw a clear night sky; the storm having passed them by.

As they walked towards the end of the channel they realized they were still some distance from the ground, apparently on the side of one of the pyramids they had seen that morning. They flattened themselves against the structure and slowly inched their way down. Ajeet, unable to flatten himself, watched the others descend. As they reached the bottom, he stepped out, his claws scrambling for purchase on the rock surface. Conall squirmed comparing the sound to hearing chalk scrape the wrong way on a blackboard. It wasn't pretty, but eventually Ajeetabbas made it to the base, sliding and scratching all the way down.

Looking up at the night sky, Quinlan determined that they were already on the north side of the northern most pyramid. He set out towards the forests of Talamh Glas, and towards their eventual freedom. Noticing Ganju's limp, and realizing that Conall would have a hard time keeping up as well, Kiwidinok decided he would have to do something if they wanted to make good time with those two. He rolled his eyes and shifted.

Conall got his camel ride after all.

Twenty-one

Brendon looked at the small cluster of trees at the base of a particularly large hill that Risteard and the other gnomes were walking towards. He looked at Bidzil and asked, "They're kidding, right?"

"Why should they be? What is wrong?" asked Bidzil.

"This is Vloorhaven? This is the homeland of the gnomes? Where are all the buildings? Where are all the people?" said Brendon in disbelief. He stood in a dark green pasture surrounded by hills and the occasional groupings of trees.

"Why, all around you, of course. Did they not tell you?" the old man said with surprise in his voice.

"Tell me what? Is it an underground city?" the boy asked.

"Gnomes underground? Of course not!" replied Bidzil. "They built it right here on the heath."

Brendon looked around again, utterly confused.

"Oh, you are in for a surprise . . ." laughed Bidzil. Fearghas smiled, having overheard the conversation.

As they neared the trees something stepped out from the brush.

"Ho there, Risteard Einion! You are a welcome sight indeed!" hailed a stocky gnome in a dark green tunic and black breeches. He carried a crossbow which he lowered upon recognizing Risteard. To his left another gnome with a pole axe also stepped into the light.

"Ho there, Dafydd Gwilym! And is that yer little brother Rhun?" asked Risteard.

"Not so little anymore," replied the second gnome who indeed stood a hand taller than his older brother.

The party approached them and Risteard shook hands with Dafydd and Rhun. "Has Cian Torin returned yet?" he inquired.

"Only yesterday. They are all safe. But there has been some treachery on behalf of He-lush-Ka," answered Dafydd. "Best ask Cian Torin for details, as I heard but snippets from me friends," answered Dafydd.

Scioldmed escorted Girvan past the three gnomes while Risteard introduced Brendon and the others. Brendon kept looking around for some sort of doorway or gateway into the hillside, but inside the grove there was only a series of broken slabs of rock and a pile of boulders, nothing more. He shook hands with the two gnomes he had just met, but when he turned back Scioldmed and Girvan were no longer there. Noticing his confusion, Bidzil chuckled.

"We are on duty, but will join you later this evening to hear of your tales, friend Risteard," said Dafydd and they stepped back into the brush from whence they had come. Risteard walked towards the stones that were sitting at odd angles. As they neared the pile of rocks he noticed that two of the slabs intersected at the top. Risteard stood by them and motioned for Brendon to come forward. "After you," he said, gesturing for Brendon to walk under the archway. The shillelagh began to glow green as he approached the arch, and Brendon looked at Bidzil who simply smiled and nodded. Turning towards the arch again he stepped forward . . .

The first thing he noticed was the delicious aroma of fresh baked pastries that had not been there before. He looked around for his companions, but they were nowhere to be seen. Laughter and movement were coming from a gap in the trees that he had previously entered, and so he ran to see what sort of prank they were pulling on him. As he walked out from the grove he blinked and rubbed his eyes in disbelief. There before him, lay a beautiful village full of stone cottages with flowers garnishing windows and pathways. Children ran and played in and around buildings bustling with gnomes of all ages. A cobblestone pathway led into the center of the village and he spotted Girvan and Scioldmed who had wasted no time in hurrying towards a large stone edifice with ornate double doors and a great wooden clock tower mounted on its roof. It was something out of a storybook, peaceful and serene.

"Lovely, isn't it?" Bidzil asked as he approached from behind.

"Yes, it is," replied Brendon.

"Caedmon Anluan perfected the magic needed to transport his people to safety, but only after they had escaped through the first realmbridge, never to return. And so, he gifted that magic to the gnomes, ever faithful companions of the aelfin people. This is what he had originally intended—a sanctuary for his people, hidden from the world, and known only to those who lived therein," he explained, a hint of sadness in his voice.

The children had stopped playing and were staring at them. Actually, they stared at Fearghas who stood behind them. Mothers began to call for their young ones as a group of gnome hunters approached from the building Scioldmed and Girvan had entered. Risteard walked up, the last to have entered the arch and gave his companions a reassuring nod, bidding them to follow him.

They were welcomed by the Home Guard, and escorted towards the large building they had seen from the tree-line. Like all of the homes and shops they passed, it had a slate roof, stone walls, and a well-built stone fence bordering a garden in front. However, it was the only structure that had a second floor, not to mention a tower. Large boulders had been set in place for the base, with smaller stones leading up to the roofline. Crossing timbers reinforced the masonry and the rich mahogany of the wood added color to the gray building.

As they passed the various homes or businesses, the inhabitants stopped what they were doing and stared at the procession, not in a rude or angry sort of way, but rather of curiosity and wonder. Fearghas kept his eyes fixed on their destination, but Bidzil smiled and waved, saying hello to practically everyone along the way. A few waved back, but most were just dumbfounded, having never seen an outsider in their life.

As they neared the doorway to the main building a small red-headed boy ran out to meet the party.

"Brendon! Brendon! You're back!" yelled Donovan with delight. He sprinted up to Brendon and hugged him with all his strength. They both began to cry a little, happy and relieved to see the other one safe. Then wiping his tears Brendon asked, "Is Conall here?"

"No, they don't know where he is. He and Kiwi haven't been heard from," answered Donovan, looking down at the ground.

"Well, don't go worrying just yet. I mean, we just got here ourselves, and I am sure they won't be far behind us," Brendon said, trying his best to sound positive.

Mr. Dabir exited the building and walked quickly to Brendon as well. "My you are a sight for sore eyes! I am so very glad to see you are safe," he remarked.

"Thank you, Mr. Dabir. I am glad to see you as well," replied Brendon.

"Welcome friends!" It was Cian Torin. "Welcome to Vloorhaven. You are well met. We have rooms for you, although they may be a bit small for some of our guests," he indicated to Bidzil and Fearghas, "But they are warm and comfortable."

They were escorted through the doors and into a spacious room with tables and chairs enough to feed several families at once, as well as a platform with a long table and chairs facing the center of the room. To the right was a set of stairs leading up and one leading down. They were taken up the stairs which led to a narrow hallway with two doors evenly spaced apart.

"This one is ours," said Donovan as he grabbed Brendon and pulled him into the first room while Bidzil and Fearghas were shown their room at the end of the hall.

The bed chamber was clean and tidy, with four small beds and four chairs to match. The interior stone walls had been plastered and painted a cheerful yellow. Dried flower wreathes hung over the headboard of each bed and the linens and bed-spreads looked soft and inviting. Brendon felt like a giant walking around the room that was designed for smaller guests, but grateful to finally be able to sleep in a bed, even though his feet hung off the side. Picturing Fearghas trying to fit on one of these beds caused him to giggle. He moved to a window that overlooked the square below, and looked out to see the children once again at play. How long had it been since he had felt so carefree? He turned with a smile and face his little brother.

"I know, right?!" said Donovan, noticing his expression. "Oh! I've got something to show you!"

"Can it wait Donny? Right now, I just want to rest," said Brendon, dropping the shillelagh to the floor and falling face forward onto the bed.

"OK, but you're gonna want to see it . . ." said the younger brother, giddy with excitement.

"Whatever it is, I am sure it is awesome. Will it still be there in a few hours?" asked Brendon.

"I sure hope so," came the reply.

"Then it can wait. Good night, Donny, I love you . . ." said Brendon as he faded into dreamland.

***

Brendon awoke to the smells and sound of a food being served. He raised himself up and looked around the room. Donovan was not there. He ran his fingers through his hair and headed out of the room and down the wooden stairs, careful to not go to fast as they were narrower and smaller than what he was used to. As he entered the Great Room he was surprised to see it was full of gnomes, conversing with one another while they ate. Mr. Dabir and Donovan were sitting at the head table on the platform, and noticed him as he entered the room, waving for him to come over and sit by them.

The food was plentiful, and looked like roast chicken, potatoes, green beans, and various breads. He sat and graciously accepted a full plate that was handed to him. He began to eat, the succulent chicken almost falling off the bones. He stuffed a few rolls into his mouth, and swallowed them down with a gulp of water, and then started in on the potatoes. He looked up to see a few of the gnomes at the tables below staring at him, and realized he had been unmannerly in his eating. He wiped his hands, sat more upright, and began to take smaller bites, remembering to chew this time. He had "forgotten to chew", as his mom would always say. It had been a long time since he had eaten a real meal, that is something that wasn't a stew or dried meat, or trail mix, or berries. It was also nice to sit at a table. He thought of how his mom used to make them eat dinner together, and was grateful for the memory.

Looking around the room he noticed that there were very few women and no children present. Those assembled all wore leather armor of some sort. There must have been eighty to ninety of the gnome hunters in all. Seated at the table just to his left were two elderly gnomes, with long white beards and bushy eyebrows. To their left sat Risteard followed by Cian Torin. An empty chair sat vacant between Cian Torin and his son, Girvan, presumably set aside for Quinlan, the eldest. Next came Scioldmed, appearing quite perturbed at having been sat next to Bidzil and Fearghas, the latter awkwardly trying to sit in a chair and use eating utensils designed for much smaller folk. Bidzil was enjoying the himself, but Fearghas seemed as though he would rather be mucking out a barn.

In time, the meal was concluded, and dishes were taken away by the staff. Cian Torin stood and the room began to get quiet as conversations died off. All eyes were on the chieftain as he spoke.

"My friends, brothers and sisters in arms, I have called you together in order to deliver some grave news," he began. "Our allies, the Saami, are leaving Talamh Glas. Furthermore, He-lush-Ka has betrayed our trust, and tried to abduct one of our guests. We can no longer count on the support of his people in our fight against the Naga. Without his help, the Naga raiding parties will concentrate on finding our location. And when they do, they will come for us in force. I have spoken with my advisors," he gestured towards the men to his left and right, "and we have concluded the only option is to close the arch and secure our borders once and for all."

The room started to buzz with conversations. Scioldmed leaned back in his chair, a smile on his face. Risteard looked down at his hands, doing his best to mask his feelings on the matter. The other gnomes at the table simply nodded approval. Bidzil, however, did not look happy, his customary smile replaced with a furrowed brow and a deep frown. He surveyed the room, gauging their feelings before he stood to his full height. The room became silent and they turned their attention to the old man.

"Cian Torin, if I may be allowed to speak . . ." he asked. Cian Torin nodded and took his seat.

"My friends, if I may be so bold as to call you such, allow me to express my appreciation for the decades of service you have rendered in loyalty to the aelfin people. You have fought to protect a land that they have all but abandoned. And for what? The memory of a kinship and alliance? The hope of a safe return of those who passed through the realmbridge?" he asked.

"No," said Risteard, "nothing so noble as that. We fight the Naga because they wish to enslave and rule any and all who are not like them. They capture and control all those who stand in their way. They remove freedom and free will from all who they conquer. And we fear they will do the same to us."

"You judge yourself to harshly, Risteard, for that is a noble reason indeed. To free those who are oppressed, to defend those in need. Is that not something that you continue to value? And should you close your doors, hide yourselves away, pretend the outside world does not exist, will that satisfy your urge to protect and defend?" asked Bidzil.

"We owe nothing to the other races!" interjected Scioldmed, standing up to make his point. "The Saami are fleeing, the firbolgs do not respond to our missives, the sagittaries have embraced th' ways of th‘ Naga, and th‘ huldrefolk,” he looked at Fearghas, “ th‘ huldrefolk have already shut their borders and abandoned us! All that we can do is survive. We lose warriors on each skirmish we undertake, and we are now desperately outnumbered. Our magic is suffering; we have but two leprechauns in th‘ entire village. We need to protect ourselves and our families. Whether or not that is considered noble does not interest me, what matters most is that we preserve the gnome race!”

There were a few murmurs of agreement. Brendon watched Cian Torin, trying to judge his reaction, but he remained stoic. Girvan shifted uncomfortably in his seat. Bidzil sat down, and buried his face in his hands. Scioldmed looked satisfied and turned his attention to Cian Torin.

“Cian, we have already given you counsel. And you have made your decision. Do not let this outsider confuse th‘ issue. You know what you have to do. Vloorhaven can be saved. It has a powerful magic, we should use it as it was intended--as an escape from Faer Ri,” he said, before sitting down himself.

“That is not what was intended. That was never a reason for its design,” muttered Bidzil.

“Oh, and how would you know, wild-wielder?” Scioldmed stood again and turned to face Bidzil. “Your magic does not work like that of any of th‘ aelfin we have encountered, nor anything I have ever read about. You live isolated from the survivors of the aelfin race, and spend your time with a huldretrow, hidden from th‘ world, toying with a magic you do not understand then teaching it to an untrained and undisciplined boy who is much too dangerous to be using magic in th‘ first place. What gives you the right to judge us, to give us advice? What makes you think you know what Caedmon Anluan intended when he created this sanctuary?"

"Well," answered Bidzil in a derisive tone, "maybe because I *am* Caedmon Anluan."

***

The room was deathly silent. Scioldmed started to say something, but a look from Fearghas stayed his tongue, and he sat down. Brendon couldn't believe what he had heard. From what Mr. Dabir had told him, Caedmon Anluan had lived a very long time ago, and as old as he may seem, it would be impossible for Bidzil to have lived so many hundreds of years. He looked at Mr. Dabir who simply shrugged his shoulders while gazing at the old man.

Bidzil arose slowly from his chair. "You are right to judge me harshly, Scioldmed, but not for the reasons you suggest. I am Caedmon Anluan. And I am responsible for the exile of my own people. I am also responsible for starting a war with the Naga. And I am guilty of abandoning my homeland and hiding away, as you say, in the company of a huldretrow. I regret what I have done. I regret my pride and ambition. And I regret that I have accomplished little to change what is happening in Faer Ri. I took pity on myself, I felt alone, and I had given up. I ignored the Prophecy of the Magi, and dismissed pleas to assist the shaman in their struggle. And yes, Scioldmed, I dabbled with the different forms of magic in an effort to understand what I had done.

"But when I completed the magic of the realmbridge for Vloorhaven, it wasn't just to prove I could do it, to satisfy my ego. I did it to protect a people who had stood by me, who had fought alongside me. It was never meant to be an escape, it was intended to be a retreat—to heal wounds and prepare to fight another day. It was a gift to dear friends, to allow them to survive and wait until a day when the winds of war would finally shift in our favor. I think some part of me still had hope that one day the Druidae would return to Faer Ri, and we would reclaim what is rightfully ours. I believe that day is here," he said, looking at Brendon.

Scioldmed regained his composure. "You can't be Caedmon Anluan, he lived hundreds of years ago. Only dragons and huldrefolk are immortal, and you are neither, despite the company you keep. What proof have we that you are telling the truth?" he said, his voice dripping with animosity. Risteard moved to intercede, but Cian Torin laid a hand on his shoulders and he sat back down.

"Brendon," Bidzil asked softly, "do you have the shillelagh?"

"Yes, it is in my room," answered Brendon.

"Would you please fetch it for us?" he asked gently. Brendon nodded and ran upstairs to retrieve the blackthorn walking stick. He returned moments later bounding down the stairs with the shaft in hand.

"Thank you, Brendon. Stand where you are if you would please," said Bidzil. Brendon stood still, holding the gnarled piece of wood.

"Mr. Dabir, is it?" he asked, looking at Farzan Dabir.

"Er, yes sir," responded Mr. Dabir.

"Where did this shillelagh come from?"

"It was an heirloom passed on to me from a dear friend, to be given to the Baird children when they were of age," replied Mr. Dabir.

"And do you know of its origin?" asked Bidzil.

"My friend said it had been passed down from father to son for thousands of years. It is said to have belonged to Caedmon Anluan himself," explained Mr. Dabir.

"And so it did. I sang many songs to that gnarled old stick, infusing it with great power over my lifetime. I gave it to my son before he entered the realmbridge, with a charge to pass it down to his son and so forth. Thousands of years have passed in your world, while only hundreds have passed in ours, yet I recognize my handiwork as if it were yesterday," said Bidzil, reverently.

Mr. Dabir and Brendon looked at each other with a hint of anxiety. *Thousands of years?*

"And how do we know it is yours? I asked for proof, not a stick!" demanded Scioldmed.

"And you shall have it. Brendon, take the shillelagh and command it to return to its rightful owner, if you please," he asked.

Brendon looked at him quizzically, but Donovan urged him to do it.

"I, er . . . I command you to return to your master," said Brendon. The shillelagh glowed green and disappeared from his grasp with a loud pop, appearing instead in the hands of Bidzil, who looked at it lovingly before setting it down.

"This means nothing . . ." began Scioldmed, but at that moment Cian Torin stood and silenced him.

"Enough. I have seen and heard enough. For now, let's assume you are Caedmon Anluan, and that you are prepared to rejoin the fight to free Talamh Glas from the Naga. What is it you propose?"

"The only way to fight a snake is to cut off its head. We don't have the manpower to take on the Naga Empire. But we can deal a decisive blow to their slave trade, while sending a message to our former allies that we are strong enough to resist," answered Bidzil.

"And what do you suggest?" asked Risteard.

"We take back Aelfheim," declared Bidzil.

Twenty-two

The next several hours were spent discussing how they would attack the city, and if it was even a viable option, considering their resources. Cian Torin explained that he had at most a hundred gnome hunters, and that would be leaving the village nearly bereft of protection. There were some older retired hunters that could be called into service, but only to protect the archway. The others were farmers, shopkeepers, and the like. Although valiant, they would not be much use against trained soldiers. Fearghas was a formidable ally, and Bidzil (Brendon wondered if they should still call him that) could perform powerful magic, but would it be enough?

While the inhabitants of Faer Ri discussed their plans, Mr. Dabir met with Brendon and Donovan, discussing the revelation of the time disparity between the two worlds.

"As I have already said, I promise you boys that I had no idea regarding the time imbalance. How could I have known?" the tired professor lamented.

"You always planned on bringing us here, you admitted so on our first day. You care more about a prophesy than you do about us. Or about our parents for that matter!" Brendon whispered in a seething tone.

Mr. Dabir paused, considering the accusation. "I admit that I have long wished for an end to the abductions, and a restoration of power to our people. It is possible that my enthusiasm clouded my judgement at times, but my concern for you and your parents is real. I had intended on training you and preparing you for years before even considering bringing you to Faer Ri. It would have been your choice. And I had assumed you would be able to return to our time, unaware that so many years would have passed," he explained sorrowfully.

"How much time will have passed when we do go home," asked Donovan.

"It is difficult to say, and would depend on how soon we locate your parents. Maybe only a few months, maybe a year. The sooner the better, of course," he answered. Then, looking at Brendon, "You may have to consider the possibility that this is your new home. I wish the reapers had not taken you boys, but it is better to focus on what we can do now, rather than dwell on things that cannot be changed."

Brendon knew Mr. Dabir was right, even if he didn't want to admit it. He nodded and, taking Donovan by the hand, walked towards the exit, leaving Mr. Dabir to stare after them as they left.

Wishing to cheer is brother up, Brendon suggested they head out and explore the village. It was then that Donovan remembered something.

"Hey, I almost forgot. Check this out!" he said. He squinted his eyes and shimmered into a golden retriever. Brendon about tripped over himself in shock.

"When? How?" Brendon sputtered.

Donovan barked, and then shimmered into his own self. "Sorry, forgot," he laughed. "I was saying that it happened on accident in He-lush-Ka's camp while I was sleeping. You see. . ." but he was interrupted by a voice from the main table.

"Did you just use shift magic?" asked Bidzil incredulously.

"Er, yes?" replied Donovan.

"At your age? How remarkable! Gentlemen, I think I have a new plan," continued Bidzil as he began to explain his idea. Mr. Dabir joined the discussion and was shaking his head. The boys, curious to know what Donovan had done to change the plans, considered staying in the meeting hall rather than going for a walk, but at that moment Girvan came over to introduce himself.

"So, this is your little brother, Donovan, correct?" he asked.

"Yes. Donny, this is Girvan. He is a leprechaun. And before you insult him, it's not like anything we have heard of back home," added Brendon.

The two boys shook hands and the three of them left the Great Hall through the double doors. Outside the air was cool and crisp, and most of the people in the village had turned in for the night. Lights in windows showed movement here and there, but it was quiet, the only sounds disrupting the tranquil evening coming from crickets and other nighttime insects. Above, the evening sky spread a dazzling array of stars forming a spiral cluster to the north, while swirls of stars appeared to flow from the cluster like the tentacles of an octopus, filling the dark expanse with pinpoints of light.

"Wow," marveled Brendon. "This beats the Milky Way."

"What does milk have to do with stars?" asked Girvan perplexed.

Brendon shook his head and changed the subject. "So how big is the village?" he asked.

"It is just th' valley, and some of th' surrounding farm land. The magic that hides us is limited to Vloorhaven Glen. Anyone that passes through th' arch cannot be seen or heard. th' buildings were transported here when Caedmon performed th' magic. It has been generations since then, but th' magic has held. Rain falls, sun shines, cold weather or hot, everything is th‘ same. But somehow, we exist slightly ‘out of phase’ with Faer Ri. Not sure if that makes sense, but that's th‘ best explanation Scioldmed could give me,” explained Girvan.

“He sure doesn't like Bidzil. . . Caedmon I mean. Or me,” said Brendon.

“Only because he is afraid of you and your abilities,” said Girvan.

“I'm useless. I couldn't do anything Bidzil taught me to do,” Brendon said dejectedly.

“That's not what Scioldmed told me. Apparently, th‘ tree back in th‘ glade you had been practicing on? He said after you left that it aged an entire lifetime in a matter of seconds. You have magic, but you just don't know how to channel it. That's why he is so afraid of you.”

Brendon looked up at the sky once more. He wasn't sure what to think, but it made him feel a little bit better knowing the reason for Scioldmed’s behavior. Looking back at Girvan, he smiled and thanked him for sharing. They continued to walk around the village, asking and answering questions about the gnomes and their customs until it became very late.

Upon returning to the Great Hall, Mr. Dabir, Cian Torin, and Bidzil were waiting for them outside, the other gnomes and Fearghas having retired for the evening. Cian Torin gave his son a hug and sent him off to bed before asking the Baird children to stay behind for a moment.

“Young friends, we believe we have come to an agreement on a plan to take back th‘ city. But it involves using Donovan's new-found talent. Mr. Dabir is of th‘ mind that you both should remain here, safe and out of harm's way. Caedmon . . . Bidzil thinks you two are up to th‘ task. I would like to hear yer point of view,” said Cian Torin.

Brendon looked at Donovan who nodded back at him.

“My dad would say 'Why dip your toe in the water if you already know you're going swimming?'” said Brendon. Cian Torin looked confused.

Brendon explained. “In other words, we may as well jump in feet first instead of hanging around wondering if we should or not when we know we’re gonna get wet eventually. Yes, Cian Torin, we will help.”

***

Conall was relieved to see the dark forest up ahead. The sun had been beating down on them all day, and they had dismounted Kiwidinok in order to give him a chance to rest. He had walked all night without stopping, and most of the morning too. The past few hours were unbearable, with nothing to shade them from the blistering sun. Now, finally, they would have respite.

The group stopped a few hundred yards into the brush and collapsed on the forest floor. Ajeet, malnourished as he was, could barely summon the strength to speak, but he had pushed himself along with the others. Ganju's leg was most likely fractured, rather than sprained, but he had also fought through the pain and continued onward, keeping his injury to himself. Kiwidinok was exhausted from carrying others and himself out of the desert. Quinlan and Conall were dehydrated, like the others, but other than that they were healthy. After a few moments rest, Quinlan decided to survey the area to be sure they were safe. Kiwidinok just waved his hand and rolled over on his side to rest.

They slept off and on for most of the afternoon and into the evening. Quinlan had foraged for some wild berries and they were able to regain some of their strength. Kiwidinok put his hand the ground was able to locate a spring not too far away. They carried Ganju to the source of water, but Ajeet was able to manage on his own. All drank deeply once again before succumbing to the numbness of fatigue. Quinlan kept watch over them that night, assuring them that he would wake another should he feel drowsy.

The next morning Kiwidinok felt strong enough to use the shift magic to heal Ganju's broken leg. It would drain him and he would have to rest for another day, but having Ganju whole again was a priority. Gently, he placed one hand on the wounded leg, while thrusting the other deep into the soft earth, his fingers buried to the knuckles in the dark, rich soil.

Closing his eyes, he concentrated on finding and binding the fibers of bones, knitting them together again. Sweat beaded on his face as he strained to complete the difficult task. If he failed to concentrate, or if he paused at any time during the process, he could damage the bone and cripple Ganju.

Eventually, after several minutes had passed, a look of relief washed over Ganju's face, and Kiwidinok opened his eyes and sat back, breathing heavily.

“Water. I need water, please,” he said. Conall cupped his hands in the stream and walked back to Kiwidinok who drank what he could and then fell asleep.

The remainder of the day they spent resting and foraging for food. Quinlan found some tubers to eat, wild onions and turnips. Before this experience, Conall would have never eaten an onion, but he was so hungry. Surprisingly they actually tasted good, even though they were raw. Ganju and Kiwidinok woke later that day and ate more of the berries and the other foraged goods. That night they slept soundly once again. Ganju and Kiwidinok took shifts watching the camp so that Quinlan could sleep.

On the morning of the third day after their escape from the royal barge they were still weak, but fit enough to venture towards the camp of He-lush-Ka, Quinlan assuming that his father and the others would be there waiting for them. And even if Cian Torin had moved on, they would still be able to recover their strength before making the trek to Vloorhaven. By the time the sun had crested the horizon, they had begun to move northwest towards the camp, Quinlan guiding them as before.

They made several stops to rest and look for food. At one point, Quinlan felt the need for real meat outweighed the fear of a fire disclosing their location, and so he caught a couple of rabbits for dinner that night. Spirits improved with the meal, and Conall looked forward to seeing his brothers again.

The following morning, they came to a large river that wound lazily through the forest. Dipping his hands in the cold stream Quinlan smiled.

"I know where we are. This is the Torc River. It flows from the Dreich Mountains into Talamh Glas Loch. As it leaves the loch it meanders through the woods before joining the Skregmore, which flows from the Skregmore Reeks!" he said excited.

"Fascinating," said Kiwidinok dryly. "So why the big smile?"

"Because I know where to go now to get to the camp," answered Quinlan.

"What? You have been leading us without knowing where you were going?" questioned Kiwidinok indignantly.

"I knew that north was safe and south was not. I knew west was good but east was not. But I have never traveled into the desert, so I had no idea where we emerged. Be happy that I got us this far and we are only a couple of day's walk from the camp," scolded Quinlan.

Ganju just stared at them both. "What did he say?" he asked Conall.

"He said 'be nice Kiwi, tomorrow night you get to eat a real meal'," answered Conall winking at Kiwidinok.

"He did *not* say that," muttered Kiwidinok under his breath as they followed Quinlan through the woods.

***

The gnomes had marched most of the day and into the night, stopping for only minutes at a time to refresh themselves. The Baird children had been given a set of leather armor, gently used and "worn-in" so it was supple and comfortable. Both had decided to use the boots rather than their sneakers, so they developed a few blisters as they got used to them. Bidzil healed them as they stopped, and told them that in a day or so the boots would be broken in and not cause them discomfort. Brendon wondered how it was that Bidzil had healed them, since he was not a shaman, but before he could ask, they were marching again.

They were back in Talamh Glas, but it would take them another three days to reach the southern end of the loch and the bridge that led to the city. At least here they were more concealed as they traveled through the woods, rather than the open hill area of the Fells of Beag Cairdas. Before they slept that night, Cian Torin had Donovan practice his shift magic and rehearse his role in the battle. Once satisfied, he wished the boys a good night's rest. Girvan and his tutor had apparently had a falling out, as he had spent the day walking alongside Brendon. It was nice to have a friend. Brendon didn't have a lot of kids back home that he thought of as a true friend. Classmates, buddies, but not a real friend. Girvan's amicability made the prospects of living in Faer Ri more appealing.

***

Quinlan returned to where the group was waiting for him.

"I didn't see any campfires, or signs of movement. I did come across tracks leading away, and several boot prints heading into camp. I stopped and turned back when I saw those," he explained in a hushed voice.

"As I said," Kiwdinok chimed in, "there are definitely life forms in the camp, but I can't tell if they are Saami or something else. Perhaps I should take a look myself," suggested Kiwidinok. And with that he shifted into an owl and silently flapped away into the night sky.

Spreading his wings as he passed over the shoreline, the breezes from over the water giving him lift and carrying him higher, Kiwidinok searched for movement along the beach. He banked to the right, and then circled around the area that Quinlan had indicated should be the location of He-lush-Ka's camp, but there was nothing to see. After examining the area for a few moments, he landed softly, soundlessly on a branch of a tall cottonwood tree, casting his large yellow eyes all around him for signs of life. He nearly missed the booted foot as it pulled itself back under a tarp. Kiwidinok listened carefully and eventually heard breathing coming from several locations in the camp. It was a trap, and the rise in their breathing patterns alerted him that they knew he was here. Why would they suspect a common owl as being a shaman? They would if the owl species he had chosen wasn't native to the area. Idiot, he chided himself.

Without hesitation, he lifted off and flew as fast as he could, a bolt of a crossbow shaft narrowly missing him. How could he have been so foolish as to land. Behind him soldiers shouted to one another calling for pursuit. He would have to hurry back and warn the others before they were caught. He sped through the night, the moon rising slowly, its light betraying his hidden friends.

Landing and shifting into himself he called to the others.

"We are about to have company. More company than we can handle. I saw no camp, just the boots of Naga soldiers waiting in ambush. Where should we go now, Quinlan?" he asked.

Quinlan thought for a moment. "Well, I hate to say it but perhaps the safest bet is to re-trace our steps and head back to the Torc River. If we see any soldiers we could always cross to the other side. They do not like the cold water, and would not follow us. We could then make our way northward around the loch and follow the Torc into the Fells. It may take longer, but they would not suspect it and other routes may very well be watched since they are more direct."

"I think that is a good plan, but we need to find out if Cian Torin is even in Vloorhaven. He, Mr. Dabir, and Donny may have gone elsewhere," said Kiwidinok. He thought for a moment, and then looked around at his friends. "I think the wisest course of action is for me to fly up to Vloorhaven and find out what has happened, assuming you can draw me a map. For now, let's head back to the river, quickly!"

They ran most of the night and into the morning. Finally, they heard the familiar sound of the river bubbling and gurgling against the banks and rocks that littered the stream. The water was almost too cold to drink, but they did so in small gulps to slake their thirst.

Quinlan drew a map in the sand along the bank, showing Kiwidinok what to look for as far as landmarks. He then explained the arch hidden in the copse of trees near one of the larger hills. This would be the hardest part, but if he found it he would have to be careful not to rush in, as they would not be expecting him. Finally, confident of his understanding of the instructions and the lay of the land, Kiwidinok shifted into a raven, and flew into the sky.

The remainder of the group started to follow Quinlan along the shore, but Ganju made sure to stir the sand before they left. He had no idea what the little man had drawn, but it didn't seem wise to leave it for anyone to discover. He hurried to catch up to the others.

***

They followed the river for two more days, having stopped to forage for food from time to time, and by evening on the third day they were within view of Talamh Glas Loch. The water was a deep blue and mirrored the beautiful autumn sky. The leaves had begun to change, hints of red, orange, and yellow here and there among the deep green sea of foliage.

They decided to make camp in a ravine near the water so they could have a small fire to cook with and keep warm. Quinlan had stalked out a flightless bird and captured it for supper. It tasted a lot like turkey, and everyone was pleased to fill their belly for a change. Ganju, with the help of Conall, told stories about his time in the service, and some of the things he had had to eat while serving overseas. Quinlan kept asking if the translation was correct, given some of the unappealing victuals Ganju had tried. Ajeetabbas on the other hand licked his lips with delight. 'One man's trash is another man's treasure' thought Conall.

Quinlan was about to bank the fire when he thought he heard something. He motioned for everyone to stay still as he turned around and peered out into the woods.

“I don't remember teaching you to build such a big fire when in the wild, Prince Quinlan,” said a familiar voice.

Risteard appeared from the brush and clasped Quinlan's hand. And then, in a display of emotion uncommon for him, he pulled Quinlan close and embraced him. Quinlan was relieved and in shock all at once, but he returned the gesture. Risteard greeted the others and then bid them to follow him. They poured dirt over the fire so as not to create smoke, and he led them out of the ravine and through a series of hills and dales until they finally arrived in the camp of the gnome hunters.

Conall and his brothers jumped for joy, elated to find each other safe and secure. They shared their stories, recounting all that had happened. Donovan shifted a few times, mostly to show off, and they laughed at Conall's description of “His Royal Majesty” being ridden by Quinlan. Mr. Dabir was worried about Kiwidinok, but after hearing about his exploits in the arena he decided his fears were misplaced. His friend was more than capable of handling himself, it seemed.

They stayed up later that they should have, but none of the Baird boys could sleep, such was their joy at being reunited. Eventually Mr. Dabir, who himself could not sleep due to the giggling, insisted that they call it a night, especially considering the big day that lay ahead of them. They were quiet for a while. That is until Conall burped and the giggling began again.

AELFIN

Twenty-three

The pre-dawn sky was slightly overcast, and the moon slid behind the clouds as Risteard, Fearghas, and Donovan crept closer to the guard house at the end of the long bridge connecting the mainland to the island city. The other members of the attack force remained several hundred yards away; the gnome hunters having split into three groups.

Bidzil and Brendon were closest with about thirty gnome hunters behind them. South of them was the second group led by Quinlan and Scioldmed, and another thirty hunters. The remainder of the gnome hunters, another fifty or so, stood ready at the command of Cian Torin. Girvan, Ajeetabbas, Conall, and Ganju remained with Cian Torin. They would be the last to cross, and would be responsible for reinforcing the other columns as well as holding the bridge.

There were only two tattooed men occupying the gatehouse on this side of the causeway. One of the men stood and stretched before grabbing his spear and walking towards the woods, presumably to relieve himself. Risteard looked at Fearghas who, nodding in understanding, slowly backed himself into the brush before heading in the direction of the man they had been watching. Looking down at Donovan, Risteard whispered, "Ready?"

"Yes," came Donovan's muffled reply. He focused on the shift magic, and in a shimmer of green he became a small raccoon. At first, he skirted the side of the guardhouse nearest the woods, then crossed the path on the far side of the building towards the lake.

As he approached the pier that led out on to the bridge, he thought he heard a muffled cry, and looked back to see the other guard lying on the ground in front of the out building. Risteard appeared behind the fallen man and waved for him to continue moving forward. The bridge seemed longer than it was the last time he crossed it, probably because of his little raccoon legs. He also remembered the eye they had seen the first time, and was a little nervous about the creature that eye had belonged to. But Bidzil assured them that he would pass by unnoticed by the beast, not only disguised, but hidden by the stone rails on each side of the structure.

He neared the first turn and paused. He thought he saw a man just ahead of him. He tucked himself into the crevice between the bridge and the rail and waited. Nothing happened. Mustering his courage, he ventured out again. The second portion of the bridge was obscured in shadow, so Donovan decided to run as fast as he could. Really it was a scurry, his legs being small and truly unable to run in this form. He also noticed he had a hard time keeping his body moving straight, rather than weaving left and right.

Eventually he made it to the third section of bridge. He peered around the corner of the rail and, seeing no one, he continued to scamper towards the gatehouse on the far side. As he neared the small out building, he slowed his pace and crept up carefully. There was only one guard who, it seemed, was busying himself with refitting his spearhead on its shaft. The man had a grinding stone nearby, and some clothe. As Donovan watched, the tattooed man took some leather cord and a knife and cut the cord to the desired length he would need to reattach the blade to the shaft. He turned to get some water to soak the leather, and Donovan got an idea. He leaped up onto the small table, took the piece of leather in his mouth and leaped off again. The man turned back around to see his project running through the doorway.

Donovan ran in between the buildings and dropped the leather cord where it would be hard to find. He then doubled back to the vacant guard house and began to look frantically for the amulets they would need to cross the bridge without the lake creature preventing them from doing so. He searched the shelves and under the table, as well as the wall behind the door. But he could not find them. Then, as he heard the sounds of the man returning he noticed the bench on which the man had sat had hinges. However, there was no time to look. He jumped up onto the table and this time grabbed the spearhead as the man entered the shack.

He looked at the man. The man looked at him. Donovan dove through the window as the man reached for him. Dropping the spearhead, he ran back up the street again, while the man, shaking his head came around to the front of the guard house and picked up the spearhead. Donovan skittered over to the side of the road. There had to be something else he could do, he needed to open that bench and see if the amulets were inside. It was an essential part of the plan.

He decided he would try something different. Climbing onto one of the abandoned homes he crawled from rooftop to rooftop until he stood poised to jump onto the guard shack. He hunched down, gathered his furry feet under him, and launched his little body across the expanse, barely making it, clawing some of the slate and mud free. He thought he would find a way to enter from the roof and get behind the guard. He started to scratch and dig at the slate and mud, tearing away bits and pieces to make an opening large enough to crawl through. He was almost finished when he heard something behind him. He turned to see two narrow-set thin slits of eyes staring at him from the edge of the roof.

The guard was standing on the window ledge trying to see what was making all the scratching noise on the roof. Donovan, startled out of his wits, let out a scream, which in 'raccoon' was more of a screech. The man, who hadn't been expecting to see a screaming raccoon in his face, also let out a scream as he lost his footing and fell from the ledge to the street below.

Donovan paused for a moment before peering over the edge of the roof. The guard was lying on his back, breathing, but unconscious. Well, thought Donovan, *that* was easy. He crawled down into the shack once again and shimmered into his human form. Lifting the bench, he found three amulets. He placed them around his neck before shimmering back into his raccoon self, and then sped off down the causeways towards the far side of the bridge.

***

Risteard and Fearghas gathered their men and, taking one of the amulets Donovan had procured, quietly sped across the bridge, their feet making hardly any sound. Brendon ran alongside Bidzil towards the back of the contingent. They kept their eyes on the city ahead, hoping not to be discovered before they had a chance to cross. Had they been seen they would have been pinned down on the bridge, unable to advance.

As they neared the far gatehouse, Fearghas gathered the unconscious form of the tattooed guard and placed him in the shack, binding him with cords. Risteard took out a hooded lantern and signaled towards the opposite shore to send Quinlan's group across. Cian Torin would follow with the third amulet once they had made it safely past the lake monster. Donovan would remain with Conall and Cian Torin until the battle was over. The younger boys protested of course, not understanding why Brendon was allowed to participate, but their arguments were ignored even though their bravery was noted.

Once the second group had crossed, and the third had begun to assemble, Risteard and Quinlan led their column up the winding road towards the plaza at the top of the island. Their plan was to attack the barracks first, and once secured, to systematically move from one section of the city to the next, rounding up the enemy as they went. They reached the first intersection and Risteard led his hunters to the right. They would come at the plaza from the south, while Quinlan would go left and come from the north. Bidzil had given them exact details of the city layout, and explained where they would create the best choke points for enemy soldiers, using their numbers against them. If they could make it to the plaza without detection, they should be able to successfully take the barracks.

Dawn was approaching, and their silhouettes became more visible against the soiled marble buildings on either side of the road. Risteard hoped they were empty; otherwise they would be fighting a battle on multiple sides, surrounded from the onset. But from the accounts they had received, the Naga housed the soldiers in the old library, having converted it into barracks. The tattooed men, on the other hand, were reported as living in the out-buildings around the animal pens north of the plaza. Brendon had remembered those pens as the first thing he had experienced in Faer Ri. Perhaps they could help free someone else if the cages were occupied.

They reached a small square where the road branched in three directions. Risteard and his men took the left this time, while

Fearghas, Bidzil, and Brendon continued moving forward. Still no movement from the buildings, and no sign of alarm. By now Cian Torin would be in place on the near side of the bridge, and would be sending patrols to back them up at the crossroads they had just passed. This should prevent them from being flanked from behind.

***

Quinlan and his men veered right at the next intersection passing a series of streets on their left leading away from the center of town. Here the decay of the city was most evident, the buildings overgrown with weeds and trees that grew out of dilapidated roofs. Broken marble support beams had crumbled and been dragged to the side of the road, covered now with moss and dead leaves. The paving stones had been unearthed by rain and erosion, jutting out at odd angles and making their approach somewhat precarious.

They continued forward until they reached a small square where the road branched to the east and to the west. Just ahead was the rearward side of the old library. It sat several stories high, with a round cupula in the center. The marble slabs were still intact, but dirty and covered with mold and trails of ivy. Quinlan sent Scioldmed and ten hunters to go and secure the two exits so that enemy soldiers could not leave from that side of the building, while he took the remainder of the force with him up the street on the left towards the pens.

They approached the enclosures slowly and deliberately; smoke was drifting from the outbuildings that butted up next to the pens, and a group of tattooed men sat around a cook fire. There were only seven or so preparing the food, and they did not seem to have weapons with them. Quinlan nodded, and his men sprang upon the tattooed men, who began to cry out in an unknown dialect. Quinlan motioned for the men to lay down, his men covered their mouths to avoid further alarm, before continuing into the next set of buildings.

What he saw there caused him pause, as everything he thought he knew of the tattooed men suddenly changed. Here, in the very same animal pens that the Baird children and others had been kept, were a hundred or so tattooed men sitting or sleeping in a large dirt ring that had once been used for livestock, but had since been enclosed presumably in order to lock up the tattooed warriors when they were not serving their masters.

Noticing the gnome hunters, they began to cry out. Fearing they would alert the soldiers in the barracks nearby, Quinlan called for them to be quiet. This is not what he had expected. These men appeared to be as much a slave as any whom they had escorted. One of them approached Quinlan, and struggled to speak.

"Sir. . . we. . . no harm, sir. We no . . . hurt. Please. . . to have us food, sir?" he pleaded, attempting to communicate. Quinlan wished he had Brendon's shillelagh so he could communicate better, but he felt he understood well enough. These men would not fight them. They were not the enemy. They just wanted to eat.

Quinlan had his hunters place the cooks into the cage as well, and left a few of them to stand guard, in case this was a ruse of some sort. They had no food of their own to spare, but instead carried the stockpots from the cook fires over to the men to disperse the contents. Quinlan hoped this would pacify them and prevent them from trying to escape. He then quickly began to reorganize his forces and head towards the main plaza. They would now be able to offer more help Risteard in his assault on the barracks.

***

Risteard entered the plaza, ducking low to avoid detection. There did not seem to be any sentries posted, or if so they were well concealed. The sun was now beginning to rise, and soon the huddled gnome forces would be quite noticeable. The idea was to capture the Naga in their sleep, so there was no time to waste. Standing to full height, Risteard scouted out the steps and entryway to the old library. The windows had been covered, and no light was to be found in any of the buildings. It was eerily silent. Just then he saw movement at the north end of the plaza, and was relieved to see Quinlan signaling to him. It was time.

Together they made their way to the entrance from opposite sides of the covered porch that extended from the building and continued down a series of step that reached from one end of the structure to the other. As they slowly climbed the stairs, the doorway nearest Risteard opened and a pair of soldiers started down the steps from the landing. Without pause, the gnomes sprinted to close the gap, Risteard whipping out one of his twin blades and throwing it with precision in the chest of the soldier on the left, while Quinlan, from the opposite side, swung his half-moon spear in an arcing motion, neatly slicing through the armor of the second adversary. They continued their pace up the stairs without stopping, their men close behind, the fallen soldiers left to bleed out on the steps.

***

Brendon watched from across the plaza, as the two gnomes and their men entered the building. So far there had been no alarm, and no resistance. Could it really be so easy? Bidzil motioned for him to follow as they ran from their hiding place behind a withering tree towards a stately building on the south side of the plaza. They had been told this was being used as the officer's quarters currently, but Bidzil explained that it had once served as a hospital. Up the wide marble steps they ran, and flung open the heavy wooden door as three soldiers were about to exit. Fearghas swung his enchanted staff striking all three men neatly across the temples in rapid succession, and rendering each unconscious. He pressed forwards down the hall, Bidzil and Brendon close behind.

As Fearghas moved ahead into the adjoining room, Bidzil took a few steps up the narrow wooden staircase to the left. Brendon, wishing to be useful, walked forward, following Fearghas to the back of the building. As he passed the stairs leading to the second floor, a door on his right burst open and men with dark hooded cloaks charged him with those eerie curved blades. There was a hint of savagery in their wild eyes as they bore down on the young Druidae.

Reapers!

Brendon had no room to run, and instinctively raised his shillelagh. It glowed brightly and began to hum and vibrate in his hands. The reapers dropped their weapons and covered their ears, screaming in pain. They were a mass of writhing black cloaks with white arms and legs twisting and churning, trying to crawl away and back into the dark of the room from which they had emerged. Horrified by their reaction,

Brendon started to back away and bumped into Bidzil who just looked at him in awe and quietly exclaimed, “Remarkable.”

Then, turning his attentions to the dozens of reapers who were squirming on the floor, Bidzil raised his hands and began to sing. Power coursed through his body and flowed into the hooded creatures. In moments they stopped shrieking, and their twitching slowed until they lay motionless on the floor.

“You didn't kill them, did you?” asked Brendon timidly, as his shillelagh stopped glowing.

“Heavens no,” answered Bidzil. “They are sleeping, and will not awake until I allow them to. Look carefully and you will see these are not Naga, they are aelfin shaman who have been tortured and abused, raised to believe the lies taught to them from birth. The reapers locate and harvest aelfin bloodlines in your world and bring them here to serves as slaves. Children taken in your world, or born to slaves in ours, are tested and then trained to be a new generation of reapers, thus continuing the cycle.”

“Can they change forms, like Kiwidinok?” said Brendon as he watched the hall behind him.

“No, I do not think they can do anything other than what they were taught to do, that is to enter your world as a spirit form and harvest aelfin descendants. I do not know if we can even help them, so dark has been their path. But should we prevail in this battle, we shall try,” said Bidzil softly.

Fearghas returned from the far reaches of the building. “There were two more. Nearly jumped out of their skin when they heard these fellows screaming. They dropped their weapons and hid under a table before I even got to them,” he said smiling.

They proceeded to climb the wooden stairs, searching for the leader of the Naga outpost, and wary for other surprises.

***

Cian Torin surveyed the far side of the bridge. Reports back indicated little to no resistance. He was concerned that they may have been allowed to enter the city in an attempt to ambush, but how would the enemy have known. His scouts had been careful to watch for troop movements on their journey south, and had reported nothing. Certainly, there existed smaller raiding parties in

Talamh Glas, but where was the bulk of the army? He decided to send a contingent of hunters to sweep the streets of the city in teams of two. He sent another messenger to Risteard for a final tally of the attack on the barracks.

The sun had now risen over the tree line to the east, and the forest began to wake from its nocturnal slumber. A flock of geese landed nearby in the water, floating and bobbing on the tranquil surface. It was going to be a clear day, without a cloud in the sky. He turned to his son Girvan and the others.

"This is perhaps one o' th' most beautiful places in Faer Ri, and I am grateful that you are here to see it with me, my son," he said with a smile.

Girvan smiled back, but the smile quickly faded replaced by a look of fear and concern. Cian Torin cocked his head to the side and spun around to see hundreds of Naga soldiers on the far bank, one of them sitting astride a large basilisk.

Twenty-four

Captain Upahasa smiled as he looked across the water at his long-time foe. His ska'utsa warriors had been tracking movements of the gnomes for the past several weeks, and so it was that as a large body of gnomes left their place of refuge in the Fells of Beag Cairdas he sent word to his men to abandon the city, leaving a few behind to watch over the reapers and the ska'utsa who were ill or otherwise not fit for battle. At most he would lose a few soldiers and a few hundred of those tattooed barbarians, but it was worth it to finally put an end to the gnome resistance.

His forces had been too late to capture the shaman camp on the peninsula, although one of his lieutenants had almost caught a straggler. But that threat was also no longer an issue. Weakened over the years, the Saami and their leader had been seen leaving the mainland a few days prior. Soon he would return to his homeland, away from the cold winters of this northern territory. Let some other 'up and coming' officer take his place, while he rose to power and position in the heart of the empire.

He pulled out the jeweled medallion from his saddle bag and placed it over his head. He had only used the medallion on one occasion, the day he had first taken over as commander of the outpost. On that day he had called for the beast to appear, acknowledge him, and perform a few other tasks to ensure the enchantment worked as he had been told. Today, however, he would command it to enter the city and dispose of the vermin that infested it. His thin smile grew into a grin and he closed his eyes and focused on summoning the leviathan.

Risteard and Quinlan walked from the barracks towards the center of the plaza, near the massive pillars of stone where Bidzil, Fearghas, and Brendon waited for them.

"We have searched th' main buildings of th' plaza, as well as th' outlying buildings. Cian Torin has sent patrols to th' homes and other structures on th' island, but so far we have not located th' main Naga force," reported Risteard.

"Yes, and I find it strange that th' tattooed men were almost all confined to th' animal pens. How many men were in th' old hospital?" asked Quinlan.

"Five soldiers, and about thirty reapers," answered Bidzil. "All are sleeping for now. With the forty or so men you found in the barracks, I fear we have the bulk of the battle ahead of us, only now the element of surprise is gone. Did you get anything out of the prisoners?"

"They would not say anything even if they knew, and I'm not sure they did not. None of them are officers, most are new to soldiering. You can tell by th' way they held their weapons, their inability to perform defensive maneuvers, and how quick they were to surrender," replied Risteard.

"What of Scioldmed, what does he think?" asked Bidzil.

"He feels we have entered into a trap, and that we should abandon th' city as soon as possible," answered Risteard. "He is making his way down to th' causeway to share as much with Cian Torin. I can't say that I disagree. Our force is barely more than a hundred, and by all accounts they should have several hundred troops occupying th' city. Our main weapon has always been surprise and ambush. Now I fear we are the ones being ensnared. I will gather up my men and prepare to leave th‘ plaza. Quinlan, you should do th‘ same. I am sorry Bidzil, but we cannot reclaim your city today.”

Bidzil looked down, “I understand. We could never hold out against a force that big. Come Fearghas, we need to awaken the reapers before we leave. I am afraid they will continue to fulfill their mission to enslave others, but we simply do not have the time to recondition them, and I cannot find it in my heart to take their lives nor leave them to sleep eternal.”

Fearghas nodded and began to follow Bidzil towards the old hospital when the ground shook beneath them, accompanied by a deafening roar. To the north of the plaza, where the island sloped down at a steep angle towards the lake, an enormous creature had emerged from the waters and placed a clawed appendage on the shore of the island. It raised its head high into the sky, its eyes level with the plaza as it focused on the gnomes that stood guard near the animal pens. Tilting its head to the right and opening its giant maw, it swept down upon the gnomes who stood paralyzed with fear, closing its jaws around them before craning its neck and swallowing them whole. Brendon was terrified, and Bidzil called for him to run to the causeway and find Cian Torin, but he was frozen in fear, his feet not obeying what his thoughts told them to do.

The creature watched as gnomes ran this way and that. It heaved its bulk onto the shore below in order to extend its reach and started to crawl up the slope towards the plaza. Showering the plaza with cold water, green patches of lake reeds falling from its back, the behemoth wormed its way forward, crushing everything in its path. The long serpentine neck continued to weave and bob, emitting an ear-piercing blast that shook trees and caused buildings to shake and tumble. Huge flippers with elongated claws dug into the sand to gain purchase as a twisted black tail flailed about in the churned-up water of the lake.

Quinlan ran towards the pen where the tattooed men were, dodging debris that was being knocked about by the monster as it swung its head to and fro. As he approached the tattooed men were huddled in a mass at the edge of one of the walls. Opening the gate, he motioned for them to follow him. They were wary at first, but eventually ran from their confinement and towards the road leading to the causeway, Quinlan leading the way in order to prevent one of the gnome hunters from mistaking their escape as an attack.

Risteard had ordered his men to retreat, evacuating the city. He looked back to see Bidzil halfway between the hospital and the massive stone circle in the center of the plaza. Fearghas was running back to the center where Brendon was still standing motionless. The creature had hoisted itself onto the slope of the hill and was raising its head to strike again. Taking out his blades he affixed the clear stones given to him by Scioldmed, and ran towards Brendon as well.

***

Cian Torin heard the roar from the other side of the island, and immediately his thoughts went to Quinlan. But he had little time to think as hundreds of Naga soldiers began to march across the bridge. A large column, five men across, and approximately twenty men deep, filled the opening of the causeway. As they reached the first turn of the structure another battalion of one hundred started to march. There were at least two other battalions that Cian Torin could see. The gnomes had to stop them from reaching the near side of thc bridge, or all would be lost.

Scioldmed came to his side, huffing and puffing. He looked as though he wished to share something, but Cian Torin interrupted, "We need to slow them down. They must *not* cross th' bridge!" A few of his men took their bows and began to nock arrows, while Scioldmed and Girvan walked to the edge of the final span. The two leprechauns raised their hands and focused on the stones that made up the causeway. The stones began to vibrate and shudder until one the size of a brick broke free of is fitting and flew towards the first row of the column striking a soldier in the chest and knocking him to the ground. Another soldier quickly took his place. The squadron leader called out and they raised their shields together as more rocks pelted the oncoming force. Arrows flew straight, but there was little that wasn't protected by armor or shield, and the projectiles careened off harmlessly into the lake, startling the geese that flew from their restful swim back into the sky.

Cian Torin looked at Mr. Dabir, who had moved Donovan away from the sight of the battle. "Can you do nothing, Magi? Lightning, rain, fog?"

"No, my friend, I cannot. I was hardly a Magi in my own world. It would take me years of study in this world before I could perform such feats. Besides, we manipulate weather, we don't create it."

Gnome hunters began to run towards the bridge from the city above, and Cian Torin ordered them to find rocks, debris and anything they could use to barricade this side of the bridge. It would come down to close quarter combat, and they would need to do something to even the odds.

In the sky above, the geese wheeled about and turned towards Cian Torin, flying low and in a narrow 'V' shape. As they came within a few yards they banked to their right, directly over the nearest section of causeway before shimmering one at a time into a heard of rhinoceros. They charged two by two across the causeway, a thundering mass of armored flesh and sharp horns. The Naga stopped and peered from behind their shields as the lead rhino snorted defiantly. Bodies flew left and right, some impaled, some trampled, as twenty or so rhinos dispatched the first column and moved to the second. The second column had turned to run, rather than be overrun by the enormous beasts, some even leaping over the railings to land helplessly into the icy depths of the lake. None ever surfaced, and all were lost.

***

Uphasa fumed as the rhinos charged his men on the bridge. He called for archers to form rank. As the rhinos neared his side of the causeway he signaled for them to let lose. A flurry of arrows sailed towards the lumbering heard. Think skin or not, they would feel the sting of these arrows. But at the last moment the rhinos shimmered into a murder of ravens. A couple of them were taken down by the hail of arrows, but the majority escaped and flew back to the far side. No matter. He had more surprises in store.

He turned to his gamekeepers. "Release the wyverns!" he cried.

***

Kiwidinok and the others landed and shifted back into human form. Next to him stood He-lush-Ka and the other shaman from the Saami. He was looking back towards the two warriors they had just lost, and then turned around to face Cian Torin.

"How . . ." began Cian Torin, but Kiwidinok interrupted.

"After I arrived at Vloorhaven and heard where you had gone, I searched for my fellow shaman. I found them paddling towards the skerries. I told them what you were doing, and that if he truly believed in what he had spent his entire life doing, what his son had given his life to accomplish, that he would swallow his pride and help. And.I may have threatened to turn myself into an orca and capsize their boats," he said, winking at He-lush-Ka. He-lush-Ka did not wink back. Instead, he dropped to one knee and bowed his head.

"Friend Torin, I am sorry for what I tried to do. And I am sorry for how I have treated you and your people. Please forgive me," said He-lush-Ka reverently. He looked up at Mr. Dabir and Donovan. "And to you young Shaman, I pledge my life in payment for what I tried to do, if you will forgive me."

Donovan nodded uncomfortably. Just then, a series of loud shrieks shattered the solemn moment, and the company turned their attention once again towards the far side of the lake. As another column of Naga marched across the causeway, large iron cages were being opened and enormous two-legged lizards with fifteen-foot wing spans were being coaxed into the air, their red scaly hides flashing in the morning sun. Long tails whipped around as they tried to gain altitude. A series of whistles from one of the men below caused them to form up and fly towards Cian Torin's position. The allies would have to find a way to defend themselves from above as well as on the ground.

***

Fearghas picked up Brendon and hurried inside the stone circle, Brendon grasping his shillelagh for dear life. Outside Risteard had done his best to distract the creature and was running and dodging between debris and shrubs. Apparently, the amulets they had used to cross the bridge no longer held sway with the creature, as it continued to climb the hill in search of victims. Bidzil had begun to sing a new song, this time pointing at the creature, but it seemed to have no effect as the monstrosity continued to advance. Setting Brendon down, Fearghas took the shaft from off his back and exited the structure to help his master. As the beast swung its head and snapped at Risteard, Fearghas leaped up and swung his staff across its scaly neck. The blow landed with a solid thud, and a crack of green light, but the beast was unaffected, its neck as thick as a bus, and as long as a football field.

The creature raised a clawed fin and lowered it on top of one of the animal pens at the edge of the plaza, crushing it and spraying more dirt and debris into the plaza. Risteard ran towards the appendage and, mustering all his strength, drove one of his twin blades into the flesh of the monster. It howled in pain, its neck arching in agony before speeding down to snap at Risteard. He jumped free as the jaws shut behind him. Rolling on the ground he got up and turned to face the creature again when he was struck by the beast's head as it whipped towards him, throwing him high in the air before falling into a heap near the stone circle.

Bidzil had changed his tactics. While the beast was distracted, thousands of vines had emerged from the hillside below and were winding themselves around its torso and lower extremities. The vines snaked towards its head as the Warrior Bard continued to sing, his face wet with the strain, his eyes alight with a green glow. Brendon felt immense power radiating from him, as he watched from his hiding place.

The vines had nearly enveloped the creature when it shook its massive bulk and released a challenging roar. Fearghas ran to Risteard to assess his wounds before picking him up and carrying him out towards the far side of the plaza. Bidzil continued to sing, and the sky began to cloud over, lightning flashing in the distance. Brendon watched as Bidzil's skin became nearly translucent, veins and arteries visible on his arms and face, his eyes now radiating an emerald glow. The vines continued encircling the massive creature who struggled to move, twisting and growing thicker with each passing moment. Fearghas returned to his master's side, and began to call to him.

"It is enough, Grandfather! You must stop! Please!" he cried. Bidzil continued to sing. The harmonies were now lost in the wind as gusts began to uproot trees and lift slate from the rooftops. Lightning flashed across the sky as clouds began to form, roiling outward from a fixed-point high above Bidzil, and moving unnaturally fast as they spread outward towards the horizon. The lake began to churn, and whitecaps formed across the dark waters. The Warrior Bard was calling upon the very heavens and earth in an effort to stop the advance of the creature.

"Grandfather, you must stop, you have embraced too much magic! You will die! You will kill us all!" Fearghas pleaded.

The old Druidae seemed to hear this last part and, with a great deal of effort, released the magic. The wind began to die down, the clouds slowed their pace, and the waters of the lake resumed their placid demeanor as Bidzil fell into the arms of his friend. His skin was still translucent, and Brendon wondered if his friend would be alright.

He was about to go to him when he heard the sound of roots being ripped from the soil. Looking out through the gaps of the stone circle, he watched as the creature tore vines that surrounded it, whipping its long neck back and forth as it freed itself from the vegetation that had restricted it. It rose to full height and hefted the bulk of its torso almost completely into the plaza, emitting another cacophonous screech.

***

Kiwidinok and the other shaman attempted several forms to prevent the wyverns from reaching the gnomes, but the creatures were big and swift in the air. No animal they could shift into was a match for them, so instead they did their best to distract and divert the winged nemeses from their objectives. Donovan, Conall, and Mr. Dabir had retreated into a nearby home, along with Ganju who had re-injured his leg trying to help with the barricade, while the gnome hunters and Ajeetabbas defended their position. More gnomes arrived from the city center, as well as a large group of tattooed men. At first Cian Torin thought he had been flanked, but his men explained that they were not a threat. They even began to help carry rocks and debris to the make-shift barricade.

Scioldmed and Girvan had concentrated their efforts on dismantling the near side of the bridge, given the Nagas' fear of water and weakness to cold temperatures. They had managed to create a seven-foot gap at the end of the causeway and were now busying themselves with deflecting arrows being sent in the direction of the barricade. Cian Torin and his men chose not to return fire, knowing that they would only waste their projectiles on the heavily armored columns.

Close to two hundred Naga were now on the bridge, hunkered down behind shields. On the far bank timber was being felled and Cian Torin knew they would be coming soon with reinforcements to span the gap, punch through the barricade, and breach their defenses. As he turned away from the battle to search for a place of retreat (when the time came), one of his men called for him to 'look out'. Cian Torin threw himself flat to the ground just as a wyvern's outstretched claws raked his back in an attempt to grab him. He cried out in pain as the creature flapped its wings to gain altitude, but not before Ajeetabbas deftly thrust his trident into the foul lizard, twisting the shaft and vaulting him over his head and into the lake.

***

Bidzil was barely breathing, and Fearghas looked at Brendon, questioning him with his eyes. He seemed to ask, 'Can you do nothing to save him?' Brendon felt helpless. He was just a kid from Michigan. He was just a boy. Not strong, not powerful, not an heir to any great race of people. He wasn't some answer to a prophecy, he had done nothing special in his life. Around him stood magically imbued stones that could take him home and away from all of this madness. The thought crossed his mind, but only for a moment. There was no way he would leave his friends and family behind, even if he knew how to use them.

Taking the staff in his hands, he fell to his knees, sobbing. If only he had Conall's bravery. If only he had Donovan's faith. If only he had his parents' ability to love. What did he have?

The staff began to hum, glowing faintly in his hands. Images filled his mind. Images of his childhood, then that of his father, and *his* father, and *his* father, all his ancestors appeared before him in a sea of faces, swirling left and right, smiling at him, trusting in him, believing in him. He felt their love. He felt their support. He watched the faces move swiftly by until they slowed and stopped on that of Caedmon Anluan. He would never have imagined Bidzil looking so young, but it was definitely him. The image looked at Brendon and simply said, “Trust in yourself.”

Brendon snapped his eyes open. He looked over at Fearghas cradling Bidzil in his arms. No time had passed, but there was no time to waste. He glanced around him at the stone circle, the only way for his family to return home, assuming they could even use them to travel again. Massive stones infused with centuries old magic. Then he remembered something Bidzil had said about having sung hundreds of songs into the shillelagh.

Walking to the center of the concentric rings, he held the shillelagh in his outstretched hands. He didn't know any of the songs of the Druidae, in fact he didn't really know the words to any song; instead he hummed. At first it wasn't a recognizable tune, but then it kind of became something he heard long ago.

The shillelagh began to glow more fiercely as he hummed louder, and then, as if turning on a switch, his mind became aware of words and music that he had never before encountered. He closed his eyes and focused on the music while concentrating on what he wanted to do. Around him he felt electricity, and the hairs on the back of his head began to rise. His arms felt light at first, but slowly they became heavy, long, powerful, the magic coursing through his body as the shillelagh began to sing another song on top of the one he was singing.

It was Bidzil's voice he heard, far off in another time and place. The power grew around him. He opened his eyes to see the hulking stones glowing green and rising from the earth. A smile appeared on his face.

***

Fearghas watched as the stones lifted from the ground and began to spin counter to each other. As they did so, they coalesced and grew closer and closer to the small form inside the radiant viridian light. The lake monster had shrunk back in fear, uncertain of the spinning, glowing mass in front of it. Bidzil, breathing ever so slowly whispered something Fearghas could not make out.

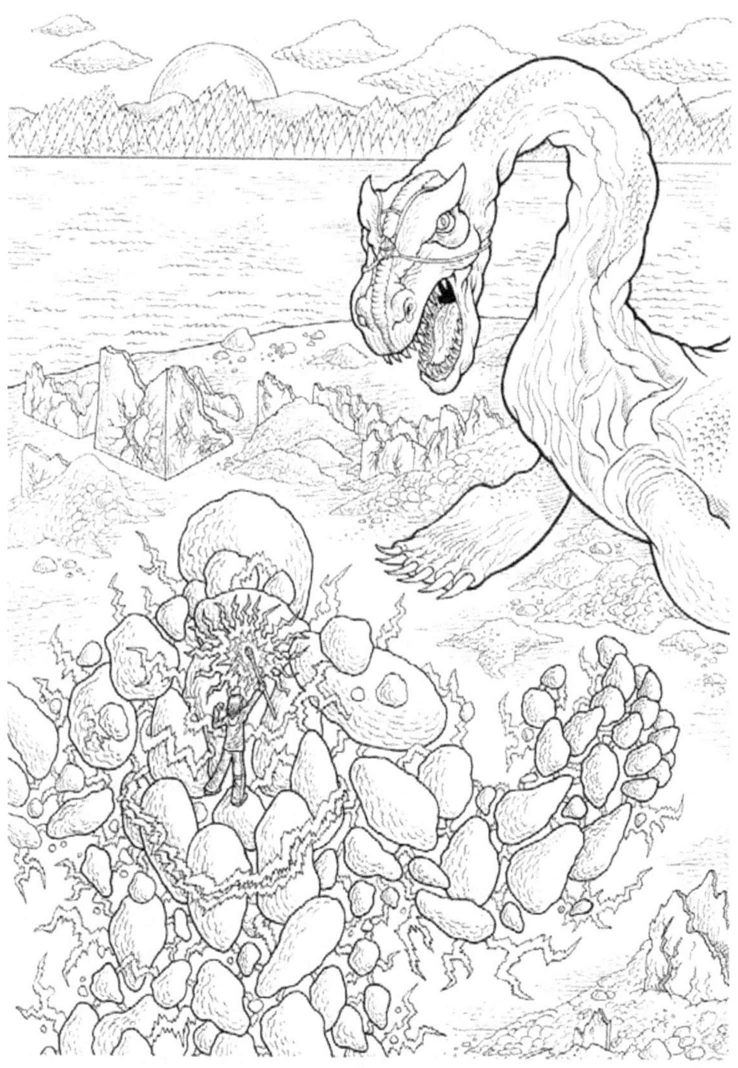

The stones began to slow as Brendon was raised off the ground. Gradually they formed around his frame taking the shape of a forty-foot stone golem who stood level with the tallest of buildings. Brendon stopped singing and rotated the shillelagh to the right as the golem moved to the right as well. The creature before him uninhibited now as the song had ended, arched its neck and lashed out at the stone giant before it, only to bite down on a ten-foot hardened sarsen sandstone forearm. Brendon shook the creature loose and swung the left side of the shillelagh forward. The left side of the stone golem in which he was encased swung its left fist and plowed into the creature's jowls, knocking it off the embankment of the plaza and sending it sliding down the slope of the hill with a thunderous crash and a cloud of dirt.

Brendon lifted his legs and began to walk, as he did so the golem walked with him. He moved towards the edge of the plaza and jumped from the embankment, landing on the neck of the behemoth. He pulled the shillelagh towards his chest as the golem squeezed the neck of the lake monster, but it rolled on its back, crushing trees and small fishing shacks at the water's edge. Brendon's golem was thrown loose as he lost his equilibrium and his left hand released the shillelagh. The creature reared its head again, but Brendon ran forward and rammed the golem into its mid-section, pushing it into the lake.

Unfortunately, his momentum carried him in as well. The water sloshed around the golem's legs, which were becoming mired in the sand and mud. The creature, seeing his lack of movement, turned its massive body around and whipped him with its enormous tail, chipping off pieces of stone and causing Brendon to lose his balance and fall to one knee. The golem fell to a knee as well.

Brendon wasn't sure how long he could keep the golem together. Also, he couldn't believe the tenacity of this beast. What was driving it? Why was it fighting them, and why now? As if in answer to his question, the shillelagh glowed again, and a thin beam of light extended from the shaft over to the creature's forehead, where a small metal amulet had been mounted with golden chains. The amulet matched the ones they had used to cross the causeways of the bridge; only this one was different, as it was covered with crimson and violet gems. Something within him urged him to ask what would happen if he removed the diadem from the creature's brow.

He had an idea. Brendon stood up and did his best to run down the beach, the golem sluggishly matching his efforts. The creature, unable to keep up on land, turned and submersed itself into the water to catch its prey.

Brendon looked over his should to see the undulating form of the lake monster following him in the dark waters. His legs were hurting, but he did not give up. Too many people depended on him right now. He neared the end of the beach as he approached a tree line on the south of the island. Lowering his shoulder, he drove his golem into the nearest set of trees, toppling them to the ground as he fell to the earth himself. The lake monster swam towards him and crested the water showering him with droplets of icy lake water and sand. It pulled its form onto land and roared challenge to the stone golem before it. Grabbing one of the tree trunks he had just knocked over, Brendon spun about and delivered a blow to the side of the monster's head. The tree splintered into pieces, the force of the blow shattering everything in his stone hands. The creature swayed back and forth before falling forward into the woods.

Brendon slowly walked over to where the beast lay and reached down to grab the chains that held the amulet, effortlessly pulling them apart and tossing the amulet into the trees behind him. Something told him this would be the end of the control the Naga had over this poor beast, and he stood up to full height to survey the damage that had been caused. He also wondered if the stones could still be used to make a realmbridge, and how he would put them back in place.

The slope of the hill was too steep for him to climb up, and so he decided to approach the city from the other side. Trudging through the forest, toppling trees as he went, he realized it would take too long to reach the other side, and so returned to the water in order to walk along the beach. It was slow going, the giant stone golem sinking with each laborious step, but before long he came to an inlet of crushed shells and was able to stand more erect and gain momentum.

Rounding the beachhead of the small inlet, he turned northward towards the bridge, only to see his friends engaged in a fierce battle, fighting to avoid the advance of a vast number of Naga soldiers and red flying creatures in the sky. Dragons? What should he do, and how could he stop them? An idea occurred to him, and he wondered if there was a song about breathing underwater . . .

***

Cian Torin's men were weary. The constant bombardment of arrows, and the winged devils from above made holding the barricade near impossible. The enemy had already placed fresh cut planks across the missing bridge section, and a large tree was being carried to breach the impromptu wall they had made. Time to fall back. Perhaps they could defend themselves better in one of the fortified buildings of the island, or maybe Bidzil could do something, assuming he had dealt with the lake moster that had attacked his men. But they could no longer hold the bridge. The shaman were wounded or tending to the wounded. Kiwidinok was the only one who still engaged the seven remaining wyverns.

He watched Kiwidinok in his eagle form circle higher and higher in the sky before plummeting to the earth to strike at an unsuspecting wyvern. It had already proved effective a few times. The creatures were strong and swift, but not bright, and if they ventured far enough away from the others, Kiwi was able to deliver a lethal attack and climb back into a safe position in the sky.

This time, however, Kiwidinok did not see another wyvern approaching from behind as he tucked in his wings and dove. As he hurtled towards his intended target, the other wyvern banked and increased its velocity. Kiwidinok opened his wings and thrust out his talons at the last moment, his momentum driving the sharp claws into the back of the surprised creature. But at the moment he struck the wyvern, the one who followed reached out for him as well.

Noticing his new adversary, he folded his wings and dove into the water to avoid capture. Kiwidinok scrambled towards the surface, wings soaked and heavy with cold icy water, he was unable to get lift and struggled to stay afloat. The wyvern threw out its wings and banked sharply, heading once again for the floundering eagle, its claws preparing to strike.

Kiwidinok thought about what form he should take, but the water sapped his strength and numbed his thoughts. He could not concentrate and felt himself slipping under the waves again. The wyvern was an arm's length away. He closed his eyes to accept his end.

At that moment, an enormous stone hand emerged from the water grabbing the wyvern, neatly crushing it before casting it into the lake. Another hand appeared holding the limp form of an eagle, and then a stone head emerged. A golem made of giant glowing stones stood up out of the water and walked towards the causeway where the Naga soldiers had begun to retreat.

With its free hand, the golem reached under the bridge and ripped apart the stone arches that supported it, crushing the ramparts and decking. Soldiers fell into the freezing waters, their heads appearing only once or twice before going to their watery grave. The golem continued to walk towards the remaining soldiers on land, which, despite the orders of their commander, dropped their weapons and fled. Without a handler to command them, the remaining wyverns flew south over the forest of Talamh Glas. The commander, alone on the beach, turned his basilisk around and crawled away.

In a matter of minutes, all was quiet. The enemy had left. Debris littered the ground and pieces of wood floated in the water. Brendon walked across the lake, carrying the lifeless form of Kiwidinok along the way. As he reached the far shore, he felt his strength fading. He lowered his friend to the ground, and let go of the shillelagh as he collapsed in a heap of rubble.

The water lapped gently against the shore, as his friends and family rushed over. His eyes fluttered and closed.

Twenty-five

Something was touching his face. An insect, maybe. Brendon tried to wake up, tried to open his eyes. So tired, yet something was touching his face. He stirred, but fell back to sleep. He needed sleep. Something touched his face again; what was it? Rain? What if it was a mosquito? Or worse, a spider?

Brendon shot up out of bed, slapping himself in the face as he opened his eyes. Donovan burst out laughing and pointed at the long blade of grass Conall used to brush against his older brother's face. Conall pretended to be sorry, but a twinkle in his eye belied his apology. Goof balls! Well at least it wasn't a spider.

"Very funny, guys; where am I?" Brendon managed to ask.

"In the hospital. Don't worry, all those creepy hooded guys were taken to another building," answered Donovan.

"How long was I asleep?" asked Brendon, as he moved his feet over to the side of the bed. He felt stiff and sore.

"About three days. But Bidzil said it was just 'Druid's Sleep', something that happens when a *bard* overextends himself," replied Conall sheepishly.

"Three days?!How long have you guys been messing with me? You'd think my own brothers would have more respect . . . did you say '*BARD*'?" Brendon looked at his brothers anxiously.

"That's what the old geezer said, but if you ask me I think it was just luck, and the shillelagh," answered Conall.

"You're just jealous because you can't do anything," said Donovan before turning into a golden retriever and trotting around the room. Conall stood up and made his way to the big yellow dog, who slowly began to back away from him. A barrage of angry threats quickened Donovan's pace as Conall chased him through the doorway and down the stairs.

Brendon noticed some clean clothes laying on the chair beside the bed. He dressed himself slowly, his whole body weary and aching. By the foot of the bed were two pairs of shoes—his tennis shoes and the boots Bidzil had given him. He thought for a moment, before choosing the boots and putting them on. The shillelagh stood propped by the door. As he walked by, he grabbed it without thinking, using it to help him descend the stairs.

As Brendon exited the building, he saw gnomes hauling away broken stone and debris. Quinlan was giving directions to a group of hunters near the animal pens. Brendon looked around for his other friends, hoping they had not been harmed in the battle. Quinlan turned and, seeing him on the marble steps of the hospital, ran to meet him.

"You look well, Brendon. But should you be up so soon?" he asked as he approached.

"I don't know, but I'd rather walk around than sit in an empty room," answered Brendon. "Tell me, are my friends alright?"

"Yes, yes they are all well. Risteard was severely injured, but th' shaman helped to heal him, along with Cian Torin who was attacked by th‘ wyverns. His back will carry th‘ scars, but he is in full health. Bidzil is also well. Like you he had to revive with th‘ druid's sleep. He awoke a day and a half ago. Fearghas has been watching over you two as you recovered," answered Quinlan.

"And what about Mr. Dabir and Kiwi?" asked Brendon.

"Mr. Dabir carried you to th‘ hospital himself, insisted on it. He felt so helpless during th‘ battle, and was so worried about you. He wouldn't have left your side had we not discovered a Chaldean observatory that needed his attention. He asked your brothers to let him know as soon as you awoke, and I assume thcy have already left to tell him," answered Quinlan.

"If they ever quit horsing around," muttered Brendon.

Quinlan looked perplexed at that comment, but shook his head and continued. "Kiwidinok is well and meeting with th‘ other leaders this moment in th‘ library. I am just heading there myself. I think they would be glad to see you," he said, taking Brendon by the arm and helping him down the steps.

They walked together across the mall. Wide gaping holes remained where the stone monoliths once stood, reminding Brendon of his permanence in this new world. As he worked his way towards the far side of the courtyard, gnomes would stop and watch him pass. It was a bit unnerving, and he was grateful for Quinlan's company.

Eventually they crossed another boulevard and climbed the steps of the library-turned-barracks-turned-library. The large oaken doors were open to allow fresh air into the building. The ground floor was constructed of the same marble as the exterior, with large columns reaching up three stories to the vaulted ceiling, arched with dark stained redwood trusses. Along the walls of the lower level, empty shelves painted a picture of destruction as the volumes once housed on this floor had been consumed by fire used to heat the barracks. A pile of charred covers and spines were being swept from the brazier grates, gray ash sifting into the air around the brooms as they worked to erase the remnants of the lost tomes.

Makeshift wooden beds and straw mattresses were being hauled out the back doors to be burned in a fire pit behind the edifice. Although the room was dusty and dirty, Brendon could tell by the ornate architecture that it was once a pristine and well cared for jewel of the aelfin capital.

Quinlan motioned for Brendon to follow him up a set of stairs in the corner of the library. The marble slabs were set in a circular formation, following the contour of the rounded tower leading to the other floors. As they reached the landing of the second floor, Brendon noticed that here, at least, some books had remained unscathed, although many of the volumes had gaps in-between them. They continued up the stairway to the third floor. Brendon was getting a bit winded, but quickly forgot his exhaustion upon reaching the top step and the scene that awaited him there.

A long iron wrought railing stretched from one end of the balcony to the far side of the room, overlooking the floors below. In the center of the room, gathered around a wide mahogany table surrounded by a myriad of high back chairs, were the liberators of Aelfheim, also known as his friends.

The chairs' occupants stood and crowded around Brendon, embracing him and congratulating him. Bidzil or Caedmon—Brendon still couldn't decide what to call him, was last to greet him, looking him in the eyes, and not saying a word. But Brendon felt love and a sense of pride from his "however many" great-grandfather. Bidzil offered him his seat while he stood to address those that had gathered. Brendon looked around the table. There were a few faces he did not recognize—an older olive-skinned man, a creature who appeared to be part man/part lion, and an older man who looked a lot like Kiwidinok, only leaner.

"Brendon, these are our new allies. He-lush-Ka, a shaman and chief of the Saami of Talamh Glas. The man in the corner," he pointed towards the lion man, "is Ajeetabbas, Ajeet for short. He is a sagittary. And next to him his Ganju Pun, who hails from your world."

Ganju stood up and nodded. "I hope you don't mind, Master Brendon, but I borrowed your stick while you were asleep. It was dreadful not being able to communicate," he added sheepishly. Not knowing what to say, and being uncomfortable with having someone call him master, Brendon simply shrugged and nodded his head.

He looked around again. Most of the others he knew, then his eyes rested on a tattooed man sitting in the far corner of the room. Noticing his alarm, Bidzil interrupted his thoughts, "Makata Moto is a friend. With the help of the shillelagh he and his people are now able to communicate with us as well. They mean us no harm. We invited him to speak with us, as he is just as involved as we are."

The sound of feet running up the steps signaled the approach of another visitor. It was Mr. Dabir, sweating and breathing heavy as he ran to Brendon and took him by the shoulders. "I am so happy you are alright," he said with a tear in his eyes. Conall and Donovan followed behind him, and all were invited to sit once again.

"I have called you together to discuss what will come next," began Bidzil. "For too long the Naga Empire has meddled in the affairs of other nations, resulting in the dissolution of alliances, the exile of my people, and the deaths of many innocents. Three days ago, we sent a message. We told them that the aelfin race is not dead. We showed them we are mighty, and we have friends. Their soldiers witnessed great power, and what they saw will spread across the empire, gaining momentum with each re-telling.

"But now is not the time to rest. We must prepare ourselves for war. Emperor Amararaja will not simply give up the city, even though the realmbridge has been destroyed," he continued, looking at Brendon with sympathy, "That was a noble sacrifice, I might add. One that few men would have been able to complete. Amararaja will seek you out, and he will bring legions of soldiers to retake Aelfheim, but we have time to prepare, and time to re-forge old alliances. For this reason, I have called this council together, the Council of Talamh Glas.Each of you and your people have a voice, and together we will decide the fate of Faer Ri.

"But first, I believe we need to renew our friendship with the firbolg to the north. Their support will slow the Naga advances. Also, we must seek the Chaldees that left Talamh Glas so very long ago. Having the elemental power of the magi will give us an advantage during the winter months and through the rainy season. He-lush-Ka has already sent for his people to come home to Aelfheim, as they too will be needed."

"My people wish to help as well," said Makata Moto. "We have been forced into servitude for most of our lives. We will do anything if you help us free our people."

Bidzil thought for a moment. "I cannot make that promise today. But should we prevail in the fight that is to come, we will do what we can to free your people."

Makata Moto nodded and leaned back.

Cian Torin stood. "We will offer what help we can for th' next few weeks, but we also must look after our own borders and our own people. But should war return to Talamh Glas, th' gnomes will be there."Risteard nodded and winked at Brendon and his brothers.

Scioldmed then stood slowly, Cian Torin's eyes gave him a disproving glance. “I would say something, if you please.” Bidzil nodded, and he continued, “I believe young Girvan has learned all he can from me. With his father's permission, I feel he would be better off finishing his training here with the Brendon and Caedmon, errr . . . Bidzil.”

Girvan's eyes opened wide as Scioldmed sat back down. He looked at his father, who looked down and then nodded. Brendon gave Girvan a “thumbs up,” but Girvan, confused looked up at the ceiling. Brendon would have to teach him that later.

Bidzil resumed, “I think that is a wonderful idea. It is time that this library was used for the purpose for which it was intended, to teach the young how to use their gifts. And though we have closed the gateway for new slaves, we have not put an end to slavery. We will continue to rescue those that are captive, and in time we may abolish the practice altogether. But today I announce the return of Caedmon Anluan, and the Dawn of the Druidae. May it strike fear into the hearts of our enemies!”

Those assembled cheered and stood to shake hands. Feeling weak, Brendon asked his brothers to help him back to his room while the others continued their meeting, drawing up plans for the upcoming conflict. Conall agreed and took him by the arm, helping him down the steps and across the grass towards the hospital.

“Brendon,” asked Donovan, “What about mom and dad?”

Brendon thought for a moment before answering. “Donny, I think mom and dad are waiting for us still. I think we owe it to them not to give up. I would much rather spend my entire life hoping for something good, than to give up assuming the worst. You have great faith, Donny. Never let it go.”

They hugged one another, and Conall grabbed them both, tackling them to the ground, Brendon protesting in vain. All around them the world prepared for war. But for now, all they felt was brotherly love . . . even if it took the form of professional wrestling.

Epilogue

The room was damp and steamy, the walls slimy with a thick black sludge. The sounds of a man being tortured from a nearby room caused the woman to wince. But she would not cry. She could not.Her husband, his health failing, needed her to be strong, regardless of how scared she was.

Outside the door of her cell a man with a golden circlet on his brow stopped to give instructions to one of the tattooed men that worked in the dungeons. The tattooed-man nodded and went to fetch something. The first man with the golden circlet then turned and looked at her through the rusty bars of the cell door. She looked away quickly, not wishing to anger or offend. Finally, she heard him walk away and she returned to the cot her husband was laying on.

Taking a damp piece of cloth, she had torn from her sleeve, and dipping it in the water the jailers had offered, she gently caressed her husband's forehead attempting to cool him in this stifling heat. Since he had fallen ill to the fever, he had not eaten and barely said a word to her, but Kaitlynn Baird was not a quitter, nor was her husband.

"Stay with me, Alistair, stay with me. Our children need us, my love," she whispered.

List of Characters, Creatures, Artifacts, and Locations

***Aelfin (Aesir)*:** Race of magic users that dwell in Talamh Glas Woods in Faer Ri. Historically a peaceful people who traded with many neighboring civilizations before warring with the Naga Empire. Refugees of the aelfin people crossed a realmbridge to Earth, unable to return.

***Aelfheim*:** Capital City of the Aelfin people, located on an island in Aeflin Loch.

***Ba'asada*:** Capital of the Sphynx Dynasty, located in the Wastes of Magadesh.

***Baird, Alistair*:** Husband of Kaitlyn Baird, and father of three boys. Works as an insurance adjuster in southwest Michigan.

***Baird, Brendon*:** Fourteen years old, runs cross country for the Bridgerton Bison. Entering freshmen year of high school.

***Baird, Conall*:** Twelve years old, loves football and eating just about anything. Will be a seventh grader this year.

***Baird, Donovan*:** At age eight, Donovan is highly intelligent and fairly athletic. He is, however, very quiet unless you talk about football.

***Baird, Kaitlyn*:** Wife of Alistair Baird, nurse and mother of three boys.

***Bards*:** Druidae who have learned to use their ability as a weapon to defend and protect the aesir (also called Warrior Bards).

***Bidzil*:** Elderly magic user who lives in the dells of Fenian Chase.

***Chaldees*:** Aelfin who study celestial patterns and the science behind the elements. They are record keepers and historians of the aesir. They spend many years of study before they are able to perform even the slightest degree of magic within their discipline.

***Cian Torin*:** Chief of the Gnomes of Vloorhaven Glen, father of Quinlan and Girvan.

***Dabir, Farzan*:** Mr. Dabir is an Iranian Magi who studied in Europe before becoming a professor. Later he moved to Michigan in order to teach at Brigerton High School.

***Druidae*:** Aeflin who study the earth, plants, trees, rocks, streams, and all creations of the Living Stone. They are gardeners, farmers, and caretakers of the land. They use their voice to communicate with nature. This discipline requires natural talent, and cannot be learned, although they can be trained to use their gift.

***Fearghas*:** Huldretrow companion to Bidzil.

***Fenian Chase*:** A series of dells and ravines carved into the hills that lead up to the northern reaches of the Skregmore Reeks.

***Findias Stones*:** White or clear labradorite gems that increase the magic of items to which they are affixed. They are most commonly used to harden and enhance the metallic properties of blades.

***Firbolg*:** Race of beings taller and wider than humans or aesir. The average firbolg is between seven and nine feet tall, with wide bodies and a hefty girth. They reside at the base of the Dreich Mountains, in a range referred to as the Ring of Steel. Once allied to the aesir, they have shut their borders to all outsiders. They are still at war with the huldrefolk, although there have been no skirmishes for nearly two hundred years.

***Garvin*:** Youngest son of Cian Torin. He is a leprechaun in training, and is valiant and courageous.

***Gnomes*:** One of the most noble of races on Faer Ri, the gnomes have been stalwart allies to the aesir. They average four feet in height, and are quick and nimble. They are farmers and shepherds mostly, but have a very capable army of Hunters which they employ in defense of their homeland. It is rare that a gnome is able to use magic, and so one born as a leprechaun is a celebrated occasion.

***He-lush-Ka*:** Leader of the Shaman of Talamh Glas.

***Huldrefolk*:** Meaning "the hidden ones", a race of creatures made by the Living Stone that resemble the land around them. Their skin and hair appear as stone, bark, or other elements of the land. While soft to the touch, their skin becomes hardened during battle, as adrenaline changes the physiology and making it nearly impenetrable. They are known for performing great magical feats as well as artistry, and once traded their goods with other races. Huldrefolk blades are among the most prized in Faer Ri. They are a finite race, unable to procreate.

***Huldretrow*:** Singular of Huldrefolk, meaning "one who is hidden and alone". This designation is given to huldrefolk who have been exiled from Jotunn Knock, or recused themselves from the family. There have been very few huldretrow in Faer Ri, most having chosen the Withering Path.

***Leprechaun*:** A gnome who is able to use magic, after much practice. They are exceedingly rare, and therefore have a special place within the gnome community.

***Magi*:** Chaldees who are able to influence the weather, predict the future, and even, according to some accounts, control time.

***Naga*:** Humanoids with a snake-like appearance in the eyes and nostrils. They are a very numerous people, and have a caste system which divides them from one another to prevent intermarriage. There are three sub groups of Naga.

***Neim Stones*:** Greenish gray shards of hardened crystal that are imbued with magical properties. These stones have been used to enhance weapons and allow them to be unbreakable. Druidae used to sing to the stones and store spells in them to be used at a later time.

***Nøkker*:** Water spirits, often malevolent with intentions of drowning their victims. Live in or around forested wetlands.

***Nykr*:** Water spirit which takes an equine shape. Also known as a Water Horse. There are tales of these spirits serving aelfin heroes, but those accounts of have been lost of the years.

***Pun, Ganju*:** Former Nepalese Gurkha and currently working security for UNESCO.

***Quinlan*:** Second son of Cian Torin, fast and alert, quick on his feet and level headed. Quinlan is considered second only to Risteard and Cian Torin in his fighting prowess.

***Realmbridge*:** A link between worlds that allows an area to be transported from one reality to another.

***Risteard*:** Cian Torin's champion, leader of the Home Guard and Captain of the Hunters.

***Saami*:** A discipline of magic employed by the aesir to study animals and nature. They are the healers of their people, and can communicate with animals. Easier to learn than the Chaldees discipline, but still requires study to master.

***Sagittaries*:** Citizens of the Sphynx Dynasty, a hybrid race with the torso, arms, and head of a man, with the body and tail of a lion. Not as fast as a centaur, but certainly fiercer. They can speak the common tongue of Faer Ri, but also have their own system of communication with grunts, growls, and roars.

***Scioldmed*:** Leprechaun of Vloorhaven Glen, advisor to Cian Torin.

***Sēra Kē Dānte*:** Mountain chain to the west of the Wastes of Magadesh.

***Shaman*:** Saami that use Shift Magic to transform into animals.

***Ska'utsa*:** A sub group of the Naga with light skin and numerous tattoos that cover their bodies from the neck down. They are hairless on their head and body. Most wear only a loin cloth, and all hunt with spear and ling knife. They are the lowest caste of the Naga Empire.

***Skregmore Reeks*:** Mountain chain on the eastern shoreline of Talamh Glas and the Wates of Magadesh.

***Talamh Glas*:** Vast woodland dominating the landscape of the aelfin homeland.

***Taylor, Kiwidinok*:** Middle-aged Shaman from Michigan. Studied biology in college and is revered as one of the greatest Shaman in North America.

***Vloorhaven Glen*:** Homeland of the gnomes. Located on the southern border of the Fells of Beag Cairdeas.

***Wastes of Magadesh*:** Once fertile farmlands of the sagittary people, now a barren and inhospitable desert.

About the Author

C.L. Hurst has spent most of his life surrounded by academics, eventually succumbing to the very career that he sought to avoid. His travels around the globe have led him to the conclusion that Faer Ri exists, and that he must be a descendant of the aelfin race, as his mind is constantly occupied with fanciful stories about fantastic creatures. He has researched the similarities of the world's myths and how these wondrous stories came to be, and is certain there is a common thread—Faer Ri.

C.L. Hurst is an educator, a coach, a husband, and a father of four boys. When not fulfilling a responsibility related to these four areas, he is traveling the world searching for more origin stories, further proof of the reality of Faer Ri. And just maybe, finding a way to return…

www.ingramcontent.com/pod-product-compliance
Lightning Source LLC
Chambersburg PA
CBHW070637310726
48982CB00001B/314